Don't L

by Phillip Kurthausen

First published in 2018 by Bloodhound Books

www.bloodhoundbooks.com

Print ISBN: 978-1-912604-93-7

Dedication

For My Wife

CHAPTER ONE

Coffee and death threats

I wake, as I do most mornings, to a death threat.

It's on Twitter, from a man I presume, although it's from an anonymous account in the name of "Frenchie". It's an *oeuvre* I've become almost amused by, one that I call "red face", as I can almost see the bursting blood vessels, like a map of Mars, on the fat face (I admit this may be unfair, and I'm not linking being overweight with violent misogyny, but it's the way I see them so suck it up) of some impotent, lonely man, with a beer and a box of Kleenex by the side of his keyboard as he types.

In this case, it's an almost text book example of the many emails, tweets, phone calls and even letters – what a misplaced joy it was to receive a letter that first time; there wasn't even any green ink to warn me of what may be inside, just nice normal blue with a handwriting style that spoke of a good education – that I've received since I began. The contents of that first letter were pretty much a longer treatise on the subject matter dealt with in the Twitter-enforced brevity of this morning's message delivered to the mobile phone lying peacefully on the bedside table. I read it again:

Hope he rots – fucking bitch fucking race traitor. I'd rape you before I slice your throat if you weren't such a fat ugly pig.

It's been re-tweeted thirty-two times by the time I read it. I block Frenchie but I don't bother reporting it. I know from experience that the police will do nothing save offer warm words and a crime number.

I place the phone on the bedside table. The most important part of the day has begun and I've made a promise to myself never to miss it unless something really important comes up and death threats don't even come close. But I can't help myself and pick the phone back up and drop a quick Instagram post, a picture of a smiling Henry with Finn on his shoulders riding piggyback as they walk along Fistral Beach. It's over a year old, of course, but people never notice these sorts of things. I caption it "lovely weekend at the beach". Take that Frenchie.

I pause at the top of the stairs and listen – no, I drink in the sounds from the kitchen below, letting it wash through me as though it will refresh and cleanse every cell in my body. The radio is the background beat, serious men and women talking about serious things, but the syncopated clanging of Henry and Finn as they attack their cereal bowls, in a way that confirms their shared genes more than any blood test ever could, is pure joy. This is the highlight of my day and I am acutely aware of it.

As I stand there listening, Lil'Bitch slyly appears from under the linen basket and rubs herself against my leg. I carefully push her away with my leg and then make my way downstairs.

When I enter the kitchen, Henry doesn't look up from his bowl or *The Guardian*, which is held down on the kitchen table like a battle map with pots of jam, marmalade and a tub of coconut butter standing in for toy soldiers and flags. Finn on the other hand gives me a big smile and in the same moment, the act of transitioning his mind from food to his mother causes the trajectory of his spoon of milk and cereal to change, sending bits of what I can see are the sugary 'o's of the cereal I've told Henry not to give him all over his face.

Henry turns and starts to move towards the sink to grab a cloth, his first instinct as always to fix things.

Finn and I both burst out laughing and for a second things are like they used to be. Then Henry is wiping the mess away from Finn's face with what I can see is a wet, dirty tea towel.

"Eww! Get off Dad!"

Henry backs off. Finn has been the boss of Henry since he learned to talk.

"Here, let me." I take the tea towel from Henry, "Use a clean one from the drawer honey," I say to Finn.

"Morning sweets, situation normal, all fuck–"

"Don't!" I cut Henry off before he finishes. I know many parents see and treat their kids as friends but I want Finn to be protected for as long as possible. The darkness will be along soon enough.

I turn the radio off and the world and all its problems fall silent.

Henry nods and raises his dark eyebrows. "He's heard worse at school and as for the Internet, that is Sodom and bloody Gomorrah."

I smile. "I know, but not at home."

Finn wipes his face with the clean tea towel. "Why are we going to Sodom tomorrow, Sarah?"

I try not to show him that I hate him calling me "Sarah" instead of "Mum" or "Mummy" as I know that this will just encourage him. Hannah says it's just a phase and her daughter went through it as well, but she was a teenager and Finn is an eight-year-old. I resolve to Google the arse out of it later.

"It's a Bible thing honey; Daddy will tell you all about it on the way to school."

Henry, a lifelong atheist, gives me a scowl that say's "thanks for that".

"Which is happening now, buddy. I have a staff meeting at nine so shake a leg."

Finn jumps down from his chair and heads for the hall with the weary resignation of a death row prisoner on the march to the gallows.

"Will you be late tonight?" I ask Henry.

He rolls his eyes and throws his palms upwards.

"Who knows? I hope not. Are you recording the show today?"

I nod and follow him out to the hallway where Finn is leaning against the wall by the front door. Before he can take evasive manoeuvres I grab him and give him a hug and a kiss on the cheek.

"Geroff!"

He wriggles away and begins to unlock the door. For a moment I think about kissing Henry but it doesn't feel right and then, to my embarrassment, I find I'm patting my husband on the shoulder like he's a pet dog. Luckily, he's too busy hurrying Finn through the door to notice.

"I'll text if I'm going to be late."

"Bye honey!"

Finn tramps down the path, head down, and just raises an arm by way of goodbye, but he doesn't look back. As soon as they both reach the gate I slam the door shut.

One by one, I turn the keys in the two mortice five-levered deadlocks, then latch the Yale lock, and finally I slide home the two heavy bolts, one at the top and one at the bottom of the reinforced frame, with a satisfying clunk of steel on steel, and then I turn and head back into the now quiet of my home.

After clearing up the breakfast dishes I make myself a strong coffee and sit at the kitchen table. I move Henry's *Guardian* and underneath is a piece of paper with a picture on it that Finn must have drawn. It's of a cartoon-type spaceship with a small astronaut figure in the cockpit. It's blasting off from a house and heading for a planet with Saturn-like rings. I pick it up and use a fridge magnet to stick it to the large silvery chrome of the fridge door. Our old fridge used to be plastered with pictures that Finn had drawn but when we got this new one they disappeared into a box somewhere, which is now either in a dark corner of the attic or more likely forms part of a sludge mountain on a landfill site.

Seeing the picture on the fridge makes me feel happy and sad at the same time. I know that Finn will probably rip it off the moment he sees it on his return from school.

I finish my coffee whilst looking out at the garden through the French doors. I know it's the time of year, but the garden looks empty and desolate, everything hunkering down waiting for the cold to pass. I tell myself that we are lucky just to have a small patch of garden in this part of London, but still I look away and as I do so I catch a glimpse of my image caught between the panes of the double-glazing. I look thin and pale. Maybe I should eat more, perhaps I'm ill? It's probably just the lack of sleep but I know myself well enough to know that before the day is out I will have Googled my symptoms. It will be cancer of course. Pale, thin and tired – cancer for sure. It's always cancer.

Recognising the trigger danger in this nascent thought I dump the coffee mug in the dishwasher and head downstairs to the basement.

It's time to put my game face on. I have an innocent man's life to save.

CHAPTER TWO

Podcast 3

"Basement" doesn't do the room justice. After the incident Henry went into full-fixing mode and when I told him I needed a place I could work from at home, he was on it, throwing all the energy he couldn't target elsewhere into architect's plans, design, materials, and three months later we had a state-of-the-art recording studio, warm, soundproof and secure.

It's bright down here, everything illuminated by fluorescent strip lighting, white walls, a pale wood floor. The paleness is only livened by the shocking yellow sofa and the framed magazine covers and awards on the wall nearest the stairs. Henry wanted it bright. I would have objected, this not being to my taste – it's like the inside of a Scandinavian designer's wet dream in its unremitting minimalism and whiteness and I prefer more homely furnishings – but Henry wanted to build a cocoon of his own design for me and I let him.

Once I've shut the basement door behind me, I turn on a small floor lamp near my desk, turn off the main lights and work in a little cone of light and the blue whiteness cast by the computer screen with the microphone in front of me. I almost feel like Philip Marlowe once the lights are dimmed. Bit too early for bourbon, though, but not too early for its replacement, work.

My chair is a brown leather Eames office chair and it's the only thing I took from my father's house after he died. It's not exactly comfortable and it causes me to shift position regularly as my backside rubs against the well-worn ridges and creases caused by the years of him sitting there, smoking cigarettes, drinking whisky and writing. I entertain sentimental notions that when I sit in it I am somehow closer to him. Nonsense of course but it's how I feel and sometimes that's more important than cold, hard reality and its disappointments.

The wall behind the desk is covered with a corkboard and is stuck with photographs, yellow sticky notes and a map of the Wirral, a place in the north that I've never visited.

On the desk in front of me are my laptop and a letter. I've read the letter already. It contained one line only, "I'm sorry", and was unsigned. I've been receiving one a week for the last twelve months and they always say the same thing, are always unsigned, but I know who sends them and I just don't care so I screw the letter up and throw it in the bin by the side of the desk.

I suck in my bottom lip, hold it between my teeth and take a deep breath, and then I flip open the lid of my laptop and open a new Word document.

I stare at the whiteness for a long moment and then I begin to dictate into the microphone, the words appearing as though by magic on the blank page almost as soon as I've said them and simultaneously recorded as a WAV file for later transmission – an old word for a new technology. I focus on the screen and then think the following three words: "engaging", "intimate", "confident", and close my eyes, and when I open them again, even if I don't feel those things I begin to talk into the microphone.

Podcast Episode 3 – by Sarah Kelly 1/11/2018

Can you remember what you were doing last Friday at 3pm? It's a struggle, hey? Now, I want you to tell me what you were doing three months ago last Friday at 3pm? Who did you speak to? Who did you call? What did you have for lunch?

Now imagine you have to recall what happened Friday six weeks ago – oh, just to add a little pressure, if you get the timings wrong you go to prison for life. Feeling a little stressed yet?

Let's recap. Here's what we know. Lauren Grey was one of those girls that everyone loved even if, and hey we're all human, you were a little envious of her. On the surface she had everything. Intelligent, she had been admitted to Oxford University to study Law, popular, she had a large circle of friends, and I'm not just talking Facebook friends here (though she never got around to joining Facebook of course), but real friends, the kind who organise a surprise birthday party (her seventeenth and last), tell you everything, and who you can tell everything to, and a boyfriend who was the captain of the school cricket team. And did I mention she was also beautiful? But the phrase that crops up again and again was that she was "adored by everybody".

But hey, things couldn't all be that good. Who has a life like that? Certainly not Lauren Grey. Her mother was a single parent and suffers with debilitating multiple sclerosis, and the reality is that Lauren, and I've checked it's okay with her mother to say this, had been helping out more and more as her mother's illness progressed. Getting home from school, doing the cleaning, making the tea for her mother and little brother. And like so many girls she also suffered with crippling anorexia and, though her friends say she was mostly cured, you can see in her photographs she was still very thin, and anorexia, hell, it's like being an alcoholic, it's always with you. Take it from someone who knows.

Did she have any bad habits? Of course she did. She smoked cigarettes, roll-ups her friends tell me, could occasionally lose her temper and chew a friend out and she had a secret tattoo of a penguin on her right butt cheek that her mum didn't know she had until she read about it in the autopsy report.

Lauren Grey was killed by the manual compression of her larynx, causing the fracture of her hyoid bones and asphyxia, on the 9 July 2006 in the front seat of her Volkswagen Golf Beetle. The car had been parked in a small car park surrounded by trees on a stretch of country park coastline along the River Dee. You can Street View the car park and if you do you'll see it's a pretty place in the daytime, as it was when caught by the Google photographers. A small tarmac patch hidden amongst a copse of birch, maple and oak trees, and beyond that a stretch of dark sand that leads to the water of the River Dee and across the river to the slate-grey hills of the Clwydian Range. A single narrow lane leads into the copse and the picture taken on one of those rare sparklingly blue winter days makes it look like somewhere you would be happy to be. But you know that at night the place would look very different: it would be darker, cast in shadow by the trees. There is only one old, lonely streetlight that leans over the neck of the lane where it meets the opening of the car park, and in the unlikely event that it was working, and more of this later, it would cast only a small cone of sickly yellow light over less than half the car park space.

It's the type of place that had on occasion been popular with "doggers" and definitely was popular with kids who wanted somewhere to park up and smoke weed. The local police had twigged to this and drove by every couple of hours to deter the appearance of the smoke-filled cars that used to be seen there a lot more, before they began this routine at the insistence of the local residents who lived near the car park.

You see, although this car park, nestled in the copse, looks remote in Google Street View, if you spin the camera round, and back out of the car park up the lane, you start to notice gaps in the hedgerows every hundred yards or so. Some are marked by concave mirrors on the opposite side of the road to the gaps. You can't see it on Street View as these gaps mark the limit of Google's surveillance powers, but these spaces are the start of driveways that lead to large houses with river views, the kind that only the wealthy can afford. If you want to get a better view, and last time I mentioned this I got a solicitor's letter but hey you know my view on that, then click on satellite view and you'll get a good idea of the size of these properties and, more crucially, their gardens. So, what we have is the appearance of isolation without the reality. This is important.

Oh, and the name given by the locals to this country copse car park? "World's End". I've dealt with the press coverage in a previous podcast but you wouldn't need a degree in Media Studies to write the headlines that followed the murder of a beautiful woman at World's End.

Lauren Grey's body was discovered on a Saturday morning, 9 July, at around 9.30am. The police later established she had been killed between 11.30pm Friday and 1am earlier that Saturday. A local window cleaner, he cleaned the big houses hidden back down the lane, Charles Brownhill, was in the habit of having a smoke and a coffee from his flask before he started cleaning the houses. He had pulled his car in next to Lauren's Beetle and noticed someone slumped forward in the passenger seat.

Charles Brownhill did what any respectable member of the public would do and he called the police. I often wonder whether he regrets that now.

The police went by the book. They secured the scene, took witness statements from Charles and made enquires at the neighbouring properties. The victim's bag was still in the car and inside the bag was her purse containing her bank cards and student ID. If the motivation behind her murder had been theft it hadn't been a successful operation. Detective Sergeant Emma Pearson also made what must be the hardest of all house calls; she visited Lauren's mother and broke the news to her that her daughter was dead and may have been murdered. This visit took place at 12.30pm.

Khalil Bukhari was in the frame straight away and for good reason; he was Lauren's boyfriend, you know, the captain of the cricket team, and the statistics don't lie. Most women murdered are killed by their partners and it's a chilling but true fact that the guy who rubs your back is the most likely person in your life to kill you. And people wonder why us feminists are angry? You'd be fucking angry if the guy eating cornflakes across from you and sending you cute emails was statistically, by a huge factor, more likely to kill you than a terrorist. But I digress.

In the normal scheme of things the police would have been putting the squeeze on Khalil big time, and they did interview him that first day, but not until 8pm that evening by which time the story had already leaked to the press. A teenage girl, Jennifer Finch, at the same school as Lauren but in the lower sixth form, and who lived in one of those grand houses along the lane, had filmed the arrival of the police at World's End and uploaded it to YouTube. From where she was standing in her first-storey bedroom you could see the top of Lauren's yellow Beetle in the car park and someone recognised the car and commented "hey doesn't that look like Lauren from the upper sixth's car" and by lunchtime, before Mrs Grey received her visit from the police, most of the teenage population of Neston knew that something bad had happened to Lauren Grey.

The reason the police didn't visit Khalil Bukhari sooner was that they had a much better suspect, Charles Brownhill. As soon as he gave his name to the dispatcher when he made that 999 call the machine's cogs began to grind and in doing so they crushed Charles Brownhill.

When the first police officers arrived on the scene and saw the purple welts on Lauren's neck they didn't need to wait for the autopsy report to work out she had been strangled. When they received the background information from the National Crime Database on Charles Brownhill they moved quickly.

You see, when Charles Brownhill was fifteen years old, he was arrested and served a two-year sentence in a youth offenders' institution. His crime? He was convicted of assaulting his then girlfriend, Michelle Taylor. The nature of the assault you can guess. They were arguing and he put his hands around her neck and began to choke her. Who knows what would have happened if Michelle's mother hadn't arrived home from work early and made her way upstairs to her daughter's bedroom, interrupting the assault? Charles had run off but it didn't take long for the police to catch up with him.

Charles pleaded guilty to GBH on a plea with an attempted murder charge being dropped. It was his first offence and he was a minor, so hence his short sentence. After his release he picked up a couple more minor convictions, marijuana related mostly, but there was an affray conviction four years ago following a pub fight (he received a fine and a suspended sentence for that).

When the police initially talked with him about Lauren it also became apparent that he had no alibi for the night before. He told the police that on the night of the murder he had just followed his usual routine of picking up a takeaway from the curry house in the village, bought a six pack of strong continental lager from the corner shop and then settled down to watch TV for a few hours before hitting the sack around 1am, roughly about the time Lauren was feeling hands close around her neck. But Charles lived alone so there was no one who could provide him with an alibi.

This was in direct contrast with Khalil Bukhari who had a strong alibi for the evening. He had been to the party. He had left early, claimed he had a headache, around 10.30pm, getting home at 11.45, where he was met by his mother, two sisters and his brother and proceeded to have a bit of a family row, almost a tradition it featured so regularly, about him hanging around with the wrong sort and his mother sniffing him to see whether she could smell alcohol, weed, cigarettes or worse, perfume. When the police first spoke with him, and it was a telephone call, which perhaps tells you that they were thinking about other suspects at this stage, he said he had been in bed by 1am. DCI Richardson followed up with a house call the next day and spoke with his family. They all confirmed his story but by then the police were fully focused on Charles Brownhill because of what his neighbour had told them and what they had found at his flat.

They didn't even need a search warrant. Charles happily invited them in. He had no idea that they suspected he was the murderer.

When the police entered the flat, they found a clean but untidy (I've seen the photographs) apartment, typical of many bachelors. It was messy and they found some adult magazines under his single bed. But what really got them interested was the collection of women's pants they found in drawer in his wardrobe. There were twenty-two pairs to be exact, different sizes and different types, lacy, big and bold, and seemingly used. Gross huh? Charles, it turns out, had purchased them on eBay and other specialist sites, who knew hey, and he could prove this with PayPal receipts, but it definitely ticked the box marked "aberrant behaviour" in the investigating officers' minds.

When the neighbour who lived in the flat below mentioned that Charles was in the habit of going out late at night on his own and he was pretty sure that he had gone out the Friday before, then the deal was sealed as far as the police were concerned. They pulled him in for questioning.

You probably saw it on the TV. He looks weird, huh, Charles Brownhill? Wears a dickie bow even though he's a window cleaner and has that hairstyle that makes him look like a more sinister version of Jimmy Savile? Someone, well hell, let's name names, it was PC Ivan Williams, later dismissed after the enquiry, tipped off the press and they were there for his arrest.

The papers went wild. Front page splashes of this odd man, pictured wearing a dickie bow whilst taking the bins out, who collected women's panties (yup, that detail had been leaked). There was blanket coverage, interviews with his former girlfriend, who, even though she hadn't seen him in twenty-seven years, gave an exclusive to The Sun, *regaling them with tales of how he liked to read pornographic magazines (this was pre-Internet times) which they ran on page three with no sense of irony. Hell, they even spoke with classmates from school who branded him a loner and a weirdo as though that were a crime.*

The fact that Charles had been held back at school and had learning difficulties and a low IQ were leaked to the Daily Mail. *It was brutal stuff, complete character assassination in the space of a few days. The guy was clearly guilty, so where was the harm, seemed to be the thinking.*

Seven days after the murder of Lauren Grey, Charles Brownhill was arrested and charged with her murder.

The Daily Mail *headline was "The Face of a murderer?", the legal fig leaf of the question mark, a laughable attempt at some form of journalistic integrity.*

Two days after the publication of that now-notorious headline, Charles Brownhill was released and all charges dropped. "Thank goodness for the question mark," whispered the lawyers.

Everything collapsed quickly. A neighbour, Margaret Highfield, who had caught an early flight on the Saturday morning that Charles found the body, had been in Spain on holiday all week, and was oblivious to the events unfolding in her street, returned and immediately went to the police and told them that she had stayed up late on the Friday evening/Saturday morning rather than grab a couple of hours sleep before her flight and had sat up drinking coffee. Her flat was on the opposite side of the street to Charles's flat and she recalled looking out and seeing Charles sat in his usual chair watching TV with a can of lager in one hand and takeaway cartons scattered by his feet. She was concerned about not missing her flight so she kept looking at her watch, pacing her kitchen, making cups of coffee. She was adamant that Charles was sat in his armchair all evening and that he fell asleep in it and was still sleeping when she left for the airport at 4am. Crucially, she testified he was there between 11 and 2am so there was no way he could have been, or nipped out to, World's End which was seven miles away. Her flat is so close she could even see what he was watching on TV, an old episode of Colombo *as it happens, and she turned over to watch the same episode. I checked, by the way, the episode was "A Friend in Deed", considered one of Colombo's most challenging cases if you're interested. As soon as Margaret returned from Spain she went to the police and swore a witness statement confirming that Charles was at home the time the murder was committed.*

But the final nail in the coffin was the forensic evidence. The results came back after Charles was arrested. They pulled DNA from her fingernails and from the passenger seat and belt of the car. The DNA under the fingernails matched one of the sequences found on the seat; there were three sets not including her own. We can assume this is the killer, but none of the DNA produced a match on the National Crime Database, meaning the individuals were not known criminals. Charles Brownhill had given his DNA to the police when arrested and convicted of assault in 1999. None of the DNA in the car or under Lauren's fingernails belonged to him.

Reluctantly, as in so many other ways he was a perfect suspect – the hair, the dickie bow, the pants collection – Charles Brownhill was released.

Without any hesitation or a remote blush at the hypocrisy, the press, who had picked away at Charles Brownhill's life until it was a bleached carcass, tore into the police.

And the police, in shame, in anger, in overdrive, went looking for the real killer.

They went back to basics and pulled in everyone who had seen Lauren the night she had died. That turned out to be quite a few people at the party.

And something else, another story, began to emerge.

The night of the murder, Lauren had attended the eighteenth birthday party of a school friend, Shona Cunningham. Her father was a big deal locally: he owned a string of hardware shops and they lived in a large house on the coast, a couple of miles north of World's End. It's a pretty impressive place, detached, white plastered walls, heavy oak doors, a maritime feel about the place and a view over the River Dee to die for.

The party, it turns out, was not the kind you'd probably remember as a kid, less a crappy stereo, cheap bottles of cider, bags of value crisps and more hired band and catering. They even had a pool, and numerous statements take time out to refer to the fact that at some point lots of the kids who attended ended up in the pool. Not Lauren though. She had arrived late to the party as she had to get her mother comfortable before leaving the house, and her best friend, Rachel Jones, told the police that she had been saving for a couple of months for her party dress, so the last thing she would do is jump in a chlorinated pool. Plus, it seems that although she liked to smoke a bit of weed and did drink, she wasn't the type to get totally smashed. She liked to remain in control. Perhaps as a consequence of growing up too quickly.

Her boyfriend Khalil was already at the party when she got there. More than one witness talks about them seeming happy to see each other, hugs and kisses on arrival, that sort of thing. At least at the start of the evening there was nothing amiss, although that was to change.

Khalil's best friend was Tom Ellis. Tom and Khalil were popular, there is no disputing it. Both looked like Abercrombie and Fitch models save that Khalil wouldn't get in that catalogue for well-documented reasons, and despite this, or because of it (I freely admit to not being up with the zeitgeist as to whether good-looking is in or not) they seemed to have no enemies. Reading the statements, there was no petty bitching, more just cool envy. I lost track of the "he was a great guy", "just nice to be around", "no way would he be involved". They were also both great athletes, Tom on the track and Khalil on the cricket field. Neither were slouches in the classroom. Khalil had a place up at Durham University and Tom was heading to Manchester.

Both Tom and Khalil had clean criminal records and yet within hours after Charles Brownhill's release Khalil was considered the main suspect in the murder of Lauren, and largely this was down to the row he had at the party and the aforementioned fact that most killers of women are their partners.

This row, which I will explore in more detail, is a key moment I think, so it bears setting out. This is based on a number of witnesses but it's still sketchy as, hey, it's a party and all the witnesses 'fessed up to having been drinking and who knows what else. I mean you're not going to tell the police things they don't need to know, right? What we know is that at some point between around 10pm and 10.45 Tom and Khalil had an almighty bust up.

It wasn't quite a fight; no punches were thrown but chests were pushed, in what my husband would describe as "handbags".

The account of the fight, although the timings differ, is backed up by two other witnesses who were in the kitchen: Jen Bogdanski, one of Shona's friends in the year below and thus on the outer rim of the friendship group, and Max Rowdon, who was with her on a booze hunt in the kitchen when it kicked off between Khalil and Tom.

And for the record, in their statements and at trial, both Khalil and Tom gave a similar version of events: that they had a falling out over some weed that Tom was meant to share but had kept to himself.

Shona and Max didn't see the start of the argument, they walked in and it was "kicking off" as Max later said. What they did witness was Tom push Khalil in the chest and Khalil apparently laugh in his face and tell him that "you're just jealous".

Both Khalil and Tom agree that the "you're just jealous" line did happen and related to the fact that Khalil had gotten into a better university than Tom. Kids huh?

Max said he thought it might get physical, but at that point Lauren walked into the kitchen and the boys stopped arguing to listen to Lauren who apparently leaned in to whisper something to them both. No one overheard what was said but shortly after Tom left the room and went to join a group smoking weed in the back garden, and this was corroborated by numerous witnesses.

Max says it was like she had this natural authority and, when I spoke with him, even after all these years, I could tell he had been a little in love with Lauren. I hope he doesn't mind me saying that, but he wasn't the only one. I've lost count of the times when interviewing her old schoolmates that they told me she was loved.

What we know is that Lauren took Khalil to one side and they had words. Max and Shona were still in the kitchen and said that a bunch of other people were too, but they couldn't overhear what Lauren and Khalil were discussing. They could tell from the body language that it was a row. Max said it was "pretty intense", Shona described it as " deep and meaningful gone wrong" and Khalil stormed out, banging into Max and knocking his drink out of his hand. This was around 10.30pm. Approximately an hour and half later, Lauren left the party as well. She left relatively early because, according to her friends, she had to remain sober and be of help to her mother the next day. No one really could explain why Khalil left early. His explanation to the police was that he had a headache. He denied that they had argued. A seventeen-year-old boy leaving a party because of a headache – you can guess what the police thought of that.

After Chris Brownhill was released the pressure on the police was intense and they began to follow up on leads they should have chased but for the gift of Charles Brownhill. The case against Khalil began to build and the first and most devastating plank in that case was what happened to Khalil's alibi. You recall he was meant to have been at home between 11.45 and 2am? Well, it turns out he kinda wasn't there at all.

Khalil's alibi was based in its entirety on the testimony of his family, not historically the most independent of witnesses.

The police checked local CCTV. There's a camera at the end of Khalil's street that belongs to a local cash and carry business. That camera overlooks the only entrance to the cul-de-sac on which Khalil's house is situated. They pulled it, and guess what? Nothing. No Khalil from 10pm to 1am and then, there it is, an HD quality moment of Khalil walking past the camera on the opposite side of the street. But at 1.30am. He even looks up at the camera as he passes, giving a crystal-clear image of his face. You can imagine the excitement in the room when the police first viewed the tape. I would bet a month's wages that someone said "bingo".

The police went back and spoke to everybody who was at the party that night and they found a witness, Jack Martindale, and he told them something they found interesting. Turns out he was the last person, that we know of, who spoke with Khalil that night and what he told them began to build the motive.

He was standing outside in the front garden of the house, smoking a roll-up, when Khalil left (he puts the time at about 10pm) and had a snatched conversation with him. He was part of Khalil's social circle; he wouldn't go as far as friends, but he was close enough to see Khalil was upset and ask him if everything was okay, and Khalil's response?

"That fucking bitch. That's all bro."

So much for Khalil not having a row with Lauren.

But a row doesn't make out motivation, does it? And okay so he lied about his alibi, as did his family, and when questioned they just said they didn't trust the police not to arrest a Muslim boy for the murder of a white girl. You may have a view on this, I do, but it's not beyond the boundaries of what a family may do. Khalil, by the way, gave up his alibi the first time the police pulled him in post Chris Brownhill's release. He said he had been walking the streets trying to clear his head.

But you know what did make out motivation? The results of the second post-mortem that established that Lauren Grey was three weeks pregnant with Khalil's child.

The motive was born. What if she told Khalil at the party, and he, a Muslim kid who had to keep this relationship secret from his family, snapped after a row with her and in the heat of his anger and frustration, put his hands around her neck and squeezed?

The police and the CPS thought this was what happened, and even though I know lots of you listening will be thinking "whoa", there's some way to go here to establish guilt beyond reasonable doubt, so, eventually, did a jury. The third nail in his coffin, and although you would expect this in his girlfriend's car, was that his DNA matched one of the three sets found on the passenger seat of the car, although not the fingernail DNA. So, motive, no alibi and DNA, the deadly triumvirate of a conviction.

Khalil Bukhari was sentenced to life imprisonment with a minimum term of twenty-five years. That was twelve years ago.

In my next podcast I'm going to present you with information that I think changes everything and establishes that there was reasonable doubt that Khalil was the murderer.

I press the mouse button and halt the recording. Podcast 3 of "World's End" is done and a few seconds later it's winging its way to Jane, my producer at Bulldog Productions, the podcast company I now work for. My colleagues and friends think I didn't return to TV news but instead chose to freelance for online content providers as a conscious choice to embrace new media, but the reality is that it was the only way I could continue to work in any meaningful way and be safe at home. It came as a surprise when this show took off and the downloads for my investigation of a long-dead case, into a seemingly ordinary murder, began to hit the tens of thousands. I guess I should be grateful for my success but I can't shake the feeling that the attention I wished to avoid is being focused on me from out there beyond my front door.

Behind me, there's a noise. I hold my breath and listen to the sounds of my house, made sinister through my silence. I know I'm being paranoid but then there it is again, a soft release of air. The kind of sound you barely hear but which you know almost instinctively is the sound of a door being gently opened. I wrinkle my nose, as there's also the hint of an unpleasant smell, something decaying or faecal borne in on the unexplained draught.

And then I can hear the birds in the back garden singing, which means that the door that has been opened is the door to the basement.

Slowly, I move my right hand from the mouse and place my finger on the panic button on the underside of the desk.

I am about to press it when I hear the familiar padding of Lil'Bitch coming down the basement stairs.

I let out the breath I've been holding and it comes with an added sob. I thought I'd come further than this, being reduced to a wreck by my cat opening the basement door.

Something is wrong with Lil'Bitch, though – she's making this noise, not a purr, something more akin to a growl, and then I see why. In her mouth is a dead sparrow. No, correction, a nearly dead sparrow, twitching and jerking unnaturally. She drops the gift at my feet. A gift I know that I will have to kill, but it's not that that causes pins and needles to blossom in the back of my head and spread to my arms; it's the fact that Lil'Bitch has been outside and she is never allowed outside because the doors to this house are never left open.

CHAPTER THREE

Fucking Zen

I don't check the front door. I would sooner forget to inhale than I would leave it unlocked. Henry and Finn have been trained not to leave the back door unlocked but I didn't check it before coming down into the basement. It's possible Henry took something out to the bins before I came down to breakfast. Possible, but unlikely.

The tingling in my arms makes me feel like I'm going to die. I know, of course, that I won't. I know the panic is producing physical symptoms that mimic impending death, but this knowledge does nothing to alleviate the sense that I am not in charge of my body, that I am floating above myself.

I watch myself as I tear off a piece of kitchen roll and wrap the sparrow in it. I know what I must do with the mummified parcel in my hand; even though it's definitely still alive, the jerking has stopped and been replaced by a slow rhythmic pump. I wish it would stop and leave me without the need to do what I need to do, but its tiny heart clings on.

Lil'Bitch keeps brushing my legs, nearly tripping me as I head to the floor-to-ceiling glass doors at the back of the kitchen.

"Lil'Bitch," I mutter. It's what I first called her when Henry brought her home from the refuge and her first act was to drag her claws down the expensive leather sofa in the lounge. Lil'Bitch had lasted until Finn started repeating it, and so a new name was required and "Moll" was born, but to me she is always Lil'Bitch, and especially today.

I caress the back door key that I keep attached to my belt with the other house keys, but already I can see it won't be needed. The door is very slightly ajar, letting in an icy draught, and I shiver but not with cold. How could I have not noticed? How could they forget? I will need to give Henry and Finn "the security" talk again this evening.

The garden is objectively small, but for this part of North London, huge. Henry wanted it modern and minimalist and so it is. Clean lines of teak line the old red-brick walls and long fingers of bamboo weave their way around them. There is a teak decking area surrounded by white gravel and a small water feature that gives out a regular *clop, clop* sound as the bamboo pipe fills with water and then hits the bucket underneath as it empties. Henry wanted the garden to be a place of relaxation. Right now I feel far from relaxed.

"Fucking Zen," I whisper to myself.

The garden is overlooked, but only just, by the third storey of the house behind the alleyway. I think it's a rental property because the bedroom window often has a national flag in it and this often changes. Right now, it's a Brazilian flag but six months ago it was a South African one.

I take a deep breath and step out into the garden. Almost immediately, my chest tightens and I feel pins and needles sprout in my wrists and crawl like jungle vines up my arms towards my heart, which I know they will strangle.

"You got this," I tell myself.

I take the sparrow bundle and place it on the ground near the disguised enclosure, which is yet more cross-hatched hardwood, this time attempting to hide from sight, I can never work out from who exactly – us or someone else who might be offended by the sight of our waste, the collection of council-issue bins.

I need a rock. Zen seems to encourage lots of rocks, I think, but looking around all I can see is white gravel, nothing even justifying "pebble" status. Christ, I can feel my breathing getting shallower. I know what comes next if I don't get inside soon: panic, pure physical and mental loss of me to that fucker inside, waiting on its chance.

I spin on my feet and look round the garden and am rewarded by the sight of a bright red fire engine. It's one of Finn's toys, but one that Henry chose because it reminded him of his childhood, a big chunk of over-engineered metal that I knew would end up crushing Finn's fingers if dropped. I bet Henry brought it out here because he knew if I came across it I would throw it away. I pick it up and feel its heft, and I know I was right, it can break bones. Just finding it places a temporary pause on the rising fear.

My heart is beating faster but I don't feel any sadness about what I am about to do, and that causes a flash of concern. And then I realise what's missing, what I need to dampen the fear. I need to take myself out of the moment.

I place the fire engine next to the sparrow bundle and take my phone out of my pocket. I take a photograph of the bird and the rock and quickly upload it to Instagram. It has to be the Earlybird filter, and I add the caption "Lil'Bitch just put me between a rock and a hard place..."

One post out of the way; if I do another at six thirty that will be enough for today, save for the comments, likes and other necessities of an online career.

I take a deep breath.

OK, better do this, I think, and I prod the bundle with my finger and feel the sparrow's tiny matchstick chest move. My phone buzzes as comments start coming in. Looking back at the house, I see Lil'Bitch sitting at the window looking out at the drama unfolding. I know I'm anthropomorphising but she seems pleased that I am doing this, that some form of compact or understanding has been reached. I could blog about this later, I think: *five ways cats are like your worst bitchy friend.*

I can hear birds tweeting and I look up and see two sparrows sitting on the guttering. Are they the family of this one I wonder? I raise my camera phone and take a picture of them.

"Don't be a dick," I say out loud, but then something strange happens: the air in my lungs disappears and my head fills with what I can only describe as toxic blood, blood that brings fear, anger and confusion.

I try and raise my hand but I find that I can't do it. What if there are people in the windows watching me do this? Filming me, laughing as I go pale and surrender to the panic.

The sound it will make if I kill the sparrow will be like ice cracking. I immediately vomit and all my veneer of bravado comes with it. I rest my hand on the bins to steady myself.

I can't do this, so I run back inside, slamming the door behind me. I don't dare risk a look back at the little bundle.

My newly decorated phone buzzes and, after wiping my mouth on the back of my jumper and then wiping the vomit from the screen, I check it and see that I have fifteen Instagram likes and two comments already. One of the comments is from an old colleague, Ben Macintyre, who is working out of the BBC's Kabul office.

Kabul is tough but nothing on Hampstead – CrazyS

"CrazyS" was my nickname when we both worked for Sky. I type a quick reply:

...now if I can just find another bird my work here is done. Stay safe Mac.

There are six other comments, all enquiring about the health of the sparrow. I quickly apply a filter to the picture of the sparrows on the guttering and cut it so only one sparrow is in the frame – the mate of the murdered sparrow? I wonder – and then upload it with the caption "all safe, garden ICU worked". No one responds well to negative posts and a happy ending is what we all crave. Journalism taught me that; it doesn't matter how shocking the news, the death, terror and fear, you have to provide an overarching positive narrative, or we will all end up hunkering down in a cave howling at the moon.

Lil'Bitch slinks off. I can't help feel that she is disappointed in me.

I stand up and lock the door. The little white bundle is still. The sparrow is probably dead, I tell myself, though I don't really believe it.

I put my iPhone on the island countertop, white on white. Why is everything so bloody white? Before the incident, when I used to go out, I never noticed the grease marks, the dust caught by sunlight that you see on white surfaces, but we agreed that with the drop in income and my being here all day, I may as well do the housework as well. I fucking hate doing it but guilt is a powerful negotiating tool especially when it's your own.

I pick the phone up and check the time. He'll be here soon.

I have fifty-four new Twitter messages and five new Instagram comments. I click through the messages whilst I wait. People are pleased to see that the sparrow recovered – heart and smiley emojis abound.

On Twitter the majority of the messages are about the case and are supportive or asking me for updates about Khalil's appeal. I give these my standard response: I'm not Khalil's lawyer, I'm just a journalist looking at this as a human story and I've not got a position on Khalil's guilt. That last bit's a lie, of course. I have a view.

And then there's the abuse. It's the usual mixture of racism and attacks on Khalil from those who think he did it, or who think that a Muslim boy dating a white girl is worthy of their bile together with the personal attacks on me, my appearance, my shitty career (it's been noticed I'm not on TV anymore) and the rape and death threats.

Frenchie has been posting again but this threat, *I'm watching you, you bitch*, is tame by the standards of the filth I usually receive.

I sigh. It's so predictable and such a waste of effort on their part. I know what real fear and danger is and this isn't it. All they tell me is that the podcast is successful; not that I need them to tell me that. 74,000 downloads for the last episode tells its own story.

The alarm on my iPhone starts to ring. My rule is to allow ten minutes from the alarm ringing to the doorbell ringing. If it rings outside that window then I reach for a kitchen knife before

I go to the intercom system on the wall to check who is standing outside the door.

But almost immediately, the doorbell rings. I check the video pad behind the door that leads to the hallway and I can see it's him but I still click the intercom and ask.

"Who is it?"

"Mohammed. I've brought croissants!"

I smile and then walk down the hallway where I begin the task of unbolting and unlocking the front door. When I'm finished, I open it, and there is Mohammed Bukhari holding up a bag of croissants. They are in a bag marked "Gigi's Deli". In passing, I mentioned what a great deli there was at the end of my street at one of our first meetings and ever since then he brings a bag of pastries to our meetings. This makes me happy.

We hug and then he steps into my house, following me into the kitchen, all the time keeping up a running commentary on how well I look, how my husband and Finn are doing, his wife Yasmin, his kids (he has two, Alesha and Mohammed – or little Mo as he calls him), what's going on at the clinic and the weather. Invariably, he is upbeat, and it's hard not to feel my spirits lift when he arrives.

Mo takes a seat at the kitchen table and tells me all about little Mo's latest scrape, hacking into big Mo's (which is what he calls himself) iPad, and how at six he thinks he has a potential future international criminal mastermind on his hands. His eyes sparkle and his words flow faster when speaking about his son, and I enjoy watching him talk like this, but I have to interrupt him and ask him a favour.

His eyes flicker to the bundle outside. "Not a problem. You make us some coffee and I'll take care of it."

Before the coffee is made, Mohammed has returned. I can see through the glass that the bundle has gone. He takes a seat back at the table and I place a cup of coffee before him.

"Thank you," I say.

"It is nothing."

"How's your mother?"

He looks away for a moment and when he returns my gaze, I can see tears in his eyes.

"Not good. I tell my patients often that medicine is an art as much as a science, and only God knows – and you know I don't believe right? – when our time comes to an end. But I can tell you this, Sarah, she will not see another winter."

"I'm sorry, Mo. When my mother was ill I felt like I was strung between two worlds. It was the worst time. If there is anything I can do please let me know?"

"Thank you, Sarah, that means a lot to me, but you are already doing so much for me and my family."

His shoulders droop and he nods and then looks away out into the garden for a moment. When he turns back, the rare vision of sadness has been replaced by his default twinkling eyes, and he slaps the table and smiles.

"Now tell me, how's your appallingly named cat? I love that little thing."

It's as though his optimism is toxic to despair and horror and they cannot survive within him for more than a moment. I envy him.

Lil'Bitch is nowhere to be seen. She is wary around strangers and usually hides whenever there is someone apart from the family in the house.

"Somewhere around; she was responsible for the fucking sparrow."

He frowns at my use of profanity and then smiles again, his large and perfectly manicured hands coming together in delight. I wonder whether his wife does them. I can't see such a ruggedly handsome man in a beauty parlour somehow.

"I thought the last podcast was excellent! We got really good press coverage of Khalil's case in *The Guardian*. Did you see it?"

"Yeah, they were chasing me for an interview, but like I said before, I think it's best I stay out of things until the series ends. I don't want to become the story."

"Sure, sure." Mo nods but his eyes flick quickly to the side; they always do when he's lying and he is an appalling liar.

"I would love to play you at poker," I say.

Mo laughs a big belly laugh. "I am too transparent for you! But maybe some more media coverage would be good for both Khalil and your career?"

How do I explain to him that my career is dead in the water and the last thing I would want to resurrect?

I sip my coffee and then fill the silence. "So, how is Khalil bearing up?"

Mo's expression changes from one of concern that he has offended me to twinkly eyed joy.

"Oh, so much better, he is so excited about the possibility of an appeal. He is a different person since you started the podcasts. You've given him hope and" – Mo waves his hands in the air – "it has transformed him. He has even stopped praying five times a day, thank goodness!"

Mo isn't what you would call an observant Muslim, in fact he has told me on more than one occasion that he thinks all religions are "scams" and he drinks and smokes – legacies, he says, of his medical training days.

"That's good. It must be hard to keep positive in there."

"I haven't the heart to tell him it will fail."

Mo looks straight at me in a way that is almost like a child saying something daring and wanting to be contradicted. I can't do that for him.

"I thought the lawyers said there were reasonable prospects of success?"

From high up in the house there comes a strained and prolonged gurgling sound. I recognise it straight away. I've inventoried every sound my house makes – it's the bathroom radiator struggling against Boyle's law. It's needed to be drained for three weeks now. I keep asking Henry to do it but he isn't the most practical of men. I resolve to fix it once Mo leaves. It's what the sisterhood would want, I tell myself.

"You know what I tell a patient when they ask me if they will be cured of their addiction? I tell them I can help them, that we will give them every tool they need to get clean, but that ultimately it is in their hands. They have the power and if they stick with it then they have reasonable prospects. This is what the lawyers are telling us. There are some reasonable prospects. They bill us and our lives turn on reasonable prospects."

He leans back in his chair, shrugs and then takes a sip of his coffee, "I don't blame them. They're part of the system and sometimes it turns and good things happen, but I see it in their eyes, there's not enough there."

For a second I find myself about to start listing, forensically, the weaknesses in the prosecution's case, but we both know the problem is the lack of any new evidence.

Instead I nod.

"Your podcast, your show though, that does offer possibilities."

"I told you six months ago when you first walked into this kitchen and sat right there." I point at the chair. "I think there is a story to your brother's case, a story that needs to be told, but I'm not a lawyer and I can't set him free. This isn't what this is about. My podcast was always an examination of a case with questions hanging over it. I'm not here to try the case."

The corners of Mo's lips turn up. "Ah, I know this but" – he raises his right index finger – "my father used to tell me that everybody has a meaning. My meaning is to help people get well, to steer them out of the maze of addiction, and your true meaning is to find out the truth. Just look at the publicity we are getting. The lawyers will make their arguments, but what keeps innocent people from rotting in jail is good people on the outside believing in them, and day by day there are more of us."

I shrug and sip my coffee. I'm not convinced. The first time we met was six months ago. Mo approached Cathy, my agent and one of my oldest friends, after reading about my investigation, a few years ago now, on a Tory MP who had been charged with historic child sex offences. Even though my politics were on the opposite end of the spectrum to this man, I knew there was something phoney about the case against him and the more I dug the clearer it was that his accuser was lying. Eventually, my pieces brought out other witnesses who could testify that the accuser wasn't telling the truth and the case was dropped. Khalil sent emails to me which were redirected to Cathy, and it was she who suggested I take a look at the case files and, once I was interested, suggested the podcast format that would mean I wouldn't have to leave the house to go to a studio.

For the first few meetings Cathy was present, but I've grown to trust this urbane and, let's face facts, handsome doctor. After he told me about his little brother's case I said I would read through the file he had brought me and that's all I could promise. I knew why Cathy had introduced him to me: she thought I wouldn't be able to resist, that it would be getting me back on the journalistic wagon. That in some way this story would be my therapy. She was right.

Mo stands up and starts pacing up and down. He's still smiling but his brow is furrowed and he raises his hand as he speaks. "You see, the appeal is not a story. It is not about his innocence; it's technicalities and is nothing but lawyers' talk. It will not set my little brother free. Only something new can do that – new evidence – and your show…" Mo wrinkles his nose and wags his finger mischievously. "It is pulling up rocks and seeing what is underneath, and I have great hope that it will flush something or someone out."

I know exactly whom he is referring to. Since day one, Mo has made it clear: he thinks that Tom Ellis killed Lauren. The lack of motivation, the rock-solid alibi and the absence of any other evidence have yet to prove an impediment to his belief.

"Well, so far we have nothing new I'm afraid."

I'm lying to him, but I don't want to get his hopes up. Mo likes to maintain this upbeat, optimistic demeanour but on more than one occasion I've caught him tearing up as he talks about his brother being in prison, and each time I've come up with some flimsy reason to excuse myself as I know he doesn't like me seeing him this way. It's just too early to tell him about what may after all be a dead end. It would crush him, and anyway, the appeal may succeed in any event.

Mo sits back at the table and then does something I wasn't expecting, and which makes me miss a breath and sends a shockwave of serotonin through my brain. He reaches out a hand and places it on top of mine and for a moment the world falls silent as I look at it covering mine completely.

His eyes, dark and heavy after his night shift, which were full of a mischievous glint a second ago, suddenly seem serious and questioning.

"I know you will keep trying. I have faith in you."

The moment hangs there, ready to turn one way or the other, and I'm at its mercy completely, ready to surrender to whichever way it goes.

My phone buzzes and then falls from the worktop behind me.

"Christ, let me get that."

I pull my hand away and I'm not sure whether it's with relief or disappointment.

Luckily, the phone isn't cracked. And the message that nearly caused it to dive off the work surface like a lemming?

It's a Twitter direct message; the picture shows a young girl, @Emmaroses2367, and is as innocuous as it gets, but the message is the opposite.

Race traitors like you deserve to be buttfucked. I'm watching – your biggest fan Frenchie....XX

I blocked him and he just set up a sock puppet account, probably will do so again. I block the fake user.

"Fuck."

"Is everything okay?"

I put the phone into my jeans pocket. "Yeah, just the usual messages of support."

Mo smiles sadly and gives a weary shrug. "Welcome to our world. I told you that you should come off those sites. They are a sewer."

"I can't, it's part of the job, and anyway it would be like burning books. I want this part of my life unfiltered."

I don't add that social media is one of the last ways that I can communicate with the outside world. Mo suspects, of course.

How could he not when every meeting takes place in my home and he's long since stopped inviting me to his house to meet his family or to lunch/coffee elsewhere? I sense he wants to talk about that, but that is a professional/personal line we haven't crossed yet and that's how I want to keep it. The last thing I want is for Mo to write me a prescription for Prozac on my kitchen table.

"Well you must not let them in here." He points to his head. "That's where they want to live; only you can allow them that space though."

I flash him a quick grin. "Don't worry, I won't. No one gets in here. These losers" – I wave my phone – "don't bother me."

But that's not entirely true. I can feel the pins and needles, the ripples caused by the barely submerged crocodile of panic, and I'm afraid of falling apart in front of him. I'm stronger when I'm alone; it's other people who make me weak.

I make a show of checking my watch. "So, your shift starts soon. I don't want to keep you from the hospital."

There is a flash of something that may or may not be disappointment in Mo's eyes.

"Yeah, I better get going."

I nod and then walk with him to the front door. I can see him looking at the locks but he doesn't say anything.

"Khalil would like to send you a letter. Would that be okay?"

At first I didn't want to communicate with Khalil. When I started reviewing the materials I wanted to come at it without prejudice, and without the emotional involvement of knowing Khalil as a person and not just a subject of my investigation but then one day Mo asked me could his brother send me a letter and how could I say no to such a polite request? But there has only ever been one letter and given the contents I never thought he would write to me again.

"Sure, tell him to go ahead."

"Thank you, Sarah, I will. Have faith."

We exchange a slightly awkward air kiss and then I let him out. I don't look beyond him as the chaos of the street's traffic, the people, the cars, all the light on this road, can still make my head spin with confusion. As soon as he steps out onto the porch I close the door shut and lock it quickly.

Back in the kitchen I make myself another espresso whilst looking at the fridge, which I know contains a bottle of Pinot Grigio.

I take the cup of freshly brewed coffee and take a seat at the table. Lil'Bitch is back, sitting on the radiator and looking at me, I want to say quizzically, but remembering my vow not to anthropomorphise mentally ticks myself off, and anyway I'm not even sure all humans act with human emotions, so why should a cat? I pull my phone from my pocket and navigate to WhatsApp and there it is, the delicate strand in the maze that may be the only way out of Khalil's labyrinth.

It's from Amy Wilder, one of Lauren's friends. I know from reading the police witness statements that she was one of the people who testified about the events of the party. But she wasn't called by either side at trial. She simply had nothing material to say about Khalil, she had seen him arrive but that was about it.

The message arrived after my last podcast:

Hi Sarah, I got your number from the website. I've been listening to the podcast and something you said about timings made me think back and well it would be good to talk.

I call her and she answers on the third ring.

Fifty minutes later and I'm lying on the couch, with a purring Lil'Bitch on my chest, and we are both about as contented as can be.

Later that evening in bed, once Henry has turned his bedside light off, he reaches for me in the darkness but I pretend I am asleep even though he must know I am not. I wait and then he removes his hand from my stomach just as I knew he would.

When I hear him start to snore I reach out for my mobile phone and send a WhatsApp message and, though I wait until my eyelids start to grow heavy, no reply comes.

CHAPTER FOUR

When

Some mornings I feel that the guilt weighs so heavily it will stop me from getting out of bed. Today is one of those days, compounded by the fact that I can't be the mother that I so desperately want to be. I love Finn more than anything else in my life. It's trite to say it but I would die for him, of that I have no doubt whatsoever. I would die for him and yet I can't find ten minutes most mornings to spend with him, despite the silent promises. I tell myself that I have a higher purpose, to help clear an innocent man who is rotting in prison, and that surely this outweighs playing with my son, but deep down I know the real reason: I don't want my guilt to poison his innocence.

I lie in bed wondering if I could just stay here, merge with the duvet and disappear forever. It would probably be best for all of us. "You knob," I hear myself say out loud, and the part of me that remains from before laughs. I never could abide self-pity and thankfully what remains of me from before still can't apparently.

It's this last thought that saves me and allows me to cast off the heavy duvet and get dressed. I do worry about the day that this may not happen and I know it's a possibility. One morning I just won't get out of bed, but not this morning.

Henry isn't in the kitchen when I descend, a fact that annoys me, as Finn has decided to engage in some impromptu painting and I can see red, blue and green paint bleeding from his notebook onto the expensive brilliant white of the Corian worktop. Finn looks absorbed in a way that I recognise from my own obsessions; his eyes are alive in a way that happens when he paints. From his first Pollack like experiments with baby food and our kitchen walls, he has always seemed happiest when painting.

He is standing on his chair, and throwing paint on the paper, and he doesn't notice me enter the room.

The mess doesn't bother me. The expensive kitchen was Henry's idea, I rarely cook and I'm not interested in "clean and tidy". A lifetime of cleaning has always seemed the antithesis of a fulfilled life but the fact that Finn is standing on his chair just one topple away from a broken ankle, or worse, makes me sharp with him.

"Finn, get down right now!"

I regret shouting immediately as I see his expression change from joy to hurt in a heartbeat. This is how childhood innocence disappears and is replaced by anxiety, I think: one remonstration at a time.

When I was pregnant with Finn I used to tell myself that I wouldn't be the type of mother who spends eighteen years acting as a health and safety monitor, that I would let my child live, explore and take risks, but the fear, nobody told me about the crippling fear that makes me everything I didn't want to be.

I take Finn in my arms and place him on the floor.

He starts to cry and at that moment Henry makes his entrance, a copy of *The Guardian* under his arm, and so I know exactly where he's been: spending some time alone before work.

Henry kneels down and takes Finn's head in his hands.

"What's wrong, my little soldier?"

Finn is bawling now, and taking big gulps of air in between telling Henry that "she" "stopped" "me" "painting".

Henry looks up at me and I can see he is thinking carefully about what to say. I imagine this habit makes him think he is being deliberate and considering but I think his students must hate it when he does this, especially when it is accompanied, as it is now, by a little nod of the head. I don't think he knows he does this, that he indicates that the issues have been weighed and that "yes", on balance what he is about to say is the distillation of his carefully considered wisdom.

"You have to let him explore his creativity, Sarah, it's an essential part of his development. You can't stifle it with" – he lowers his voice – "your anxiety issues."

Twelve months ago I would have told him to stuff his issues where the sun doesn't shine and probably would have left the house to meet up with Cathy for a coffee, but not now. Guilt has my tongue.

"I'm sorry, you're right."

Henry inclines his head towards Finn. It's an instruction and I obligingly obey, "I'm sorry, Finn."

Finn's sobs have slowed in speed and I bend down and kiss him on the top of his head. And as I do so he puts out a chubby hand and wipes away the tear I hadn't even noticed was dripping down my face.

Henry doesn't seem to notice. "Come on, son, it's time for school. Let's get ready."

When Henry and Finn have left the house, and once I've bolted the door, I run down to the basement. Nothing kills anxiety like work when it's going well. With work, there is no suffocating panic, no shrinking of my universe down to a tiny place in my mind surrounded by the rest of me going bad. It's all gone, because this podcast will change everything. I am going to set Khalil free. You see, it's all about timings.

Podcast Episode 4 – by Sarah Kelly – 8/11/2018

I want to talk about timings. "When" is our watchword for this episode.

The police, you will recall, put the murder at taking place somewhere between 12 and 1am on the Saturday morning of 9 July 2006.

Khalil initially said he was at home with his family. His sister, brother and mother all gave evidence to the police when questioned the first time that this was the case. It was only when presented with the video evidence that their statements fell apart. At first, you, like me, may have looked at this and thought uh huh, that looks fishy, why would they feel the need to lie to the police?

Here's what Mohammed, Khalil's brother, has to say about this:

"We knew that something had happened to Lauren and we knew that the boyfriend is always the first person to be suspected. We asked Khalil where he had been and he said wandering the streets. We panicked. You have to know what times were – are – like for Muslims in the UK. We are the bad guys, always suspected and never trusted, and we knew that although Khalil would never do such a thing, people would be blaming him so our first reaction was to protect him. We thought it wouldn't be long before they caught the real killer so no real harm would be done."

Mmmm, I know what you may be thinking. These guys just constructed an alibi for someone in their family who may be guilty of murder and they are saying they didn't think any harm would come of it – gullible, stupid or something much worse? The police and, as it turns out, the jury, thought it was a combination of all three.

But remember 2005, the year before the murder, the Tube bombings, the second group of bombers on the loose, Jean Charles de Menezes? These were febrile times and if you and your family, however unjustified, felt you were being targeted, who knows how you might have reacted? And even if you are not with me on that, one thing I am sure of is the fact that he lied about being with his family does not make him guilty of murder.

The prosecution, as you can imagine, went big on this element of the case. It wasn't helped by Khalil's second version of events, namely that he wandered the streets, worrying about his row with Lauren and that in this time he saw no one, spoke to no one and couldn't even precisely provide details of where he walked (he said he was in a bit of daze and had also been drinking and smoking weed). The details he could remember were sketchy and, as for timings, he was all over the place. The one place he could remember passing was a 24-hour garage on the way home. This garage is on the main road that runs between Neston, where the party took place, and Heswall, where he lived. His defence team got hold of the CCTV footage from the garage and studied it, eventually pulling up a grainy forecourt video that shows someone on the street passing the garage at around 1.15am.

The defence say that the blurry figure passing the garage is Khalil. The importance of this is that walking on foot at an average pace would mean that to get to the garage from World's End would take most people forty-five minutes. Khalil was by all accounts stoned and drunk and, if my limited experience is anything to go by, you don't speed up when this is the case. But taking the most conservative estimate means that if the murder happened in the time slot between 12.30 and 1am, then Khalil in all likelihood didn't do it, as he couldn't have made it to the garage forecourt in the time available.

This is a big deal as it narrows the time frame right down. Suddenly the prosecution has to show that the murder was done in a much smaller time frame, 12–12.30am if Khalil has to have time to walk to the garage, and that's problematic because of the dog walker, Jess Phillips.

Jess lived in one of the houses down the lane and on the night of the murder she took her pet labradoodle, Mazzy, for a quick walk in order for her to do her business. She took her usual route, turned right out of her driveway, walked a hundred and fifty yards down the lane, turned right and, unusually on that night, she walked into the car park of the World's End. Why do I say this was unusual? Because she would never go in at a weekend if there were cars in the car park; it was just too likely that there would be doggers or kids doing drugs. But not on this evening. On this evening she could see there were no cars in the car park, so she and Mazzy wandered in, Mazzy did her business and then they wandered out again, heading back home where Jess fixed herself a cup of hot chocolate before bed.

And the time of this walk? Jess is adamant it was at midnight. She was listening to Radio 4 and she set off just after the first headline after the midnight news. She says the walk took her a total of about fifteen to twenty minutes.

You see the problem for the prosecution? If the murder took place between 12 and 1am but Khalil wasn't at the scene, and nor was Lauren, between 12 and 12.25, then if Khalil was outside the garage then he couldn't have been at World's End after 12.30 (and at an average pace, never mind a stoned kid's pace, it's more like 12.10).

This doesn't even take into account the fifteen minutes he would have needed to meet her, kill her and then pretty much sprint away before getting to the garage.

What did the prosecution do? They just said the defence couldn't prove the figure in the dark coloured hoodie passing the garage was Khalil. It could have been some other kid in a dark hoodie passing this suburban garage right at the time Khalil had said he was there. The image was grainy and even though both sides paid tech experts to clean up the data and blow it up, it remained inconclusive. I've seen it and played it back maybe fifty times and I have some sympathy for both sides. There is five seconds of a young man in a dark hooded top and jeans who walks past the low brick wall that marks the boundary between the garage and the pavement. You can't make out his face, he's got his hands in his jean pockets and he looks like his head is down. The witnesses who were asked confirmed Khalil was wearing a navy blue hooded top and jeans the night of the party, and the prosecution didn't challenge this point in their case.

You can't conclusively say it's Khalil but you can't rule it out either, and what are the chances of a similarly dressed kid passing in front of the garage at this time of the night? I should mention that this garage is on a country road and it gets traffic, sure, but pedestrians? In the thirty minutes either side of the "Khalil" figure appearing, there were only two other pedestrians, walking together: two girls who called in to buy cigarettes. That's the kind of evidence lawyers sniff at, but hey, I'm not a lawyer, and if it were my money, I'd put it on the figure in the video being him.

We'll never know what the jury made of this. All we'll ever know is that they convicted Khalil after less than four hours' deliberation.

So, timings didn't help Khalil, but timings were also relevant, and to the advantage of Tom Ellis when the police questioned him. His interview was conducted by a much more junior officer than the officer who interviewed Khalil, by the way, a pretty sure sign of how the police viewed things if you ask me.

Tom said he stayed at the party after Khalil and Lauren left, and he got messed up according to his version of events, and it has to be said there is a lot of supporting evidence to back this up. Five witnesses say they remember Tom being at the party till the bitter end, somewhere around 3.30/4am. Memories of the exact time are, as you may have expected, a bit hazy on this point.

A bit more geography: the party was held at Shona Cunningham's house. She was a school friend of Lauren's. It's a beautiful new house, think glass frontage, a pool and a view over the River Dee to the dark Clwydian hills of North Wales. Below it is a coastal path that runs the length of the Wirral peninsula, some twenty-six miles. If you walk out of the garden of Shona's house there is a small earthen path; nothing official, just the route she and her family use to access the coastal path. Once you hit the coastal path, if you turn right and keep walking you'll get to World's End.

If you walked fast, say really fast, about four mph, you would reach the World's End car park in one hour fifteen minutes. As Khalil left the party at some time before 10.45, at the latest this means he could have walked there and reached the car park in the murder time frame. But it's also a good reason why Tom was never really considered a suspect by the police. How could he have made it there and back to the party given the witnesses who saw him there during the course of the evening?

The first of those witnesses was Mark Whatmough, known to the gang as Whatto. I've checked with him and he doesn't mind the description I'm going to give him: he was the go-to man for weed. Apologies to Mark's mother here; he's a successful GP now by the way. He recalls having a joint with Tom in the garden at around 11.20. How is he so sure? He had just realised he had run out of booze and papers and Tom suggested they drive to the local off-licence, but Mark got bummed out when he realised it would be shut as it had gone 11. So who said drugs are bad for your short-term memory? Mark turns out to be one of our more precise witnesses.

Other witnesses at the party are sketchy – they remember Tom being there, but try and pin any of them down and it's like trying to catch air in a fishing net.

All, that is, except Amy Wilder. She was a friend of Lauren's, one who coincidentally didn't help Khalil's argument that he was a model boyfriend as she testified at the trial that he had frequently rowed with her about the clothes she was wearing, who she was seeing and that theirs, contrary to Khalil's case, was a tempestuous relationship (I'll come back to this point). She could place Tom in place and time at the party. What are the two busiest places at a party? It's always the kitchen and the toilet, and this party was no exception. Now this house had three bathrooms (well, four, but the parents' master en suite was locked as was the bedroom; parents aren't all daft when they go away for the weekend).

A few minutes before midnight, Amy told police she was banging on the door of the downstairs bathroom, having repeated the same desperate banging on two bathrooms upstairs – but on each occasion she got the same answer: go forth and multiply.

So she did. She walked past the crowd by the pool, now thinning as the night got colder, and she made her way to the bottom of the garden. Down here there was a shed, an old swing and then a hedge, and beyond that the scrubland that ran down to the coastal path.

She adopted the position and answered the call of nature and was also multitasking, checking her messages on her mobile phone, hence how she was so specific on the time. She was anxious about battery life and checked it, when a voice in the darkness said, "Hi Amy" and that's when she noticed Tom sitting on the swing smoking a cigarette. She said she got the fright of her life and told him in strong, robust terms what she thought of him scaring her like that. And then she stormed off, leaving Tom sat on the swing. She told the police that this was at exactly 11.56pm.

And that was that. Her statement was just one of the many reasons why Tom was never considered as a suspect, and why should he have been? Sure, there was the argument in the kitchen with Khalil and Lauren, but so what? There was nothing linking him to the actual murder.

But Amy has been listening to the show and she has been in touch with me. Yesterday she sent me this email and I'm going to read it out for you. It changes everything:

"I thought I had to get in touch as I've been listening to the podcast and I always thought Khalil did it. I sort of still do but in fairness to

him, to his family and to me, I have to mention something about my statement I gave to police.

"When I gave my statement to the police it was exactly as I remembered it and was in response to my questions. They wanted to know how I knew what time it was, and I knew as I looked at my phone. They wanted me to be sure it was Tom, and it so was, and they asked me lots of questions to make sure I didn't make it up to help Tom. I didn't, I just told it like it is. Except of course that I didn't tell it exactly like it was. I didn't tell them that I was wearing black denim jeans and converse pumps, I didn't tell them that Tom's voice seemed heavy somehow and I still don't know exactly what I mean by that but it was. I didn't tell them that there were no stars in the sky because it was overcast and I didn't tell them that there was a bike propped up by the shed."

A bike.

You can go, easily, fourteen mph on a bicycle. In that time, for example, you could cycle the five miles to World's End along a coastal path in less than thirty minutes, say by 12.30am, and then back again in a similar time. If no one saw you leave or arrive at a busy party then it could look like you had never been away.

Of course, this may never have happened. But no one ever considered whether it was a possibility. And if someone else had the opportunity and if that someone was one of two people who the victim had been involved in a heated discussion with earlier in the evening, then wouldn't that have to cast some doubt on Khalil being the murderer? Wouldn't it have at the very least warranted more than the most junior officer on the murder enquiry taking Tom's witness statement?

I click the mouse and press the pause icon on the computer screen, stopping the voice recording. What I'm thinking of doing is not illegal, I think, although I'm no lawyer, but it is kind of unethical. I breathe in and then lower my head so my lips are nearly touching the microphone head. I click the record icon.

"So here's the deal: the police missed a trick but opportunity is nothing without motive. Next time on 'World's End: Pick One' I am going to give you motive."

I stop recording and save the WAV file to the hard drive and then immediately send a copy to Cathy.

She's going to be thrilled and the download figures for the next podcast in two weeks are going to be huge. I've basically named someone I think is the murderer and will be telling people why he did it. There's only one problem: I have no idea what Tom's motivation could have been for killing Lauren Grey.

CHAPTER FIVE

Hornets

I came late to the podcast world. It was Cathy who suggested it, as a way of getting "back into things slowly", which is how I recall her putting it. This was about three months after the "incident" and I know her and myself well enough to know that she saw that I needed something to work on to keep me sane. This was also around the time people were starting to ask questions about why I never seemed to leave the house.

Turns out podcasts are tremendously straightforward to do and I was good at them too. Once a broadcaster, always a broadcaster.

The way it works is like this. I record the podcast on a Wednesday and send it to my producer, Jane, on the same day. At this stage it's just a rough recording, me, my notes and a microphone, pretty much. I record directly onto my computer. I initially started with scripts, just reading them out, but it came across as stilted so now I just jot down the main points I wish to get out onto a legal pad and then start talking. The conversational style is key to making the listener feel as though you are talking directly to them.

Jane is a producer who I first met back when I was working at Radio Oxford. She now freelances, and she cleans the sound up, adds music and some effects and sends it back to me to check I'm happy. This is within twenty-four hours of me sending her the file with my recording on it. It's invariably great, and even if I have to make some slight tweaks, the final version is with Jane by Friday at the latest. She sends it to Bulldog Productions, a start-up trying to franchise a US model, and they add the ads and get it online by Saturday at six o'clock.

Saturdays are a busy day for Henry and Finn. There is Tae Kwondo in the morning, then Spanish lessons and usually a party or two to fit in before dinner so, I can often find myself alone for the whole day, sometimes longer.

The Saturday the "Timings" podcast goes out is one of those days.

Henry and Finn are at a party. I say party, but it's a Harry Potter themed garden event and Henry has already texted me saying we will have to take out a loan if we ever plan to hold a party for Finn's upcoming sixth birthday. The costume we hired for Finn cost £50 alone and the gift, an Xbox One educational game involving zombies and algebra, appeared on a suggested present list we received by email three weeks before the party. Not that I was thinking of the cost when I saw Henry's texts, but rather the fact that I can't foresee Finn having a party here anytime soon and the guilt made me hate Henry a little more for being insensitive in this text, which I know is entirely unreasonable of me, which has the effect of heightening that anger. Poor Henry – he never will realise life is unfair. It's the product of an expensive public-school education, a sense of invincibility and, although I mock him for it, there's no doubt part of me is envious of that confidence overcoat that shields him from life's more bitter truths.

As they won't be back till eight*ish*, I settle down on the sofa with a glass of Pinot Grigio and my iPad. Lil'Bitch wanders into the room and joins me, flopping down and then snuggling up against my thigh where she purrs as though powered by the warmth of my body.

After the podcast drops I like to check out the social media reaction. When I started the podcasts there was some initial interest based upon who I used to be, and the fact I'd been out of the public eye for a year without any explanation but for my press release at the time, stating that I wanted to spend more time with my family. But the initial download figures were nothing spectacular. What changed that was the power of social media. People began to get hold of the idea that Khalil was the victim of a miscarriage of justice and this small group were tweeters. The more they tweeted the more traffic flowed to the podcast website, and I called in a favour from some of my old BBC colleagues and did a couple of Skype interviews on the phenomena of podcasts and real-life crime cases. After that it became a snowball travelling downhill.

With the attention, of course, came some that was unwanted. The majority of emails, tweets, and even old-fashioned letters I get are supportive of the podcast and what I'm trying to do with it, but there is the darker side: people who are convinced of Khalil's guilt, either because of the facts as they see them, or worse because of who he is, a young Muslim man who was dating a pretty white girl.

I can deal with this though; it's a small price to pay for doing my job and frankly I have experience of real-world violence, so its puny online cousin can't even kick sand in my face as far as I'm concerned.

I hit Twitter and start browsing the podcast series *#worldsendpickone*. I called it that after something Mohammed had told me when he asked one of the police officers who arrested his brother about the reasons he had been arrested and his answer was "pick one".

Straight away I can see the number of tweets this episode has generated are substantially up from the usual amount. People are talking about the timings, swapping stories of how quick they can cycle five miles, and lots of them are saying they could easily, even if drunk, do the distance quicker than I estimated and that Tom is definitely in the frame.

There is a small and regular group of tweeters, the *#fitups*, who think the police framed Khalil and they are going crazy about the police not asking Amy whether there was a bike there at the time. Some think this is evidence of a deliberate omission, and the non-fitups think that this proves the incompetence of the police, and there is a lively debate going back and forth.

A third group think Amy has made the whole thing up because she was having a thing with Tom, or maybe he rejected her. This group are arguing with another group who think Tom set up the row in the kitchen in order to get Khalil to leave the party so he could try and make a move on Lauren. I won't lie, I love this speculation and the power of social media to get people thinking and talking. The thing most people are talking about is what I know about Tom's motivation and what the big reveal in my next podcast will be in a week's time. I've taken a risk and the thought of that is intoxicating. I would never have been allowed to do that in the mainstream media. Why did I do it? Maybe it was Frenchie's taunting emails or perhaps it was Mo's faith in me flushing something out, but at the moment I don't really care why. I gulp down my wine and replenish it with more from the bottle on the coffee table, and the more I drink the less I worry about what I am going to say and the more excited I feel about the success of this podcast.

I drink half my glass. I don't need to worry if I don't find anything more about Tom anyway as I don't have any intention of publishing anything untrue. If I don't flush anything out then on my head be it; I'll just say I don't have anything in the next podcast. No harm done. Some people will gripe and I may lose some listeners but there will be more listening anyway. I giggle out loud and Lil'Bitch looks at me with disgust and then leaps down onto the floor.

I finish my wine in a gulp.

"Go on, sod off then, Lil'Bitch!" I shout after her, which causes me to break into a fresh fit of giggles.

And then amongst the Twitter notifications popping up comes one I recognise – it's a new account with a familiar name, @FrenchDuck1044. He has been resurrected with a new twitter handle.

I read his tweet.

@frenchduck1044 Just bought you a ticket to the murder rape train choo choo you can join Khalil on there.

I don't know whether it's the wine – let's face it it's the wine – but before my brain can intervene I type:

@therealskelly replying to @frenchduck1044

Rape isn't funny and neither are you. Why bother? No date on a Saturday night?

As I hit send I can see him in his bedroom, dirty laundry on the floor, squirming with delight in a plastic chair as his computer delivers a bite. I expect invective so am surprised to get a coherent response:

@frenchduck1044 replying to @therealskelly

Bonsoir Sarah mon cherie. Simples. Because you want to free a murderer. He is guilty he should pay. All the guilty should pay.

It's like my fingers are working independently of my mind.

@therealskelly replying to @frenchduck1044

He might be innocent. Reasonable doubt maybe?

@frenchduck1044 replying to @thereaskelly

He did it. The jury knew it and you, yeah you know it. This is not a game.

@therealskelly replying to @frenchduck1044

How can you be so sure?

@frenchduck1044 replying to @therealskelly

He did it, it's plain as a pikestaff to us.

"Pikestaff" is an unusual word to see these days and I revise his age limit – over forty-five I reckon.

@therealskelly replying to @frenchduck1044

Us?

@frenchduck1044 replying to @therealskelly

There's a lot of us, out here, watching, listening and waiting.

@therealskelly replying to @frenchduck1044

If it annoys you stop listening. No need for rape/death threats.

I can see our exchange of tweets is being re-tweeted in huge numbers and I sense I might actually make progress with this man and, let's face it, the wine spurs me on.

@frenchduck1044 replying to @therealskelly

You don't listen to anything else we say. You feminazis only like weak men, minorities, gays, you don't want to hear what we have to say but you will. #freespeechbitch

@therealskelly replying to @frenchduck1044

Most people on here agree with me.

This last tweet gets re-tweeted in support, a lot.

@frenchduck1044 replying to @therealskelly

U are not the many. U liberal elite. U kill us. U traitors to us. We are the many, you are the few and we are coming.

@therealskelly replying to @frenchduck1044 I am with justice that's all, what's the problem with that?

@frenchduck1044 replying to @therealskelly

Khalil killed Lauren, Muslims rape white women and your type don't care. It's you who are the racists. Every culture matters but ours.

@therealskelly replying to @frenchduck1044

This is islamophobia. I should block you.

I pause as tweets role in one after the other saying "block the racist".

@frenchduck1044 replying to @therealskelly

I am the hydra Sarah, you know that already though don't you. Go ahead do it to me. I'm coming.

So, I block him.

A few seconds pass and *beep*, a Twitter notification. It's from @Deliahflow98; she's been one of the most positive tweeters in support of the show.

I gasp.

@Deliahflow98 replying to @therealskelly

Guess who? Your blood will lube my dick.

And then @Corbynslovechild, another enthusiastic re-tweeter.

@Corbynslovechild replying to @therealskelly

I'm coming for you and your kids fucktart. We are many and watching. Frenchie Duckie go quack everywhere.

Ping. Another notification; more abuse from a previously friendly account. I stop checking after five more similar messages. I block all the sock puppet accounts. It must have taken him days to set them all up and engage with me and others on a regular basis. Frenchie clearly has a lot of time on his hands and a real grudge. I consider calling the police and just as quickly dismiss the idea. The police would want to ask too many questions and I know that the accounts will be impossible to trace. It's why Twitter is so beloved of the anonymous sociopath.

The upside is my tweet exchange is being re-tweeted at a staggering level and already requests are flying in for interviews. I guess that's what a bit of mystique around my disappearance from public life and my newfound fame as a crime reporter can do. But I'm not doing them. I am in control of my career and who gets access to me now. I will not be public property again.

I check the time. 7.15pm. Finn and Henry are normally back by now but I don't want to send a text just because they are 15 minutes late. That would be crazy. But the fact is, Frenchie's Spartacus moment has freaked me out a little bit.

I check my emails. There is a lot of congratulatory stuff and I can't say I don't enjoy reading that, so I do – well, only the ones from people I want to like me.

The BBC is really after me and there is an email from my old editor at News London; he wants me to come into the studio "if I feel up to it" (what does he know?).

There's also a Facebook message from Hannah. She's been monitoring my Twitter feed and has seen Frenchie's attacks. Seeing her message arrive blows away the digital poisons cloud surrounding me. Hannah is, aside from Cathy, the friend I feel closest too. Part of that of course is how similar we are: she is two years older than me, lives in North London (Islington), is accordingly house rich but cash poor, shops at the same places I do, likes the same music, reads the same paper online (*Guardian* natch), has a child the same age as mine (a girl, Natasha) and most importantly, she is also outside inhibited, a phrase we came up with together when drunkenly exchanging messages about being housebound. In her case, her husband left her after having an affair so it's so much worse for her, but having someone I can confide in, who understands, has made life these last six months bearable. We "met" on Mumsnet in a thread dealing with agoraphobia, a word we have both vowed never to repeat.

Are you ok with the trolls my little fucktart? xxx

I text her back and tell her I've had tougher steaks than these guys.

These men and their threats, do you think it is because they were starved of the teat as babes? :-)

I type quickly but delete a "LOL" as I know it both ages and shames me:

It's the lack of sex, it's been scientifically proven to cause being a total wanker.

The reply is classic Hannah, and makes me genuinely laugh out loud:

Christ, if that's the criteria I am the queen of wankers, actually I quite like that, it's going to be my new twitter handle. Listen I have to run, gotta burn some pasta for Tash. You sure you ok hun?

I assure her I am.

It's nice to be wanted and cared for. I check the time again. 8.20. When does a little late become a worrying late? Ten more minutes and I'll send a text. I don't want Henry to think I'm falling apart.

And then with a ping an email drops into my mailbox and as it drops so does my heart.

It's from Toby Grey, Lauren's little brother. I say little; he was little when she was murdered twelve years ago. Now he's eighteen.

I open it.

Hey Sarah,

You contacted my family before you started broadcasting your podcast, do you remember? I do. I gave an interview to you over the phone and you promised me something in return, you promised me and my family that if anything ever turned up that pointed to someone else killing my sister you would tell us first. I was comfortable with you exploring the case, as you know I'm training to be a lawyer, and I was happy for you to investigate as we only ever wanted Lauren's killer brought to justice but I've just had my mother on the phone for the last 30 minutes sobbing. You know Tom was a friend to us all after Lauren died and he's still in our lives and now we find out that he had the time to be involved, and if we wait another week, a cliffhanger to you, torture for my family, we get to find out why he may have wanted to kill my sister. We won't be waiting with baited breath or excitement for your revelation, we will be waiting in dread, terror, confusion and misery. You should have told us you were going down this route and now you should tell me straight away what you know about Tom and why you think he had any motivation to murder my sister.

This isn't a game or a documentary for us, it's our lives and you are ripping open old wounds. Contact me if you know something. We deserve to know.

Toby Grey.

I shut my eyes.

"Fuck, fuck, fuck!"

How could I have been so stupid and insensitive? I start to shiver and then tears are running down my face.

I flop back into the couch and then suddenly the doorbell is ringing and I'm in a foetal position and the bell rings and rings and rings but I'm not opening that door, not ever again.

CHAPTER SIX

The waterline

I shut the door.

Henry and Finn are gone again for the day and won't be back till six. It's just me and Lil'Bitch and my hundred thousand podcast subscribers. There's been a somewhat leap in listeners since the last podcast, helped by all the publicity and the fact that PixieDixie, a millennial Instagram and Twitter goddess with a following of over two million, re-tweeted the abuse I was receiving under *#everydaydigitalrape*.

I spent all of Sunday in bed. Henry insisted on it after the trauma of Saturday evening. He and Finn had stopped off at a Leon's on the way home – that was why they were late – and Henry's phone had been dead so he couldn't text me. He told me that Finn kept saying, "Mummy is going to be worried." He feels proud that our son was so empathetic but I feel nothing but shame that our six-year-old is so aware of how pathetic I am.

When I didn't answer the front door, Henry had known immediately something was wrong. He had put Finn back in the car as he didn't want him coming with him; he was scared of what he may find and I feel such guilt that my son was left in the car, such shame that Henry has to think like this about me. He had run down the alley at the back of the house, climbing over the garden wall before letting himself in with the keys to the patio doors. He found me curled up on the sofa sobbing. There was a pool of red wine on the carpet and I tried to pass things off as me just having had too much to drink. Henry was happy to play along – it saved us both an awkward conversation – but a day in bed recovering from "my hangover" was the medicine Henry insisted I take. He took Finn to see his mother in St Albans and I lay unsleeping and corpse-like under our goose down duvet, warm, secure and safe.

When, later that evening, he had returned, he tentatively asked me if everything was okay as though he was stepping out on a rope bridge strung across a bottomless abyss and I gave him, and me, a pass and said it was because I was on my period and I swear I could see relief flood into his eyes as he realised we weren't going to have to talk about the real reasons for his wife being a total basket case.

Instead I emailed Hannah and told her what had happened with Toby and how this had caused me to collapse and how this sort of thing happened all the time since the incident.

Hannah took some time to respond; she often doesn't reply straight away. She has her own life of course, but when she did reply, it was with her usual knack of making me feel better immediately.

You fucked up. Do it better next time, call them and explain the position. You didn't kill his sister, you are finding out who did. Call him, make it right, you can do that right?

I can do that.

That night I sleep well.

When I emerge, the light of the day has been almost bludgeoned to death by the early arrival of a thuggish dark sky and I realise that I have slept deep into a wintery Monday morning.

I had waited under the covers for Henry and Finn to leave. I even pretended to be asleep when Henry came into the room to say goodbye, and that pretending must have turned into the real thing. I check my phone; it's 11.30am. I am the lazy slut I always suspected I was and this thought carries a sting of comfort. Is there anything more satisfying than the warm, sick embrace of guilt?

Guilt and shame can give you a hangover as sure as booze can, but in the same way, they start to wear off as a new day begins. I type a quick response to Toby Grey.

Dear Toby

I am sorry about the shock you and your family must have received hearing the show on Saturday. I should have warned you.

You know that my show is about the unsoundness of Khalil Bukhari's conviction and not a police investigation. As such I am not making any allegations against Tom nor suggesting that he killed your sister but rather I am attempting to show that the police and the CPS focused on Khalil at the expense of all other possible explanations because they needed a quick arrest after the Charles Brownhill debacle. One thing I can tell you now is that I do not know the identity of your sister's murderer and if I did, or if I had evidence of this, I would tell you right away. However, that does not mean that in the forthcoming podcasts you will not hear things that may be difficult as I will be focusing on other possibilities to the one that the police pursued. I am sorry if this causes you or your family distress but it is my journalistic duty.

I will always remain a friend of you and your family and have nothing but the greatest of respect for how you have handled the situation you have been thrust into. I do this partly to honour your sister's memory and to ensure that she receives the justice she was not granted in life.

Yours sincerely

Sarah Kelly

I click send and sure, I feel a little bit dirty, but this is my job, I tell myself, and I even manage to half believe that if I don't think too deeply about it.

Although this old Georgian terrace looks and feels modern inside, the bones of it are old and rickety and despite the heating having clicked on at 7am– as it does every morning – it's still cold after several hours of battling against a chill that seems to have tightened around the house like a fist. I grab one of Henry's old jumpers from his wardrobe and put it on before even attempting to descend into the colder parts of the house below the bedroom.

On the hall landing I hesitate because there is a noise coming from the other bedroom, the box room, next to our bedroom. It sounds like someone, or something, shuffling. I step closer and very carefully, and quietly, place my ear next to the door. There's nothing and then there it is again: a scraping sound and the scrunching of papers as though someone is taking their time to step in a certain way to avoid making a sound.

There is someone behind the door; as I think this, goose bumps sprout all along my arms. Maybe they didn't leave after all, and perhaps Henry is clearing the room of boxes like he is always promising.

"Henry?"

My voice catches and crackles; it is the sound of fear and the voice of a victim and I hate it. I won't be that person. Hannah and me swore to each other that even though we are trapped inside we wouldn't be timid within our own, admittedly restricted, environments.

As I think this, part of my mind makes an unconscious decision and I'm almost surprised to see the door opening in response to a fierce push from me.

There is a screaming sound, a sudden, violent movement and something large and black flies straight at me.

I cover my face with my hands and it hits them square on, hard and heavy and then, making a noise of terror and fear, hits the ceiling. The pigeon, for that's what it is, is a city bird, oil-slick coloured and full of sores. It lands on one of the boxes piled in the corner of the room. They mostly contain my books. Henry likes the minimalist look and books don't really fit into that scheme, so this room is filled with boxes containing all my "nick-nacks", as he calls my lifetime collection of books and pre-family material. The pigeon immediately shits all down the side of the box.

Its crimson eyes regard me with fear and I wonder whether it can see the fear in mine. At least I now know where Lil'Bitch is getting the birds from; the window is open. Henry must have left it like that to let some air in the room. He's always complaining about the dust in this room setting off his allergies. Christ knows how long it's been left like this.

"Go on then, shoo," I say to the pigeon.

It hops from one leg to another and defecates once more.

Feeling foolish, I point at the window.

"You need to leave. You know, outside? Female pigeons – or male – await outside! Whatever, it's a diverse city. Go on."

The pigeon shows no sign of moving.

I take a step forward and it backs away until it's near the wall. I could, I suppose, try and grab it and throw it out of the window but all I can see happening is something involving feathers, shit and the likelihood of a dead pigeon.

"The way out is there." I point to the patch of grey sky framed by the Velux window.

I swear the pigeon looks up at the window and then it hops from one foot to another again.

"I'll take that as an acknowledgment."

But it doesn't move.

I'm talking to a pigeon and it is trolling me. I decide against trying to grab hold of it.

"It's your lucky day, pigeon, I need coffee."

I retreat and close the door behind me. Henry can put a mask on and get rid of it later.

I walk down the stairs to the second floor. On this floor there are two more bedrooms and a family bathroom and I can't resist taking a look in Finn's bedroom. He's obsessed with *Star Wars* at the moment. His duvet has a picture of the Death Star, Darth Vader and Obi Wan Kenobi on it, and all available shelf space and every horizontal surface is covered in plastic figurines and *Star Wars* related books. It is like stepping back in time to my bedroom in 1984 and it brings me a sense of closeness with him that sometimes I struggle with when he is actually here. I sit down on his bed and then lie down, stretched out, face first, smelling the sheets, smelling my boy. The emotions this brings are almost too much for me at times, the sheer love and with it the almost crushing fear about what the world, about what adults, will do to him and his innocence. I think of Finn and then Khalil, sitting alone in a cell. What does his mother feel? This last thought is what stops me from spending the rest of the day on his bed and somehow, despite the heaviness I feel, I move my legs and get off Finn's bed.

I close the door and head downstairs to the real world.

The stairs lead to the hallway and from here I can turn right to the kitchen and open-plan living area, or left to the front door at the end of the hallway. I head left, I always do. Henry is on strict orders to lock the door from the outside, but I decide to check just in case he forgot. He never does of course and the door is locked. But one thing he can't do from the outside is slide the two bolts home. I do this and the noise of them slamming home is as satisfying as the first hit of a cigarette when I used to smoke.

On the way back to the kitchen I stop for a moment next to the closed door. The door that leads to the dining room. It's a plain, waxed pine door, old and worn, with a dark iron door handle and lock. Standing here makes me feel colder than anywhere in the rest of the house but I know it's not the temperature that makes me shiver here and at least I'm not shaking so that's progress.

Suddenly, from behind me, there is a loud bang on the front door. It's a man's knock, I can tell, a man who means business and expects the door to be opened. Men knock on doors like they demand to be let in. Even Finn knocks on the door like this.

I hold my breath and slowly, so as not to be heard, turn around and face towards the door. There is no glass of course, that would be a weak point, a culvert under the castle, but there is a spy hole. I'm not moving that way though; instead I slide, as quiet as a mouse – a scared, terrified mouse – my socks slipping on the oak floor like ice.

There is another urgent barrage of heavy knocks.

The ball of tension in my stomach escapes and with a moan I run back into the kitchen, hoping he won't hear my muffled footsteps. Once there I check the video camera feed on the intercom. There are two cameras: one is positioned just below Finn's bedroom window and gives an overhead view of the man standing fifteen yards away from me, on the other side of the door, and the second camera is at doorbell level with a fish-eye lens which gives me a slightly warped face-on view. The man is big, gym sculpted and bald; his shiny head speaks of nightclubs, the smell of cheap alcohol, fast food, sweat and violence.

His round face looks angrily at the camera and I know he knows I'm watching him. He's wearing a black leather jacket that stretches tautly against his back, barely restraining his bulk.

I have no idea who he is. I'm not expecting anyone or any deliveries and Henry knows better than to arrange anything without informing me of the exact time I can expect someone to be appear at the threshold.

I rationalise away, my rational brain providing me with the ordinary explanations one by one, but each "it's just a market survey, pollster, canvasser, tinker or dishrag seller" is eaten alive by the rampaging, adrenaline-fuelled beast called MURDER AND RAPE that kills everything I can throw at it.

The man mouths "fuck" and then kneels down on his haunches and shoves something through the letterbox. Once he's satisfied it's through, he gets up and retreats down the path, leaving the gate open, and then disappears from the camera's frame.

I wait thirty seconds to make sure he's not returning and then run to the door. There's a plain brown manila envelope on the mat.

For a few seconds I stare at it like it's alive and could bite me and then I tell myself to stop being so fucking paranoid, and this thought makes me snort out loud with derision at my own weakness.

I pick it up; it's addressed to me and carries a return address of a street in the city. I tear open the envelope and remove the crisp white letter within. There's an embossed font declaring the letter is from Fingersmiths Solicitors.

Dear Mrs Kelly

We are instructed by our client Tom Ellis and hereby give you immediate notice to cease and desist from making further defamatory comments in respect of our client.

On 8 November 2017 you broadcast an episode of your weekly podcast (title World's End:Pick One), and made comments which we and our client consider to be untrue and defamatory, namely that our client was implicated in the murder of Lauren Grey.

As you are fully aware, our client co-operated fully with the police investigation and as a result of that investigation the police concluded there was no material evidence to link him in any way to that murder. He was, and has never been, a suspect in that case and your attempts to link him to the murder are without foundation in law or fact.

The real culprit, Khalil Bukhari, is currently serving a life sentence in HMP Strangeways, a fact which of itself makes your assertions defamatory and providing a clear cause of action in libel against you by our client.

You have defamed our client by raising matters that do not even amount to circumstantial evidence but rather are pure speculation on your part. This has been done as far as we can see for no legitimate reason, as it clearly does not relate to the appeal process currently being undertaken by Mr Bukhari and therefore we can only conclude that the motivation for such comments is for entertainment and the furtherance of your professional career.

We have sent a copy of this letter to OFCOM and our client is at this stage reviewing his legal options which may include a claim in damages or injunctive relief. We insist you make no further such allegations or unfounded insinuations linking our client to the murder of Lauren Grey. We reserve, to the fullest, all our client's legal rights.

Yours sincerely

Howard Beard

Shit.

I place the letter down on the worktop. They are right of course, I probably have defamed him. I'm no legal expert, but I've certainly speculated on his involvement and hinted at it on the podcast. But I don't feel any guilt about this, I do about everything else but this, in fact. Instead of guilt I feel something else, I feel my journalistic senses tingling. I've lifted a stone and things are moving. Tom Ellis may not be involved, and I have only raised the issue to highlight the focus that was paid to Khalil Bukhari, but one thing I do know already from my research is that Tom Ellis is one twenty-four carat gold-plated shit and I'm not wasting any sympathy on him.

Mo brought a file to our first meeting. I can still remember his excitement as he spread the contents of his canvas shoulder bag over my kitchen table; it was the breaking of nervous tension for someone who was finally being listened to. It was strange watching this urbane man, whose hands usually wielded a scalpel, become twitchy, words tumbling over each other as they fought for prominence. I've seen it before of course; it's the rush of finally having an audience willing to listen, and I witnessed it on many occasions during my professional career, that moment when the frustration of being ignored, denied, is replaced by a voice being heard, and that listener is feeding their hope. It's an intimate moment as well, from subject to journalist, in much the same way as patient and doctor.

Mo had been working on the case since his brother's conviction and, together with what he and the family could raise and donations from the local community, they had funded the legal bills for Khalil's so far unsuccessful defence and appeals.

As part of the legal process Mo collected an enormous amount of information on everyone at that party the night Lauren was killed and there were thick lever-arch files filled with, on the face of it, reams of printouts of social media screenshots detailing the online lives that those kids had gone on to lead. But by far the most interesting information concerned Tom Ellis. Right from the start Mo told me that he thought there was something too good to be true about Tom and so, it appeared, it was the case.

Tom's lever arch file was the first Mo handed to me and he told me I had to read this before any of the others. And so I did, and as I read I learned about Tom Ellis.

At school Tom was a good guy, so it seemed, never in trouble, excellent grades, a brilliant sportsman. Mo had a private detective interview his teachers. They all said he was a model student save for one. The teacher in question was his English teacher, Mr Cartwright. He told Mo's investigator about an incident regarding George Orwell's *1984*, one of the set texts for that year's A level exam. In a classroom discussion about the book they had talked about the use of metaphor and in particular the phrase Orwell uses when O'Brien tells Winston "if you want a vision of the future, imagine a boot stamping on a human face, forever."

Apparently, Tom's reaction differed from the rest of the class. In the midst of the discussion of why this was so terrifying Tom had commented, "Depends if you're the one wearing the boot or not."

A glib remark maybe? But one the English teacher said left a deep impression on him as no child he had taught had ever said such a thing. He felt it important enough to recount it over ten years after the event.

But aside from that there was initially very little to suggest that there was anything fishy about him. Tom came from a good family with no reports or evidence of any dysfunction. There was certainly nothing in his background to suggest he would be capable of being a killer.

Setting aside an old teacher's recollections (and this was an English teacher who generally tend, by their nature, to be unrepentant romantics in my opinion), where things began to get interesting was in the stuff Mo dug up that happened a long time after the murder. All of it is completely irrelevant to the legal case of course, and therefore inadmissible, but fascinating to the journalist and amateur student of human behaviour which I, as most journalists I know whether they care to admit or not, happen to be.

The murder took place in 2006 and in the years since the murder it is fair to say that Tom Ellis has led an interesting life.

He had been in the combined cadet force at school and when he left the sixth form, instead of going to Durham University where he had secured a place to study PPE, he joined the army. This was late 2007 and he would have known that there was a high chance of him being deployed to a combat zone. This happened to him and he served two tours in Iraq and one in Afghanistan. He was eventually invalided out in 2009 after being blown up by a roadside IED. He got off lightly with a perforated eardrum, two of his colleagues were seriously injured and he was honourably discharged at a captain's rank.

Our war hero went on to join a property investment company, Wheeler and Sons. One of the eponymous "sons" was a fellow officer in his old unit and fixed him up with a job when he hit "civvy street". He went on to make, lose and make back again a small fortune in the turbulent times after the global financial crash. He found time to marry his wife Emma, a cousin to the same son who had set him up with a job. Life seemed to be working out for Tom.

On the day of Tom's marriage to Emma, Khalil was in the fifth year of his life sentence with an early parole date fixed for 2025. Tom and Emma had their only child, Ben, in 2016. All this is easily found on the Internet and Mo had screenshots of it all, local news sites reporting on the injured war hero, wedding photographs, Facebook entries, the works. I wonder whether the work of a private detective is easier in the days of social media or whether it will make them redundant, as we are all detectives these days? Henry won't go to a dinner party, when we used to go out to dinner parties that is, without Googling all of the guests in advance and making a long list of assumptions based on their profiles as though the truth of who we are online bears anything more than a passing resemblance to the real "us".

But this wasn't the real juice; the real juice was that in June 2016 Tom Ellis was arrested after a complaint of domestic violence. He had turned up drunk at the family home, started shouting to be let in and then, when Emma opened the door, he got into an argument with her. This is confused and I haven't seen the police report but somehow Emma hit her head and had to be rushed to hospital. A neighbour called the police and he was arrested soon after.

And the weird thing is, he wasn't charged. To this day Tom Ellis has a clean record. Mo's private investigators got the details of the arrest from a neighbour who had witnessed the drama, and then from a special constable who had been on hand when the arrest took place. "A bog-standard domestic" is how he had described it, which probably tells you as much as you need to know about the ubiquity of male-on-female violence in the UK.

Why wasn't he charged? I don't know, but I can guess that Emma chose not to press charges. It's not unusual for the victim of spousal abuse to not co-operate but here's the thing, was this the first time Tom Ellis had walked away from justice?

All inadmissible evidence, but the lead wasn't a dead one. Firstly, it gave us an insight into Tom's character and secondly, just maybe Emma would speak to us. This was a false hope, however, despite both me and Cathy attempting to contact Emma by phone, text, email and in Cathy's case actually door-stepping the poor woman. The most we had got was "I've got nothing to say, if you continue to harass me I'm calling the police", which Cathy had received on the doorstep.

But the third thing, and the most important thing this gave me, was the confidence to pick up Tom's lawyer's letter, tear it up and throw it in the bin. Tom Ellis is a wife beater and a coward when it comes to legal action. His job in the city is high profile, lots of networking required – the regimental tie and pride – and the last thing he wants is a court case, so Tom Ellis and Fingersmiths are just going to have to go and fuck themselves.

Feeling empowered, I say "yeah" out loud. Lil'Bitch, as is usually the case, is my only witness to this defiant moment.

"You know it, Lil'Bitch," I say to her and she blinks. I take this as an acknowledgement, and it's the best I'm going to get.

I crack open my laptop and open up Outlook. I have a motive to discover in time for the next podcast in five days' time.

I type:

Dear Emma,

I know that you have ignored my requests to give me an interview before and that you have been very clear in this but you should know, unless you already do, that in my last broadcast I mentioned new information about the night that Lauren was murdered. Specifically, Amy Wilder has given a statement to the effect that when she saw Tom shortly before midnight there was a bicycle nearby. The significance of course is that Tom can now be at the murder scene in the relevant time frame. I am making no accusations but I will be revealing further information in the next podcast which will cast serious doubt on the safety of Khalil's conviction.

I hesitate, as I don't like lying to get a witness to co-operate but in the spirit of empowerment, fuck it.

I want, need, your help and I think you may know something about the character of your husband that may shine a light on this case. I want to give you the opportunity to do this before that podcast goes out as I anticipate you may receive more media enquires if you stay silent.

This is approaching blackmail and is certainly bordering on harassment but the scales are easy to balance: one rich middle-class woman's embarrassment versus a potentially innocent man rotting in prison. In for a penny, I think, and continue typing.

And one last thing you should know, as it is relevant to this case in every way: Khalil Bukhari's mother Yaminah was diagnosed with incurable liver cancer a month ago, and she has been given six to nine months to live, so as you can see anything you might know about what happened, to you or to Lauren, could mean the difference between her seeing her son on the outside before she dies. Please contact me.

It is so shitty, but I hit send anyway. The way I figure it is that I can do things the police can't, and who knows, maybe an innocent man will walk free?

Being a shit makes me thirsty so I make myself an espresso. There's something about the ritual of grinding the beans, Ethiopian in this case, smelling the freshly ground coffee, spooning it into the holder, patting it down and then the satisfying chug of the machine as it forces hot water through the coffee mix, that I find at once relaxing, and at the same time it is an act that symbolises everything I love about my life at this moment, at the beginning of what is looking like is going to be a dark century.

My Mac pings.

It's an email from Emma; it's short and to the point.

I've given you my answer already, I will not be changing my mind. LEAVE ME AND MY FAMILY ALONE. And STOP your fake news it helps nobody.

I can't say I expected anything different but I am disappointed nevertheless. I wonder if she has actually listened to my podcast and then find myself snorting out loud. Of course she has listened, I'm talking each week about her husband and the murder of one of his friends. Who wouldn't be able to listen to that?

Back to the coffee, and this is my favourite bit. I hit the button and the machine starts to chug and then the water is pouring out of the machine. Solitary pleasures, I think, and feel slightly sad.

But this is where social media comes in and as soon as I have made my coffee I take a seat at the table and WhatsApp Hannah.

Speaking with Hannah is like bathing in cold water after the heat of Twitter, Facebook and all the other social media channels. It is the joy of real connection versus the superficiality of the instant. As well as our "averseness to the outside" we have other things in common too: we both studied English at university (me at Bristol, her at Manchester) and we both adored Sylvia Plath, both had major crushes on Patti Smith and Thom Yorke and on politics we were even more simpatico. We chimed. And perhaps the most important thing of all, something that Hannah first mentioned a few weeks after we first started swapping messages – she too was trapped. She told me after inviting me to meet up for a coffee. She only lives a few miles away in Crouch End, not far from Hampstead, and she invited me to her flat. I put her off, made up an excuse and I told her, I just came out with it: "I can't leave the house". I hadn't told anyone before. Even with Cathy it was unspoken, a topic we skirted around. She had replied, "Thank God, I HATE leaving the house". It was an invitation and so easy to open up to her, to tell her without the shame I feel when talking to people I've known all my life, my friends, that I too was frightened, no that's the wrong word, prevented by myself, from leaving the house. Her reply was "Hell is *Homes Under the Hammer*", a reference to the daytime TV show of your nightmares and one which I became too familiar with in the early months of my confinement. I decide to WhatsApp her.

How's your day?

A few seconds and *online now* appears on the status bar.

Hannah: Three coffees, four cigarettes, but it's been 6 days since my last Homes Under the Hammer.

Me: HA! I'm cold turkey for 27 days now.

Hannah: Yeah but you've gone full dirty, Colombo, TJ Hooker, Magnum PI, and I hear on the grapevine that Murder She Wrote is your new fix you sick bitch…

Me: Guilty as charged. I can't get enough of La Lansbury. How's Tash?

Hannah: Good, got into a tizzy at school with another girl who claimed she would marry Harry Styles but Tash wasn't having that oh no, a call from the school entailed. All sorted now. How's tricks your end kidda?

Me: OK, the show is really taking off and guess what?

Hannah: You did it with the pizza delivery boy when he dropped round your Hawaiian?

Me: I would never order a pizza with fruit on it, I'm not a barbarian dahling.

Hannah: Get you posh Hampstead types, it would need to be pomegranate or dragon fruit.

Me: I left the house, nothing massive, just the back garden but hey progress!

Hannah: OMFG that's amazing. No panic attack, no skiddy knickers, actual real outside. I am as proud as I was when Tash did her first potty. Seriously that is amazing news. I am going to have an extra cigarette and a large wine to celebrate, maybe even a sneaky Homes under the…

Me: NO!!!! I won't be responsible.

Hannah: OK I'll summon up my will power and fags and booze it is. Listen sorry to do this but have to run. Gotta work call in 1 min and I really can't afford to fuck up a job that allows me to work from home, such times to be alive and be an agoraphobic ha!

Me: Go on I'll catch you later and never mention the A word again!

Hannah: Will do and just so you know I am like super mega proud of you.

I finish my coffee. What I should do is start writing the next podcast script but the god of procrastination is helped out by the fact that I don't have a goddamn idea of how to proceed, and the house is filthy and really needs a clean. I regret getting rid of the cleaner we had but it seemed too much what with me being at home all the time and our income reduced, so now I do it and it is the perfect excuse for not writing, so I don my marigolds, dig out the Dyson and head upstairs.

The cleaning, and by this I mean a good clean, not a real full-metal-jacket let's-do-this-thing clean, but also not a quick whizz around with a duster, but the weekly clean, takes me three hours. Today I manage it in two hours forty-five minutes, a fact I put down to the music choice for today's clean, Daft Punk and Goldfrapp, the higher BPM's propelling me around the house like a superstar cleaning DJ.

When I slump back down at the table with my second coffee of the day, I can see my phone notifying me I have thirty-five new emails. Hoping Emma has changed her mind, I open the mail account. It's amazing how our eyes are drawn to the most important things first – it's because they evolved to recognise danger, the Sabre-toothed tiger stalking us in the dark – and my eye is drawn amongst all the emails to a subject line that makes my stomach ball into a terrified knot of tension.

Subject: Finn is such a lovely boy

I click and open the email.

You blocked me on Twitter diddums. Can't stand another point of view or does the truth just hurt that little bit too much?

Fury and fear hit me like a tidal wave and I type a response.

Touch my child and I'll fucking kill you. Where did you get my email address you sad sack of shit?

With a whoosh it's gone before I, or my common sense, can stop it.

Ping. A reply almost immediately.

Ha, you don't like it when people poke their noses in eh! Such a hypocrite, you liberals are all the same, you don't like it do you? Or maybe you do? I've seen your pictures, you used to be hot before you had that child. I wouldn't touch you now – I bet no one touches you now.

Common sense struggles with an urge to throw my phone across the kitchen table, and luckily it wins. I go straight into the settings and block his email. How long will it take him to get another account, a minute, less?

"Fuck." I say it loudly enough that Lil'Bitch, lounging on the kitchen radiator, turns her head to look at me quizzically.

"Yeah, yeah, I know."

I blow out through my lips, making a raspberry sound. I used to do this all the time as a child, especially when my mother told me that I'd never get a husband if I made this noise. It makes me feel better right away.

Ping.

I look down at the screen. xcalibur5yt@hotmail.com has been replaced by traitorsgate45657@yahoo.com. The subject line is "You can run but…"

I delete it and block the new address. Before I've even done this, *ping*, another email, this one from Frenchiefindyou3456@gmail.com.

I delete it and then another ping, like a bang on the door. Subject line, "I'm not going away". It follows the rest into the junk, and then there's another, and this time I hesitate because of the subject line which makes my throat constrict in panic. It's titled "Outside Now" and there's an attachment.

I click to open the email.

What a lovely house you have Sarah.

I download the attachment, oblivious to every Internet warning.

It's a JPEG file and it opens in my photos app.

My hand goes to my mouth as I recognise my front door. Red gloss paint shining in the low November morning sun. I can even see the copy of the local paper sticking out the letterbox; I heard the paperboy deliver it earlier this morning.

Something clicks and kills the fear. I hear a snarl and realise with surprise that it's coming from my throat.

I yank open the top kitchen drawer and I pull out the biggest bread knife in there, and I charge down the hall and I get to the front door and then I'm pulling back bolts and then my hand is on the latch and all I need to do is move my hand an inch and the door will click open but I can't because what if he is there? I lift my hand off the latch and slowly I back away from the door.

CHAPTER SEVEN

Marigold

"What did the police say?"

Cathy is standing in my back garden smoking a roll-up cigarette. I'm sipping coffee, standing on the threshold, and pretending I don't want to join her.

"They sent round a special constable. He took a copy of the email, said they probably wouldn't be able to trace it and that in any event taking a picture of someone's door wasn't a crime. He even said it was a little like a more modern version of knock and run he used to play as a kid. I think he was trying to reassure me."

Cathy tips her head back and exhales a plume of smoke.

"Did he think it could be, well, you know?"

I shake my head but say nothing.

Cathy is looking at me suspiciously and then she points the tip of her cigarette at me so that embers fall like dying fireflies to the ground. "You didn't mention it did you?"

"It wasn't him so there was no reason to mention it."

Cathy drops the fag and grinds it into oblivion with the heel of her leather boot.

"That is so fucking typical of them for not having a crayon to join the fucking dots. And" – she jabs her fagless finger at me – "of you for not telling them. How do you know it wasn't him?"

I want to tell her everything, her more than anybody, and the act of not telling her causes adrenaline to flood my nervous system, making me feel shaky and sick, but more powerful than that is the shame I feel. It easily swallows the adrenaline and I know I won't tell her.

I know because it wasn't him, the man who attacked me twelve months ago; it couldn't possibly be him.

"It's just a troll who got hold of my address. The man who…" I hesitate, searching for a word and plump for "attacked" as the real word I want to use couldn't ever come close to the terror, the vulnerability, the shame, the fear, the clinical detachment and the banality of the survival, so why bother? "He wouldn't play silly knock and run games and why would he risk getting caught over something so trivial?"

Cathy looks unconvinced.

"You should have told him about it. They could have" – she throws a hand in the air – "cross-checked their databases or whatever it is that they do these days."

"For weirdo men who give women a hard time on Twitter? We're going to need a bigger database."

She giggles. "Yeah, yeah, *Jaws* and sexual violence. You know there's a whole theory that *Jaws* is actually all about men's fear of the vagina?"

This is too much and we both collapse into hysterical giggles.

Cathy comes back into the house and slides the French doors shut behind her. I slip in behind her and turn the key in the lock.

"You should block them all you know, or just come off social media altogether; it's a fucking cesspit out there."

I shrug.

"I can't, it's all of the outside I have at the moment and I need that."

"You shouldn't have to put up with it, rape and death threats, fucking stupid men and their violence."

"But it's just the world isn't it? It's always been this way, it's just now they can express the thoughts in their head anonymously. Most of them would never dream of acting on it, you know that. Social media is just one long boring, drunken uncle's pub rant sometimes, that's all. The rest of the time it's this fabulous place where everything is and can be discussed; it's the most empowering thing that's happened in my lifetime. And real violence? I know that it comes from real fists, not," – I hold up my phone – "bedroom warriors like fucking Frenchie here."

Cathy backs off. She knows I hold the trump card here and to my slight shame I just played it.

"So, we have an episode to write and you've set us a pretty big task: to come up with a possible motive." She raises a finger to silence me. "Which is not defamatory and supported by evidence, and you have until I return from your bathroom to do it."

She stomps out of the room without a backward glance.

I look at the papers spread on the table and then back to the blinking white, empty screen of the Mac on the kitchen table.

The fact of the matter is that I have nothing.

I sit there trying to think of an angle and suddenly a piercing scream rings out. It's Cathy and for a second I can't move – terror holds me fast like gravity – but then I will my legs to push me up from the chair and I'm running before I can think and then I'm out of the kitchen and then in the hallway and I put my shoulder to the bathroom door, crashing through and into a disgusted-looking Cathy.

"Look at my fucking shoes!"

They are covered, as is the bathroom floor, with stinking, brackish water that is pouring over the toilet rim.

"Christ, let me get a mop."

"A fucking mop? These are Gucci trainers!"

The doorbell suddenly rings, stopping us both in our tracks. We exchange a look.

I don't want Cathy to think I'm mad. Eccentric is how I think, how I hope, she sees me at the moment but it's the middle of the day, she's here and the doorbell has gone. To not answer the door would be to make real all her suspicions about my self-inflicted hermitage.

"You clean yourself up. There's a clean cloth under the sink. I'll get that."

"Are you sure?"

"Of course." I smile and hope she can't see the panic in my eyes.

A deep breath. I check the spy hole. It all looks okay, it's just a workman in a fluorescent jacket, but why do I still feel like I am standing on a cliff edge and about to throw myself off? A deep breath. I do it, taking the air deep down, and before I can tell whether it's helped I slip the latch across and open the door.

"Sorry love, we've got ourselves a fatberg and it's backing up the sewer. I'm going house to house warning people there may be some flooding."

"A fatberg?"

He nods insouciantly like it's just a matter of time before your house turns into one that's just floating out there in the sea of the city.

"Grease, fat, waxy deposits, you know, er, feminine products." I swear he looks at me accusingly here, the cheeky fucker. "They build up, layer by layer, and when they are big enough they block up the sewers."

I check his name badge again.

"And that's why my toilet is overflowing with shit, is it, er, Peter?"

I hear a giggle from behind me. It's Cathy. I hope she's left her shoes in the bathroom.

I put Peter in his late thirties; he was probably one of the last Peters. It's not a fashionable name anymore for sure.

"We are throwing everything we've got at it, pressurised hoses, men on breakers, but it's a big one this one. It's even got a name."

"A name? What, like storms and hurricanes get now?"

"Yeah, council thought it would raise awareness about the bergs, encourage people not to throw their shit – sorry, their stuff – down the bog."

"And what's the name?"

"Marigold."

"Marigold the fatberg?"

"Yeah."

Behind me, Cathy starts to laugh uncontrollably.

"It's not funny. These bergs are a serious business."

"I know, you should see my bathroom floor. When will it be clear?"

Peter scratches his nose in a way I am sure he learned on the job; it's a professional nose tickle, a precursor to bad news.

"Well that's just it, we're not sure. Marigold is proving a bugger to get rid of. I'm going round the street warning people that there could be Marigold-related incidents for the next week or so until we shift it, and any other mini bergs that may be down there."

"Well thank you for letting us know. What sort of incidents might we expect?"

He sniffs and the little bubble of snot that had formed above his moustache pops.

"Oh, you know, the usual stuff, toilet and sewer issues, water on and off, foul odours. The gas these things give off is fucking awful, 'scuse my French."

French. FrenchieXX. French Duckie.

I look at him again. He could be anyone; it's easy to forge an ID. All you need is a computer and a half-decent printer. But I look along the street and can see the orange work tents and other men wearing similar high-viz tabards. *Don't be so paranoid*, I tell myself.

I go to shut the door but he has hold of it and instantly the fear leaps from its hiding place in my stomach.

"Hang on." His right hand goes to his pocket, and I pull the door harder, but he shows no sign of letting go. "Leaflet. I've got a leaflet for you."

Peter sticks out his filthy hand, in which is a yellow leaflet marked with biohazard symbols.

I take it and finally he lets go of the door.

"If you need anything the number is on the back," he says to the door, as it slams shut.

Cathy, sans shoes, thank Christ, is sitting on the stairs red-faced with tears running down her face.

"Marigold!" we say in unison and then we're both laughing hysterically.

But soon the laugher ebbs away.

"So what are you going to do?"

"About Marigold?"

Cathy shakes her head.

"No, about Tom Ellis? You said you were going to give a motive in the next podcast. Without Emma what do you have?"

We both know the answer to that question.

The answer is I have nothing and we sit down at my kitchen table to discuss a way forward. Two hours later we still have nothing and when Cathy leaves it's with a promise from me that I will have something by the morning.

That evening, whilst watching *The Great British Bake Off*, one of our family rituals, I tell Henry about Marigold. He rolls his eyes and says it must be due to the fast food places "upriver" dumping their cheap grease into the system, and that this is the problem with the city, one part infects the other. I go to say something else about Cathy's shoes but he shushes me as the judge on the show begins to taste a contestant's soufflé.

I don't tell him about the police visit. He couldn't take anymore. It would be like stepping on palm fronds covering a black pit.

Henry takes Finn upstairs to read him a story, and then I know he will probably go straight to bed himself. Once he's gone, I WhatsApp Hannah.

How are you and Tash doing Fucktart?

She replies straight away.

Hey Fucktart No.2 – she's in her poster phase, her bedroom looks like the inside of Smash Hits, you remember that?

I type quickly and silently.

I do yes, Finn is still on Star Wars – same as me!

WhatsApp tells me she is typing and I greedily anticipate her response, it's warmness so contrasting with the cold bed that awaits me upstairs.

I fear our Farrow and Ball mumps breath or whatever it's called will be forever scarred by the Blu-Tack outbreak – when she changes allegiance to the next boyband the walls will look like a smurf with smallpox… How are Finn and Henry?

Finn and Henry? How are they, I truly don't know how to be truthful with my answer so I avoid the question.

Finn is still the most beautiful boy, I spend all of my time thinking I've failed him.

I know what you mean – every time I tell Natasha not to do something I worry if my nagging will leave her with deep psychological scars which she will take out on some unsuspecting boy or girl in a few years time – but seriously Finn will be fine, you just need to make him loved when he is there which I know you will do. And Henry? Dare I ask?

I pause, thinking of the right words, ones that don't make me feel like I am betraying him all over again.

Still nothing – I just don't know how to be intimate, since the incident. He wants to but I'm not sure how I feel about that anymore.

Is there someone else?

Not here, not now, but there is a ghost but I can't tell Hannah about that, I can't tell anyone about that.

God no! I'm a born again nun!

Not even that hunky doctor?

I don't recall telling Hannah about Mo, but there have been so many drunken texts exchanged between us I often wonder what else I may have told her that I just can't remember.

I hear Henry's footsteps from upstairs, he will be walking from the en suite and climbing into bed, wondering where I am.

No! That's work. Listen I've got to go – work calls. Take care and I'll text you later.

The reply is almost instantaneous.

Take care Fucktart No.2

CHAPTER EIGHT

Faith

When Khalil was jailed, Katy Perry was number one with "I Kissed A Girl", I hadn't met Henry yet and Finn was five years and a reckless evening and two bottles of Cabernet Sauvignon away.

I couldn't even tell you whether there are still number ones never mind what the current one is today. Which is what I am thinking when I read Khalil's one and only letter to me. He sent it to me shortly after I started looking into his case.

Dear Sarah

I wanted to say thank you. Thank you for agreeing that I could write to you, and thank you for taking an interest in my case.

It's been twelve years since I was put in this place. I would like to tell you that time for me has passed easily here, that I have found some focus, found God, found anything of value here, but I am afraid I cannot. I don't even have a poster of Rita Hayworth on the wall.

When I first entered prison I still believed in things. I believed in God, not in a particular creed, though culturally I always will be a Muslim, but I believed in a plan, a design for us all. I also believed in other things, things you may think quaint. You may laugh, as my brother does when I mention this, but if I told you I believed in English justice and a sense of fair play I would not be lying to you.

When I heard the verdict at my trial I still believed that someone would realise that a mistake had been made, that someone watching, someone who hadn't been paying proper attention, would see an error had been made and would make themselves heard. "I'm awfully sorry there's been a terrible mistake" and then we would all go home. For a long time I waited, expecting that voice. Even when my appeal failed I didn't lose hope, no, not hope, a belief that things would be put right and the ship righted.

On the third day I was in here, whilst queuing for food a prisoner standing in the queue behind me – they never found out which one – jabbed a prison-made shank, a sharpened biro case, into my calf. I heard a prison guard laugh as I screamed.

As I lay in the hospital ward recovering I didn't doubt that all this would be cleared up. Daada-Jaan, my grandfather, a retired lawyer in Islamabad, who loved this country and its ancient institutions, would write to me, assuring me that British justice was the best in the world, "not like the corrupt bhenchoods judges we get here".

Daada-Jaan wrote every month; often the letters contained yellowing pages from an old Halsbury's Statutes *which he had torn straight from the book in his own small library. There would be sections of the Homicide Act underlined and notated. All out of date and useless, but to him, they were sacred texts and if only he could arrange the words and clauses in a certain way, if the spell could be formulated just so, then the magic would happen – "open sesame" and the doors of this cage would spring free. Every month one of these letters would arrive and he always ended them the same way.*

"Believe Naadaa."

Naadaa means innocent one in Urdu. He believed in justice, he believed it would be served.

He died three years ago, and I wonder, as he lay dying, did he still believe or was his belief the last thing to be eaten by his cancer?

And with his death I think my belief died, or so I told myself.

Others have tried to fill the gap where that belief used to be. I see it here every day, the men with big dreams and visions, who sell those dreams and visions to others who have none. When I was first in here, the dreams were big scores, life-changing jobs but over the years things have changed and the dreams are bigger, eternal life, seventy-two virgins, everlasting paradise. When you have nothing to believe in, then believe in something bigger than yourself: redemption and sex.

I thought my belief had died but these things, like religion, are hard to remove. I still believe that someone will call time, that a flag will be raised, that someone will hold up their hand and ask, who really killed Lauren, we must find out, the guilty must be punished, a great wrong has been done. Are you that voice Sarah?

I have seen, we have all seen, what can happen with the media when they get involved in a case. I don't expect the same results here but I believe that you will make it happen. I hope you can see the difference. It is faith.

But there is a difference with my faith now; it has become personal and hidden deep even from myself. I can't think of it, I cannot live it, not for me the waiting for the call that never comes; every moment lived through the prism of that expectation, and its non-arrival crushing the spirit. I have seen what that does. I saw what it did to my grandfather and so I won't be listening to the podcast, I won't be waiting on news, I will be living my life in here, reading, listening to music and surviving. I hope you do not think this rude but I will not be in touch again and I won't be waiting to hear from you with good news or bad.

One last thing. I know Mo thinks Tom Ellis was responsible for Lauren's murder. He has told me about Tom's life since we were at school. I just can't see it, he loved Lauren and I can't believe he would be responsible. But then I know that's what everybody said about me when I was convicted.

Have faith, Sarah. I do.

Khalil Bukhari

I put the letter back in the folder. Faith that something will happen. I don't have that faith. If you want to make something happen you have to do it yourself. Even if it's just pushing a small pebble over a cliff face, causing a bigger stone to move, you can hopefully cause an avalanche if you are lucky.

I don't have the motive but what I do have is the time, the context. I need to throw a pebble.

I dial Cathy's number. Whilst the phone is ringing Lil'Bitch looks at me, unblinking, from the worktop. She shouldn't be up there, Henry would go apeshit if he saw her there, but I just haven't got the energy or rather the inclination to shoo her down fifty times a day. In truth I admire her stubbornness and desire to get up to a height where she can see what's going on. I stare back and then Lil'Bitch blinks once, jumps down and heads out through the cat flap.

"Lucky bitch," I say out loud.

"Nice to hear from you too," says Cathy.

"Sorry hun, I was talking to the cat."

"Not necessarily an improvement in the saneness stakes than calling me a bitch."

I giggle. Cathy always lightens my mood.

"Listen, I think I have a way forward."

"Don't tell me Emma cracked? Have you got a motive?"

"Nothing that good but I've got enough for the next podcast."

"I'm all ears; blow me away SK."

"Islamophobia."

There is a pause on the line and I can hear a noise that I know is Cathy tapping her lighter on something. She always does this when she is thinking.

"Islamophobia," Cathy says, enunciating each syllable as though it were a particularly juicy item on a fancy restaurant menu.

I don't know whether this means she likes my idea or not.

"I like it. You know I wrote an article for *The Guardian* on Islamophobia and media representation. Basically, I just copied and pasted a load of Daily Heil headlines and wrote 'duh' underneath."

I did know it, of course. I banked on it.

"I was thinking that this investigation took place at a time of increased Islamophobia. Did that skew the investigation; did it affect the witnesses' testimony? Remember this all took place in the summer of 2006 – the year after the tube bombings, de Menezes, you remember what it was like. Maybe Khalil was doomed from the start."

"I like it. I bet I could get *The Guardian* to let you write an opinion piece on this week's episode."

"And I haven't mentioned the best bit."

I hear Cathy make a sucking sound; that will be her taking a drag on the e-cigarette she uses in the house.

"Go on."

"I can prove that the prosecution's main witness is an Islamophobe. How do you like them apples?"

"I'm Eve and I'm ravenous. What have you got?"

What have I got? Guilt, shame and something else much more valuable. I have information.

I got the information from Mo of course. His team of PI's had dug it up but it was after the trial and was useless for the appeal as it didn't classify as appealable new evidence. But for the show? Well, let's face facts, it's dynamite. I wasn't sure I would ever use it, but without the motive I promised, what can I do?

CHAPTER NINE

Shiver

I push away the plate. The shiny Danish pastries on it remind me of the eyes I saw in my dream.

Mo looks amused.

"Are you on a diet? My wife, she is always dieting. I say to her, Yasmin, you look great already and what can you expect after having four kids!"

He laughs uproariously and pats his knee. It's grossly sexist and if it was one of my male friends I would be pulling him up over it, but it's said with such love and warmth which comes off him like a furnace that I find myself letting go and just laughing with him. With him I don't police my own mind and it's refreshing.

"No I am not. I'm just not hungry right now, I had a rough night to tell you the truth."

The laughter is gone, replaced by a look of concern that I think is genuine. I've seen a lot of concerned looks over the last year and you'd be surprised how many are just pasted on as a matter of form.

"Is it the troll? I can see on Twitter how he abuses you. You should let me do something about it."

I'm touched that he wants to help. Maybe it's in his character; he's a doctor after all and he's also dedicated the last twelve years of his life to helping free his brother from prison. And it's not just time – he let slip in one of our first meetings that he had re-mortgaged his house to fund Khalil's legal fees and the costs of the private investigators he's had on the case.

"What could you do?" I ask him.

He frowns.

"Maybe nothing, maybe something."

I shrug. There's nothing he can do, trolls live under bridges for a reason. I change the subject.

"Why do you do it?"

He looks perplexed. "Do what?"

"Spend all this time, this money, on this case. It's been twelve years. Don't you ever get disheartened?"

There's a look on his face like a shadow cast by a passing car and then it's gone.

"You know I'm not a believer, right? Allah, God, all sky fairies to me. You work in A&E for a week and any faith you did have left will soon be kicked out of you, trust me. But what being a Muslim means to me is family. Family is all we have. When you're dying, lying in that bed covered in green sheets, plugged into a machine counting out the last moments of your life, you know what people call out for? It's never God, trust me, they always call out for family. That's whom they want near them in those moments because that's what they know in those final moments. That all this life is about is the people you love and who love you, even if that love was dead many years before. An old lover, husband, wife, someone they haven't seen in fifty years; that's who they want to be near them. And we all understand this. That's why people jump on planes and travel halfway around the world to be by a bedside. We understand that need. But you see people understand it when it's far, far too late. Working as a doctor I've seen it a thousand times, the regret of words unsaid, deeds not taken, and what I've realised is that those few moments at the end of life, when things become clear, they are always there, but hidden out of sight by the promise, the illusion of more time to come. People live their lives like it's a credit card, putting off reality whilst they spend their time like they can afford to waste it. I won't do that with Khalil. I will spend it now letting him know each moment that he's my brother and that I love him."

He leans back in his chair as though this – the most intense I have seen him be since I have known him – has cost him serious effort.

"And as for his guilt. He's my little brother, I've known him all my life. He couldn't kill anyone, especially not Lauren. He loved her."

"You know that's what a lot of murderers' relatives say."

"Do you believe he killed her, Sarah?"

The question almost shocks me. If I'm truthful it's a question I've usually thought of as entirely irrelevant. I couldn't possibly ever know. All I was interested in was the story of how a young Muslim boy could have become the focus of a sloppy police investigation and potentially been the victim of a miscarriage of justice, so I'm almost surprised to hear it's my voice saying, "No, I don't think he did it."

Mo smiles sadly. "He didn't do it. My brother couldn't hurt anybody. Thank you, that means a lot."

And then he reaches over and takes hold of my hand and the sensation that this sends through my body, every part of it, makes me shiver. I close my eyes and feel tears coming so I blink hard and then slowly move my hand away.

When I open my eyes Mo is looking at me with an amused sadness.

"Are you ok, Sarah?"

I nod.

He starts to say something but reconsiders and although I want to ask him to continue – so much – I know if I do he will, and that I'm at the absolute limit of my strength right at this moment and with one push I will fall.

"Okay," he says, and stands up. "Don't worry. I'll let myself out."

I let him, but as soon as I hear the door slam I rush to it and slam home the bolts and slide the catch down on the industrial-sized latch.

"Shit," I say aloud. I need to speak to Henry, and not in the language we have developed since the incident, the unspoken code of something unsaid, but directly, and soon.

If I could only find the right words, put them in a sentence. I know they are out there. I can make things right again, but I've been silent, the words hidden in the darkness. No longer, I tell myself.

Instead I do what I always do. I WhatsApp Hannah.

You know that hunky doctor?

As usual there is almost no delay.

Yeah? Did he take your temperature in the old-fashioned way?

I blush even though I am alone.

No, but I think we just shared a moment, he made me shiver with a look.

This reply takes a little longer:

Well he does have eyes to die for, will you do anything about it?

I hesitate but then type:

No, I wouldn't hurt Henry.

An instant response ... *again*...

That cuts. Hannah, cruel and truthful, but the only friend I can rely on for this necessary combination. She doesn't know the details, no one does, but she knows I hurt him, and that I carry around a house-sized load of guilt as a consequence.

The doorbell interrupts our WhatsApp conversation but it's only Henry and Finn back from the park, so I don't jump out of my chair as I would have done had I not been expecting the doorbell to ring.

I can see Henry looking exasperated, phone in one hand, Finn holding on to the other. The phone means he will have rung out for pizza as he doesn't want to cook, and I never do.

I tell Hannah I will ping her back and go and let them in.

Finn is grinning and his pupils are dilated which can only mean Henry has given him sweets.

"We are getting pizza!" Finn shouts.

"As a dessert?"

Henry gives me the look that I know is his warning not to go there. "It was that or I was leaving him in the park," he says under his breath. "I ordered you a margarita, is that okay?"

I shrug.

Finn dodges around me, running towards the kitchen, and I turn and start to go after him. "Don't run darling." Then my foot clips something heavy and slips and I fall heavily, landing on my arse, hard.

"Fucking bastard!"

I look up and see Finn staring down at me in shock.

"I don't mean you, darling." But the truth is I do. I tripped on his fire engine that he dropped behind me as he ran. I see his eyes fill up because the truth is you can't lie to children, not really. He knows I, his mother, meant it and this kills me in a thousand new ways.

Henry shakes his head. "You'll be okay," is all he says.

I extend my arms. "Come here, Finn, I'm so sorry. I love you."

"No you don't, Sarah," he says and he picks up the fire engine and runs off up the stairs.

"Outstanding work. Another day in paradise."

I glare at Henry but bite my tongue; I owe him too much to rise to this.

"I'm sorry, it just came out. Listen, why don't you and Finn get the pizzas? I'll skip dinner as I've got work to do."

Henry juts out his bottom lip like a naughty schoolboy.

"Ah yes, your murderer and the doctor, the two most important men in your life right now."

Silence. I give him my silence.

CHAPTER TEN

Podcast

Podcast Episode 5 – by Sarah Kelly – 15/11/2018

Imagine this. You're a student studying in the UK. You love it here, the language, the relative freedom of the society compared to your Catholic upbringing, the diversity and cosmopolitan big city. You're at home here, no, you've found your home here.

Each night you study a little and then maybe meet some friends for a beer, or one of your group – an eclectic mix of Spaniards, Portuguese, Brazilians, French and Arabs – will cook something, usually a traditional dish from back home. Everyone likes that and it also eases some of the homesick pangs. You live in a small place for sure, but it's warm, it's safe and secure, and to be fair the room doesn't matter because you live here, in this city, this supranational entity that is bigger than the small country it is nominally the capital of, grander, a place of limitless possibilities and hunger, always needing more young people like you to be fed into its ceaselessly demanding maw.

You love it.

Each morning you and your friends who you share the flat with have the same ritual. You get up, and whoever gets to the radio in the kitchen first tunes it in to a local station; you all agree on Capital. It makes you feel like Londoners even if sometimes the music is laughably terrible and inauthentic. Breakfast doesn't exist beyond a cup of coffee and maybe a piece of fruit, the city is awake and you need to move, always be moving in the pulsating energy of people making, creating, talking, the endless talking that never shuts down. Even when you sleep you can hear the background noise of a billion city conversations.

This morning, the morning everything changes, is no different to any other in the city except in one respect. You partied a little hard the night before and have overslept so you wake an hour later than usual, but it's okay because your first lecture isn't till 12 so you have plenty of time to walk to the Tube and then take the Northern Line before then. So, you make a coffee and as you drink your espresso you look out of the window of your first-floor flat.

It looks like a mild day, or it would if you were English. In this weather, what would pass for nothing more than a cool spring day in your country, you have seen English girls wearing bikinis in the parks, laughing and drinking as their pale mottled skin contracts against the weak sun.

You shiver involuntarily and as you leave the flat you grab the coat that your mother bought for you just before you left to come to this country. Mother knew you would feel the cold; she always knew how you felt, usually way before you knew yourself.

You zip the coat all the way up and open the door, letting in the chill air that masquerades as summer in this latitude and chuckling as you think of the sights this will bring out at the campus today.

Before you step out one more time, the last time, into an English day, you lean down, pick up and then strap on your backpack full of text books. It is heavy for sure but you are strong and the day promises much, so you hardly notice the weight as you slam the door shut.

Even though it's past rush hour the streets are still busy, full of people charged like frantic electrons circling the nucleus of the city. You smile, you enjoy being part of this greater mass, maybe the most chaotic, supreme expression of civilisation yet. You are looking forward always and thus you never look back, never see the man with his worried, tense face, some thirty yards back whose eyes have never left you since you left the flat.

Today is your lucky day: the bus you catch to Brixton Tube Station to get you to Kilburn turns the corner to your bus stop just as you arrive. You board the bus. A few seconds later the worried-looking man boards too and he takes a seat three back from yours.

The journey passes quickly. You've got your headphones on listening to some funk carioca. It reminds you of home.

Then your luck changes. As you hop off the bus you can see that Brixton Tube Station is closed. Something to do with the bombings two weeks before. Your mind wanders to the horrific events of that day, images of bandaged faces like risen mummies from the depths of the city.

But the bus hasn't moved; maybe your luck is holding?

You jump back on and the driver gives you a knowing wink. The city has felt like this since the bombs: strength in each other, the fear pushed out to the periphery of vision.

The next station is only a few minutes away and when the bus pulls in you see it is open. Stockwell is only one stop along so no harm done. You can still make your appointment in Kilburn.

You pick up a copy of the Metro *in the station and then flash your Oyster card at the barrier. Running down the escalator – dimly aware of the people behind you doing the same – you can hear a train pulling in below.*

The train is on the platform waiting for you to arrive as though it's always been there. You spring on and take a seat next to a glass partition. One of the better seats, as no one can sit next you on one side.

Three men board and take seats nearby. It's only then that you notice one of them is looking straight at you. You've been here long enough to know this is a breach of Tube etiquette. Maybe he is a foreigner?

And then a man is shouting behind you.

"He's here!"

You turn and can see the man is pointing at you, and another three men board the train, but these men aren't like the others, these men are carrying guns.

You stand up. What is going on?

Seconds later, eleven bullets are fired into you.

Remember those weeks? Remember the fear? They say terrorists win if we let them terrorise us. I cry bullshit to that. Of course they terrorise us and our reaction to them terrorises us, but we understand it don't we? The febrile time, that sense of the other coming for us, living amongst us whilst it plots our downfall. It led to the death of Jean Charles de Menezes on that July morning in 2005.

I said I would give you a motive for Lauren's death but I can't give you a Cluedo-type motive, not yet, but what I can say is this: I think the motivation for the investigation's focus on Khalil Bukhari has to be looked at in the context of those weeks, the start of this miserable century, and that this isn't just some political rant but rather it played out directly in leading to the conviction of Khalil Bukhari.

Listen to this. It's an extract from the police recording of a phone call received a week after they released Charles Brownhill. If you know about the case you'll know the name. The recordings a bit scratchy but you'll get the gist:

CALLER: Hello, is that Detective Richardson?

RICHARDSON: This is DCI Richardson, who's calling?

CALLER: I'd prefer, well (coughs), not to say right now, but you're the police woman investigating Lauren Grey's murder?

RICHARDSON: Police officer, but yes, that's me. But I really need your name, Mr…?

CALLER: (nervous laugh) I saw you on TV apologising to that chap you arrested, the weirdo with the dyed hair. I don't want to be on TV but I do have information.

RICHARDSON: I can assure you that anything you tell us will be treated in confidence but I really do need your name, sir. You can appreciate in an enquiry like this we get many nuisance calls.

CALLER: I'm no crank, I can assure you, but I do need to tell you something.

RICHARDSON: I–

CALLER: I was there on that night, at World's End. I drove past and I saw him.

RICHARDSON: Who did you see?

CALLER: The murderer of course.

RICHARDSON: (pause) When?

CALLER: The night she died.

RICHARDSON: Can you describe him?

CALLER: Of course. Six foot tall, muscular, late teens to early twenties and a Mohammadian.

RICHARDSON: Pardon?

CALLER: A Muslim.

RICHARDSON: Okay. And what did you see?

CALLER: I saw him walk into the bushes as my car approached the World's End car park.

RICHARDSON: And what time was this?

CALLER: Around 12.30pm.

RICHARDSON: Were you alone?

CALLER: That's all I have to say. I just want to be of assistance.

THE CALL ENDS

So, this call lands and you know what, I spoke to a friend of mine, ex-Met Police, and he told me that on a big enquiry, one that generates significant press interest, and this case most certainly did do that, you can expect upwards of a hundred calls from well-meaning souls who think they can help but don't, often disturbed types who just want some attention and the occasional troublemaker who just wants to spit in the well for the sake of it.

Timothy Bowden, albeit Richardson didn't know it then, turned out to be the opposite. He was the piece of prosecution gold in the dirt.

This was potentially a breakthrough in the case and confirmed what Richardson and the murder team were already thinking – that Khalil Bukhari was their number one suspect. The trouble was that it didn't amount to evidence; it amounted to precisely nothing without the witness giving a statement.

And here's where the police caught a break. I had assumed that they would have some sort of tracking device on the phones. They did, but then so did everyone else. It was called ringback but of course the caller had disabled it.

When Richardson told the team about the call it was WPC Langley who came up with the idea of speaking with her list of "customers". WPC

Langley was the beat officer for that part of the Wirral, the coastal stretch between Heswall and Neston, and she was familiar with World's End and the type of late-night visitor it attracted, the "dope heads and the doggers", as she told me when I spoke with her last week.

When she heard the tape recording she realised she didn't need to speak to anyone else but suspected straight away who had made the call.

Enter Timothy Bowden. A doctor, fifty-three years of age, married to a local justice of the peace and known to WPC Langley as "Naughty Timothy" due to that moniker being given to him by a local prostitute, Dana Reed, who used World's End as her office and who, one summer's evening, when Langley had stopped her patrol car and shone her flashlight into a badly parked Ford Mondeo and asked, "Is everything okay in there?", had replied, "Don't worry about me, I'm just finishing off Naughty Timothy."

On two further occasions Langley had had cause to ask Naughty Timothy to move along or she would arrest him for a breach of the peace, and each time Timothy Bowden had been almost overwhelmingly polite and correct in his manner and spoken to her like he was speaking to a sommelier offering him an array of options from the wine list.

Richardson and Langley visited Timothy Bowden at his practice and although Langley was coy on this point I think it is safe to say that they persuaded Timothy to put his name to a statement by referencing how unfortunate it would be if details of his proclivities made it into the public domain.

He agreed and he took part in a line-up two days later when he picked out Khalil from a group of six Asian men.

There was a problem with this line-up. The area was so demographically white that the police had to bus in Asian males from Liverpool to take part in the line-up. The Bukharis were one of only two Asian families in Heswall and although he denied it under cross-examination it was likely that if Timothy had ever seen a young Asian boy in his teens before then, it was highly likely to have been Khalil.

But the evidence was allowed in and on 3 September 2008 Timothy Bowden, when asked to identify the man he saw stumbling from the World's End car park on the night of the murder, raised his right hand and pointed at Khalil Bukhari in the dock.

Trials in England aren't filmed but I've seen enough movies, read the court transcript and spoken to people who were in the courtroom, so I know how a pointed finger at an accused man goes down. This is someone without an axe to grind choosing, in the knowledge of what this means, to place a person who denies being there at the scene of the crime in the time period when the murder was carried out. Boom.

So, what did the defence do? They played the man.

Timothy Bowden, on the face of it a respected member of the community, doctor, parish councillor and family man, was a swinger and habitual user of prostitutes. The police knew this and it didn't take a lot for the defence to find out his history. You see, the doctor had a nom de guerre in the swinging world and was well known in the local swinging community as Doctor Dick. Okay, stop the sniggering back there.

Unfortunately for the good doctor, who had thought that the only way of covering up his other life was to give evidence, the opposite happened. The defence went for him. The attack line was how could he be trusted if he led a secret life frequenting dogging sites like World's End. But Naughty Timothy/Doctor Dick hit the defence barrister's line of questioning for six; turns out his wife knew all about it and occasionally, although you get the feeling it was like going with her husband to reluctantly watch the football, partook herself, if the weather was nice. The jury lapped it up, his urbane politeness in the face of what must have come across as dirty tactics by Khalil's QC. When he finished his evidence one of the journalists wrote that you could see the jury felt that there was only one sordid person in the exchange between Doctor Dick and the lawyer, and it wasn't the doctor.

Timothy Bowden came out of it looking like what he is: just someone wanting to do his duty, someone who, as the prosecution pointed out, had no axe to grind.

But what if he did?

Back to Jean Charles de Menezes, shot in those febrile hot weeks in July 2005. Just after 7/7, another failed bomb attempt, the country was on high alert. Nightly news bulletins showing pictures of Asian men wanted for murder, terrorist plots – you might remember the fear.

Once the police had Khalil picked out in the parade it was a matter of record that they didn't pursue any other leads. They had their man as far as they were concerned. The defence tried to attack the doctor; they focused on his peccadilloes and they failed.

What they didn't know and what we now know is that Naughty Timothy did have an axe to grind, maybe not with Khalil but with Islam in general.

I've got hold of some old screenshots. When I say old, they are MySpace account pages. For those of you who don't remember, MySpace was like a Neanderthal predecessor to Facebook. In full disclosure, I can tell you that these were acquired by a firm of private detectives working on Khalil's appeal. They purport to show an account in the name of Reginald de Chatillon. That name by the way is the name of a Grand Master of the Knights Templar, a monastic order who participated in the Crusades.

The account is message after message of Islamophobia, one after another, equating Islam with terrorism and blaming all Muslims for the actions of terrorists.

Here is a typical message; it was posted on 2 September 2008. That's the day before Timothy Bowden gave evidence. I have to give a trigger warning here; this could upset some of you so here goes:

"Mohammed fucked nine-year-olds and slaughtered Jews and non-Muslims for Arab imperialism. The bombs in London, Madrid and New York are just more of the same. Islam is fascism."

And there's more of this stuff, well, lots of it, and I'll be posting it to the website if you want to take a look, but you've been warned. The account is long dormant but it's there in the fossilised record of the Internet, dead but not forgotten.

And you've guessed where I'm going with this: Reginald de Chatillon was an anonymous account but only if you don't understand that accounts have signatures. With MySpace it was associated email accounts. Reginald's account was linked with an email address. It was just a Hotmail account, sweetipeie26454@hotmail.com, *but here's the biggie: that email is also linked to a current Facebook account, that of one Timothy Bowden. So, no axe to grind? Take another look. If the defence had had this evidence would the jury have been so keen to believe Naughty Timothy?*

But maybe they would have ignored it. He had an issue with Islam, so do a lot of people, and that doesn't necessarily make him a liar.

But what if I could show he lied? Here's how the prosecution should have done it. Timothy Bowden was asked on the stand whether he knew Khalil Bukhari. I mentioned before that there just weren't that many Asians living in the Wirral at that time. He said, "No" and everybody believed him, but he lied.

For two years before he was arrested Khalil Bukhari went to Timothy Bowden's house every day five days a week.

He had a paper round you see. He didn't know that one of the houses belonged to Timothy Bowden – it never came up at trial – but listen to this. It's a tape recording I made of a conversation with a man called Gerald O'Brian (he runs a newsagents in Neston), and Khalil worked for him for three years before the murder.

GB: I remember Khalil; he was a nice kid. For what it's worth I always thought he didn't seem the type who would commit a murder, but they all say that afterwards don't they, ha ha!

Me: So on his round he delivered to Timothy Bowden. He had a house in Little Ness near World's End?

GB: Yeah he did. Naughty Timothy took him The Telegraph.

Me: And did Timothy Bowden know Khalil?

GB: Know him? I couldn't say, but I know he left him a Christmas tip, I remember he brought it into the shop, coz of what he said.

Me: What did he say?

GB: It stuck with me. He said, "Can you give this to the Mohammedan boy who brings me my paper?"

Me: When was this?

GB: Must have been the Christmas before the murder, so Christmas 2005.

Me: And did the police ever ask you about this?
GB: Nobody has until now.

Timothy Bowden never mentioned to the police, the CPS or at the trial the fact that he knew Khalil Bukhari.

I would like to ask Timothy Bowden about this. I think it would throw some light on the case. Maybe he would, with hindsight, admit that he knew Khalil and that when he picked him out of the line-up it may just have been because that was the only Asian face he was used to seeing, but the trouble is I can't do that, ever. Timothy Bowden died eighteen months ago.

Does this matter? Well, take away the line-up evidence and what is the difference between Khalil and Tom Ellis as suspects?

Next time I promise I'm going to look at motive and I never break a second promise.

CHAPTER ELEVEN

Fatbergs

The podcast goes out every Friday at 9am. This one is no different. Each one lasts, with music and ads, exactly thirty minutes.

At 9.32 the phone begins to ring.

I ignore it and focus on making coffee and Googling a recipe for dinner that I hope will make Henry happy, but at 9.45 I see it's Cathy calling so I pick up.

"Oh my God, you've really rattled some cages with this one, hon! The studio has been bombarded. Twitter is in meltdown – Naughty Timothy is trending in the UK!"

Lil'Bitch jumps onto the kitchen table and rolls over, offering her belly, or rather demanding that it be stroked. I oblige and am rewarded with a purr.

"Islamophobia is so hot right now," I say, but Cathy ignores the *Zoolander* reference, which disappoints me as our relationship runs on the fuel of throwaway pop culture references.

"I know right, and this opens up a whole can of worms. Loved the Jean Charles de Menezes angle; really put the audience in there as a victim of racist police behaviour. You absolutely nailed it. *The Guardian* want a follow-up piece, today if possible."

"I don't want this to be clickbait for them. I'm going to have to say no."

I hear Cathy light a cigarette. She always does when under stress, and not agreeing with her always causes her stress.

"I think you should reconsider, I really do, hon. We need to ride this wave."

"I don't want to do it." I'm curt with her but I know she won't give up if she thinks there's a chance I can be persuaded.

"What do you want, hon? What's the purpose of all this, then? And don't tell me it's just about justice for Khalil."

She's right, of course it's not all about Khalil. I can see how it might be seen as therapy after what happened and I stay silent as I know this is what Cathy and others think it is too, and there is a certain degree of perceived moral value in that, as well as just enough remaining superstition and fear to make people, even Cathy, not want to ask too many questions about my mental health. Mental illness is also hot right now, but not so hot people want to stare at the subject for too long. So I say nothing and the silence allows her to reach the obvious conclusion.

"Don't answer, I get it," she says.

She's wrong though. I don't do it for therapy. I do it as redemption.

"Okay, well look, you handle the calls. You can do the article if you want as part of the production team. I'm good with that."

A pause.

"I might well do that, and Sarah?"

"Yeah?"

"Take care of yourself. And I just want to tell you that you're doing an awesome job there."

"Thanks Cath, you too."

I click *end call*, feeling like a total fraud.

Lil'Bitch takes a nip at my hand, as it's been absent from her stomach for too long.

The doorbell goes and my heart, as it always does, goes *pop* like a balloon pierced by a shiny pin.

"Get a grip Sarah," I whisper to myself and then I check the video monitor. It's Peter the council engineer. He mustn't have noticed the CCTV camera on his last visit because he's scratching his arse with his right hand. I make a mental note not to shake his hand if proffered.

When I open the door it is with relief that he doesn't go for a handshake.

"Hello, Mrs Kelly, I was here last week."

"Hello again. The fatberg, yes I remember. Hard to forget it really, Marigold."

"We're calling it Adele now." He leers as though he has just dropped a Wildean bon mot.

I don't laugh and his leer drops faster than tools at five o'clock.

"It's only a joke, like."

"Bit misogynistic though, eh? Why didn't you just call it Pete instead?"

Peter looks down at his large stomach straining against his fluorescent tabard and then back up at me. He looks hurt but I doubt he will make the link between his own feelings and naming a fatberg after a woman; men like Pete never do.

He's blushing and I'm marvelling how I can be so strong with him yet still be like a frightened mouse when the doorbell rings. Sometimes it feels like I have a hundred different version of 'me' inside me at any one time.

"Sorry, I didn't realise you were one of them sort."

"And what sort is that?"

Peter, briefly, defiantly looks up and whispers, "A feminist," before dropping his gaze again.

I can't help it but I burst out laughing.

"Oh, I'm sorry, it must be a confusing time for you what with women having a vote and being able to get jobs. Anyway, what can I help you with?"

He looks back up and this time I can see in his eyes that there's something else there, something I've planted, but I don't feel guilty about it one bit. It's hatred. It's a look I've seen flash across the faces of countless men in all my places of work, usually around the same time a woman says something clever or asks for something: an assignment, a raise or respect.

"I was just going to tell you, tell all the rezzies, like, that the water will be off this afternoon till about five whilst we get a more powerful jet on Ad – on the Berg. Hopefully that will shift it."

"And what if it doesn't? What happens then?"

Peter brightens up.

"That's never happened; we can guarantee everything is going to be alright."

And he believes what he says, I can see that.

"Okay, well thank you for letting me know, Peter, I appreciate it."

This seems to perk him up some more and he beams at me again, but almost as soon as the corners of his lips reach their zenith they are plunging back down as he remembers me scolding him.

"Yeah, see you later, miss."

I close the door and walk back inside. Lil'Bitch follows me, rubbing herself against my legs and almost tripping me up.

True enough, when I try the taps in the kitchen nothing comes out. A little wave of panic washes through me as it occurs to me it's only 10am and Henry won't be in until six and I can't go all day without water. I grab the fridge door and pull it open.

"Fuck!"

There are no beautiful fresh bottles of mineral water with condensation running down them as I had hoped.

"This is like Ice Cold in frigging Alex," I say to Lil'Bitch who clearly doesn't get the reference.

The corner shop isn't really on the corner of the street; it's maybe half a mile away at the end of the street and it may as well be on the bloody moon for all the intention I have of leaving this house.

I try the taps again and am rewarded with a chugging sound like my father's old Austin Allegro used to make on a cold morning, but no water.

I wasn't thirsty before I was told the water was off but now I feel my tongue turning furry even as I think about it. Sometimes I hate my brain; it often seems that it's a fifth column waging an inside war against my best interests.

Work, I tell myself. *Distract yourself and this psychosomatic thirst will go away. Want to bet?* fires back my traitorous grey matter and supplies me with an image of melting ice as a reminder of who is in charge.

I pop open the laptop and bring up a new, fresh Word document. The cursor blinks back at me, daring me to start writing.

Motive. I promised my listeners a motive. But without Emma helping me I can't see how I can make any progress. And then it hits me. I promised a motive, not Tom's motive.

There were other guests present at the party. What if one of them had a motive, a spurned suitor, a jealous but quiet watcher of Lauren and Khalil that the police investigation missed at the time? *Think*. But of course nothing comes. How can I be expected to find evidence of that if the police hadn't turned anything up? I lick my lips but my tongue feels dry and I have to swallow to bring some spit to my mouth, which is patently ridiculous as by my reckoning it's only been less than an hour since I had a cup of coffee.

It's not my job to find a suspect, I remind myself, merely to cast doubt on the conviction, which seems to me to have been a lazy job by a police force desperate for a conviction after falsely accusing Brownhill.

My fingers hover above the keyboard and then I stand up and try the taps again. Nothing but that gurgling sound, balls!

I open the fridge again. There are two bottles of Sancerre in there, cold and crisp, waiting to be drunk.

The clock on the cooker says it's 10.10am.

No, I'm not going that route, so I close the fridge door and sit back down at the table again.

The cursor blinks away, mocking me.

Maybe a quick Internet browse will help spark some inspiration. Even as I think that I laugh out loud at my pathetic attempt at such self-deception.

I launch Twitter and within five seconds wish I hadn't. My Twitter feed is full of abuse way beyond my normal high, female-journalist-with-an-opinion quota. Being abused on Twitter is something I'm used to but the volume and sheer vitriol takes my breath away.

The balance used to be that one in ten tweets I received would be abuse from trolls, but the mention of Islamophobia in my last podcast has added jet fuel to the already seething hatred that surrounds my account.

The abuse is easy to deal with. I simply ignore it. The dialogue with Frenchie was an aberration and one I shouldn't have let happen.

"Never explain, never complain," I say out loud to Lil'Bitch, who has padded back into the kitchen and is looking at me from her position below the fridge door. "And no you can't have any treats. I've only just fed you and you're getting fat."

I give my stomach a little squeeze; she's not the only one getting fat. Before my self-imposed exile I used to run every evening after work. That's gone now and despite trying to work out every day with an app on my phone, the promised seven-minute miracle workout hasn't succeeded in stopping a ring of middle-aged blubber developing over what was once a firm and taut stomach.

A thought gate crashes me – *what if this is why Henry won't go near me anymore?* – but I know that's not the reason, in fact Henry used to moan that I was too thin and that he missed the curves I used to have when we first met, when I was padded by the side effects of my drinking days.

My phone beeps but it's a different tone from the usual text or email alert. I pick it up and there's an unfamiliar yellow box in the top corner of the screen. I recognise it as a Snapchat alert, although I haven't used it since before the incident. What if it's him? He was the last person to contact me on Snapchat. I have to know and I click it and the Snapchat app opens. But it's not him, it's worse.

I'm looking instead at an image of Finn at the school gates. He's wearing the grey jumper and blue trousers I dressed him in this morning. The image is close up, as though taken through a telephoto lens or the photographer was close. My heart thumps inside my chest and I stifle a scream.

The image stays on the screen for six seconds and then goes. It feels like a thousand years.

I call Henry immediately.

The phone rings out. He never answers when he's at work. I leave a message. I call his office number. Mandy, the school receptionist, answers.

"Hi Mandy, it's Sarah, is Henry there?"

Mandy's tone is always the same, flat and professional even when she must be able to tell from my voice that I am panicking.

"Hello, Mrs Kelly, hang on for one second," I hear her tapping keys and I have to fight the urge to scream *Come on you fucking bitch!* and then: "I'm awfully sorry but Mr Kelly has a free period now and I'm not quite sure where he is. Can I take a message?"

"Yes, tell him to ring me back the moment he gets in."

Fucking Henry!

I ring Finn's school and get another receptionist.

"Hello, Gladwell Primary, how can I help?"

"My son, Finn Kelly, he's being watched. Fuck, he's in danger."

I hear a sigh.

"Mrs Kelly, could you calm down and speak more slowly. What danger?"

I want to scream at her, tell her she's a cunt endangering my son, but I breathe.

"I've just received a photograph on Snapchat from a paedophile who has taken a picture of my son as he was dropped off at school two hours ago. I need you – what's your name?"

"Ologo."

"Listen, Ologo, you need to go and get my son out of his class now and make sure he's safe right now. Will you do that for me?"

A pause. I get ready to scream as I can almost hear the sound of the jobsworth part of her brain battling common sense.

"Well, how do I know you're his mother? We take data protection very seriously here."

"Listen, my son is in fucking danger, right now, so you can worry about his data protection rights once he's fucking safe, do you understand?"

Even as I am shouting I realise what a terrible mistake I've made; she's going to come back at me with some shit about respecting staff and their right not to be spoken to like this, and then she will put the phone down and time will have been wasted and what will these lost seconds, lost because of my temper, mean for Finn?

I bite my lip as I hear Ologo take a sharp breath.

"Let me see. What did you say your son's name was again?"

The past tense cuts me.

"His name is Finn Kelly." I try and recall what classes Finn has on a Friday but I can't remember even though he's probably told me dozens of times in answer to a procedural "what did you do at school today honey?" and I feel the old guilt weigh down on me. "Will you please go and find him, Ologo? Please."

Computer keys are hit.

"Okay, Mrs Kelly. I have found your son's class. It's Spanish with Miss Velazquez. Let me see what I can do, but please be clear if you talk to me like that again you will be most sorry."

There is a click and then all I can hear is background noise – distant shouts and calls of children lost in their carefree day – and I want to cry but I can't.

A minute passes and I see an incoming call from Henry but I don't answer, as I can't risk severing the line or missing Ologo's return.

Henry's call ends and then is immediately followed by Henry ringing again.

My heart leaps as I hear a door slam near to the phone.

"Hello, is this Mrs Kelly?"

It's a man's voice. He's going to tell me something awful has happened to Finn, I know it.

"Have you got my son?"

"Yes, I have him here safe and sound. Ologo mentioned something about a photograph?"

"Let me speak to Finn first."

My voice cracks as I talk.

"Darling, are you okay?"

"Yeah, course. What do you want, Sarah? Everyone laughed and Miss Velazquez asked me to say 'I"ll be back' in Spanish and I didn't know and Ben was laughing and the others joined in."

"Oh nothing, just" – I feel relief replacing adrenaline and my thoughts, without their adrenal supercharge, begin to tumble and collide – "me being a bit of a fuss pot. And when you go back to class you can tell that teacher that I'll be back is hasta la vista. I love you Finn."

"Whatever."

The phone goes down and then I collapse on the kitchen floor.

CHAPTER TWELVE

The gates

Finn's deep rhythmic breathing reassures me. It's the sound of contentment and rest. If he had been tossing and turning, his breathing shallow and agitated, I wouldn't have shut the door and gone downstairs.

Henry is loading the dishwasher with the plates we used for the takeaway food we ordered. He insisted I wasn't up to cooking after such a stressful day and he ordered in Chinese food. The old me would have laughed off his presumptions of firstly me doing the cooking and secondly that I was too delicate to handle what had happened, but it's like reading a history book about the First World War. I know it happened but I can't really remember the touch and texture of the old me.

"Did you speak to the police?"

Henry doesn't look round, he just carries on loading the dishwasher. I notice he isn't washing off the sticky remains of the rice first.

"Yup."

He volunteers nothing else and so I know he's pissed off with me.

"And what did they say?"

Now, he turns around and he holds a dirty plate up and points at me with it.

"What did you expect them to say, Sarah? There's no evidence and where do we start when there's so many suspects? If we narrowed it down to those who've sent you death threats we'd still be left with hundreds of possible suspects."

His face is set in the expression I think of as "disgusted". It's a look I never really saw on his face until the last year. Since the incident it's there a lot, even when he's not aware of it and is actually trying to be nice. I wonder whether I have a similar look; is he looking at me right now thinking she is disgusted with me? And what happens when we only have these looks? Does resignation replace disgust? And when that happens do we split up? But I can't think of that because we can't split up, I won't let it happen, I can and will control this situation.

"They checked the CCTV cameras that cover Merton Street from there. Nothing for the time when I would have dropped Finn off. They said they would send a patrol car by over the next few days, at dropping off and picking up time."

He moves towards me and goes to place his hand on my arm but I pull back.

"You didn't keep a copy of the picture – well I guess you can't – so I wonder, is it possible that you somehow…" Henry pauses and gives me his "understanding and concerned" look that makes me feel the fury ignite in my stomach.

"Don't," I say to him.

"You've been under so much stress. I know you don't sleep well, and with all the pressure of the show, maybe you transferred some of the stuff in the show on to your natural maternal concern and saw something that was real to you?"

I shake my head. "He's not going back to school."

Henry's face flushes an angry red and he jabs the plate at me again.

"What do you suggest?"

I try to ignore the jibe and tell myself to focus on achieving the result and to keep my features in a neutral expression.

"We could move schools. I don't know, maybe home teach for a bit?"

"No! He's not going to be locked up in here like you, afraid to go out because of something you caused! I won't let that happen to him."

He shakes the plate and I watch a piece of mangetout fall to the floor and land next to his foot.

"We need to catch whoever sent that message, that's what we need to do. If the police can't help then we need to do it ourselves," and as I say this I jab my finger at him to emphasise the point.

He snorts, a gesture that makes his face screw up and look meaner and older.

"It could be anyone. You've got a lot of enemies. These trolls are everywhere. I told you what would happen if you did these podcasts, it just stirs people up. It's an open invitation to them to waltz into our lives and into our home."

Is Henry referring to the "incident"? If I ask him directly he will deny it of course, so we do what we always do, ignore it, not so gently float around the subject.

"It's Frenchie, I'm sure of it."

"So what? It could be any of them. They are legion, aren't they? I've seen your Twitter feed. You are public property and if you keep up with this podcast there'll be more. You have got to stop this. Why isn't being a mum to Finn" – he reaches out his hand and awkwardly takes hold of mine – "and a husband to me enough for you?"

I bite.

"How is this my fault?"

Henry snatches his hand away and I can see he is trying to say something but rage causes his mouth to flap hopelessly, as the words murder each other before making it to his mouth.

"I only want him to be safe," I say.

Henry's words reach a truce with themselves and charge at a mutual enemy.

"He's not going anywhere. And if anyone has put him in danger, it's you with this stupid fucking podcast, winding up fascists and fucking nutters. You! Your fault. Just like–"

He stops himself but the attack has been made.

"Why don't you say it?" I whisper.

He wants to say it was my fault. I can see it in his face and I realise part of me wants him to say it too, and if he does, this will break something for sure, but maybe it needs to break. He raises the plate and I can see it in his face; he wants to throw it at me.

And then his face changes. Disgust is replaced by something worse: fear and helplessness. I turn and look and see that Finn is standing at the kitchen door. Christ knows how long he's been there.

Henry puts the plate down on the counter and quickly walks over to the door and picks up Finn.

"Come on, son, you've had a long day, you need your rest."

Finn looks back at me from over Henry's shoulder. His big brown eyes are full of tears. All I can think is that I'm failing in every way to protect those I love, or am supposed to love.

After they leave the kitchen I take the plates out the dishwasher and wash them down with water from the tap before careful reloading the dishwater plate by plate. Only when they are lined up in their racks do I close the door.

When I get into bed the duvet wall is firmly in place. I think about stretching out a hand to reach for Henry but then I hear his breathing. It's shallow and full of tension and I know he's pretending to be asleep.

Instead I get out of bed and go to the bathroom. Once in there I take my mobile phone out the pocket of my dressing gown and text Hannah.

It's a simple message:

One of the trolls took a picture of my boy at school. I need help.

I wait but there's no reply. I type the same message to Mo and hit send.

A reply comes within thirty seconds; it's from Mo.

I'm on it. Will call tomorrow.

When I go back to bed Henry is still faking sleep. Maybe it's because I know Mo will help, but I fall asleep straight away.

CHAPTER THIRTEEN

This is a call

Something happened and I'm not sure if it is a good thing or a bad thing. I received a voicemail message.

I replay it again.

The voice is one I have never heard before but had already imagined. It's thinner, reedier than I had conjured up. I had imagined a booming baritone to go with the booming temper I was sure he had, but he fails to live up to my imagination.

I hit "2" again.

"Message received Monday 8 November at 8.32am: 'Hello. Is that Mrs Kelly? It's Tom Ellis here and I would like to talk, clear the air so to speak, keep lawyers out of it, eh? All they do is eat up money. So please call me back when you get this message. It's important for both of us'."

He doesn't sound threatening at all. He sounds desperate.

I don't call him back straight away. Instead I wander through the deserted kitchen amongst the remains of Finn and Henry's breakfast blitzkrieg. I shake a fallen packet of cornflakes, checking for any stragglers, but it's just corn powder. The butter which has only recently replaced the "healthy spread" lies melting in the middle of the table covered in the dust of toast fallout.

"Protect and survive," I whisper out loud, thinking of the 1970s UK government pamphlet on how to survive a nuclear attack.

The house is quiet and even Lil'Bitch is nowhere to be seen. Henry must have already fed her otherwise she would be rubbing up and down my leg right now, trading purrs for food.

I open the fridge and grab some yoghurt. I locate the muesli box hidden under a copy of *The Guardian* and pour a generous helping into a bowl with the yoghurt.

I eat and enjoy the silence. I often wonder if part of my not leaving the house is the fear that the sheer sensory overload of the city would wipe my brain clean like an electromagnetic pulse. The silence is like a warm duvet and I relax into it.

The buzzing of my mobile phone breaks the peace. I look at the display and see that it's Mo trying to call me. I let it ring out. My feelings towards Mo are complicated. In working on his brother's case, I realise now there was always an unspoken dynamic, that I was helping him, but now with my cry for help a new rhythm has been sounded and I'm not sure how it will play out. So I let the call ring out whilst I debate whether the late-night decision to involve him stands up to my daylight, rational self.

By the time I finish my cereal and drink a cup of coffee I've made my decision and I go down to the basement.

It's even quieter down here and cooler too. I feel nervous as I set up the computer system and the recording equipment but when I put on the headset all my nerves vanish. It's as though I'm a different person, stronger and more real, grounded less in my incorporeal fears but in a purpose that feeds me.

I dial the number and within three rings there is an answer.

CHAPTER FOURTEEN

The hunt

Cinnamon rolls, crisp with iced toppings, lie on the table like a map of the galaxy.

Mo reaches for one of the dark swirls and, with obvious relish, pops half of it into his mouth in a bite that screams mindfulness more than a million self-help tapes. As he chews, his eyes scrunch up with enjoyment; here is a man truly in the moment.

I can't help but watch him and take my own pleasure in his simple delight. I wish I could lose myself in this way but "I" am always there, commenting, criticising, judging as to whether the moment measures up to what it could be.

Whilst he eats I take out my phone and take a picture of the plate of pastries. It will make a good 'Gram post later.

"Thanks for coming over, Mo. I'm meant to be helping you, not the other way around."

He puts the other half of the pastry down on the plate in front of him and then rubs his index finger along his moustache, sending a flurry of white icing sugar down towards the table.

"I love cinnamon rolls but if I keep eating them I'm sure to get fat, ha! As for my help, it is the very least I can do after everything you have done for Khalil and for my family."

"But…"

He raises one of his large hands.

"Your child was threatened, your family." His eyes narrow and then flash with anger. "And to attack your family is to attack my family. That is how I see the world Sarah, family is everything and you do everything you can to protect them. The police" – he waves his hand – "don't want to know because no one was hurt and your persecutor will think he is safe and he will continue to threaten you. I read the emails and posts you sent me. Disgusting garbage from a sick mind. No, not a sick mind, for that would be excusable if he were ill, but a mind allowed to think he is untouchable and protected, that he can strike out in the darkness with impunity, and make no mistake, such a person is dangerous. The more they get away with the further they go. I've seen the results on my rounds."

An image of Finn, lying prone and lifeless on the pavement outside of the school, flashes into my mind. Mo must see this expressed on my face.

He reaches his hand towards me and it hovers above the cinnamon roll galaxies.

"But that won't happen here. We are going to hunt this Frenchie down and stop him from harassing your family and allow you to concentrate on setting Khalil free. Yes?"

I nod and muster up a faint smile. It's hard not to believe this gentle bear of a man and the calm assurance he gives out.

"Good! This is settled then."

I can't but help think of Henry's limp response to the threat to our child and compare it with Mo's certainty and strength and how he makes me feel. He makes me feel stronger, he adds to my sense of self. And Henry, how does he make me feel? I push the thought to the back of my mind.

"How will you find him?"

Mo's hand descends and plucks another roll from the plate.

Before he puts it in his mouth he smiles with his eyes.

"Hunters follow tracks. He will have left some, you can be sure, and we will hunt him down. But this is for another day," he takes a big bite of the roll and his eyes roll up in pure appreciation of this moment, this sensation and I envy his ability to take pleasure when and where he finds it, "will you join me? They are delicious and you must save me from getting fat."

I shrug. "Why not?" I pick up one of the rolls and take a bite. He's right, they are delicious.

Later that night as Henry sleeps upstairs, I WhatsApp Hannah.

Hi, are you around? Big news!

Her status changes to online almost immediately.

*Yo girlfriend, tell all, just enjoying (****?!) bath time here.*

I quickly type.

We are going to hunt Frenchie down.

Her answer doesn't come straight away, in fact it doesn't come even after a minute, which is a lifetime in a WhatsApp conversation so I send her another message.

You ok?

Her reply pings back straight away.

Sorry! That is fucking fantastic, who is "we" though?

I type quickly: *me and the handsome doctor.*

Do you have any idea who Frenchie could be? Isn't it impossible to track down these trolls?

We don't know yet, Mo is helping me, I think he is going to get his private investigators to track him down.

There is a noise from the stairs. It's a squeak I recognise; it belongs to the third step up from the hall. I strain my ears. I can't hear anything else but I have the distinct impression someone is standing outside the door.

I tell myself not to be stupid but I know all the noises of the house. I have lived them every day for over a year now and they are as familiar as my heartbeat, and so when something changes, however imperceptible, I notice it before I can identify it. And something has just changed, and the air feels thicker as though someone or something has added to it.

Hang on, Hannah. Think Henry may be outside listening.

Fucktart you ok?

I don't reply; instead I carefully raise myself from the sofa and, breathing and moving as quietly as I can, make my way to the closed lounge doors.

I stop when I reach the door and listen. At first all I can hear are the usual rhythms of the house, the central heating's slight hiss and gurgle, quieter since the last service, but still there as a chugging back beat to the melody of the movement of air through the house, the delicate drafts and mistrals of window edges, keyholes and Victorian brickwork. But then, there, another sound, regular, the sound of suppressed breathing, as though someone were trying not to be heard.

What if it's not Henry? What if it's Frenchie or someone worse? What if it's him, returned to finish the job he started twelve months ago? I look around for a weapon but nothing but the table lamp presents itself so I bend down, slowly, and unplug the lamp. I gather the cable in my right hand and hold the lamp base in my left, poised to strike.

I use the fingers of my left hand to grip the doorknob and then gently I twist it until I feel the click of the bolt come free. As soon as that happens I pull the door open and get ready to bring the lamp smashing down on the head of Finn who is standing there, a blanket in one hand, his red fire truck in the other and a look of terror and confusion on his face.

I sink to my knees, dropping the lamp and then enveloping him in my arms.

"Are you okay, my love?"

I pull back, terrified that I've scared him, but he rubs his eyes.

"I just wanted a story," he says, and the tremble in his voice causes such depths of self-loathing and fear that I'm infecting him with my anxiety that I want to run screaming as far as away as possible to protect him from me.

Instead, I take his hand; it feels so small and delicate it could break my heart.

"Come on, I'll read you one. What about *The Very Hungry Caterpillar*?"

He pads alongside me as we mount the stairs.

We reach his bedroom but before we enter Finn pulls on my hand.

"What is it, my sweet?" I ask him.

He looks up at me with his dark eyes, so full of innocence.

"Can Daddy read it to me instead?"

I shouldn't feel envy about my son wanting his father to read to him instead of me. I shouldn't but I do. It's an honest request from my little boy, a boy who doesn't feel reassured by his neurotic mother. I kneel down and bring my face close to his.

"Daddy's asleep so it's me and you tonight. Is that okay? Daddy can read to you tomorrow."

He sucks his bottom lip in.

"Suppose so."

I get him into bed, tuck him in and then squeeze next to him.

Way before *The Very Hungry Caterpillar* has formed a cocoon, Finn is asleep, and although I should rejoin Henry, I feel sleep dragging me down into an abyss of exhaustion I can't resist, and then I'm gone.

CHAPTER FIFTEEN

Who is he?

"Who is he?" I ask.

Mo is back at my kitchen table and this time he has brought Chelsea buns and a blue cardboard folder. He cocks his head to one side and then smiles. The wrinkles around his eyes have been joined by bags and dark circles that speak of a sleepless night.

"Your tormenter, the stalker of your children and of you, is a twenty-three-year-old student of economics, one Marcus Evans. He lives with his mother in New Cross and works at a call centre in the daytime dealing with PPI complaints."

Mo opens the folder and tips its contents onto the table. It's a series of black and white photographs all of the same man, a scrawny twenty-something with bad skin and patchy facial hair.

"This is Frenchie?"

I look up at Mo. He has just begun eating one of the Chelsea buns, and he nods vigorously, causing a flurry of icing to fall and land on the table.

I fan the photographs out across the desk as though I'm in the CIA or something. I'm not going to lie, it gives me a subversive thrill looking at the images of this normal-looking young man. He looks like a student who should be out protesting about something or another, not knowing that I am observing him, and I can't help but wonder if this is how he feels. It's power.

"How did you find him so quickly? Is it legal?"

Mo chuckles and I can see he's enjoying this. It must be a break from being a surgeon, and perhaps it counts as light relief to him?

I dismiss the thought as uncharitable; he's the only man helping me right now.

He licks his fingers as he talks.

"I wish I could tell you we tracked him down through some tricky software or satellites or something but the truth is rather more prosaic and certainly legal. We used Facebook."

"How?"

"Pretty simple really. My cousin ran a search against all of his usernames and we got lucky with the variant FrenchDuck1066. You'd be surprised how many hits there were. People tend to use their online names like their real name, habitually, and that's what we got. Dating profiles, chatrooms, even newspaper below-the-line comments sections. None of it was useful though, as it still only had the 'Frenchie' tag line variation, except one, a user profile on Breitbart. This was a Frenchie1066. We looked back through his comment history and found one posting about the London Bridge terror attacks; it referred to his local paper, the *Hampstead & Highgate Express*."

"That's our local paper."

"Yes, and the link was to an article on the attack calling for solidarity and unity, and underneath the article was a comment by a reader calling the author a 'cuck'." He sees my confusion. "A cuck is an alt-right term for someone who has been cuckolded by the liberal media, but the important point is that posting on the local paper has to be done through a Facebook account. Now it could be a fake account of course, but when we checked the user, Marcus Evans, it showed up some interesting results. Take a look at that printout there."

It's a screenshot of a Facebook page. The profile picture is the same man as in the black and white shots, but he's wearing sunglasses in the Facebook profile.

There are a series of posts but it's the one at the top that catches my eye. It's dated three months ago and it contains a link to my first podcast, and Marcus has commented on it. The comment is "Another liberal cuck – time to bring Frenchie out again, 1066 and all that!"

"It must be him, but can we be sure?"

Mo runs his fingers through his thick black hair and then sits back, putting his hands behind his head in triumph.

"I'm sure."

"We should give this to the police."

Mo doesn't answer right away, and in the sudden silence the noise of the house, the grumbling pipes, the creaks of wood that never settle and the sound of air on the move seems amplified.

"I wouldn't do that," he says quietly, all trace of humour having left his face.

"Why?" I ask, but I know why. I just want to hear it, have my thoughts justified by their articulation from another.

"It's all circumstantial. You'd never get a search warrant on this basis, and even if you did, so what? His messages might not even amount to a criminal offence and I don't trust the police, and neither should you."

"What are the alternatives?"

Mo looks up and goes to say something but then stops short.

"You were going to say something?"

He breathes in deeply and looks at me again.

"I have a cousin, he's… let's say he's the black sheep of the family. He could speak to him, in a kinetic manner. Nothing too serious but enough."

"You mean beat him up?"

I look at Mo and his expression is one I don't recognise. It is serious and there is a hardness difficult to reconcile with the man who brings me pastries.

"He threatened your child. It's what I would do if someone threatened my family," he says in a matter-of-fact way.

Mo looks up at me again to gauge my reaction. I think he is expecting shock and horror at his suggestion but the truth is I had already considered this as an option. Christ, how I would love to give into that rage and really, what else will do but physical violence when someone threatens your child? But, and I wish I could say it was because I'm a good person, the reality is that I am frightened of getting caught, and that would mean being removed from the house. Instead, I put forward an alternative.

"That's brilliant, Sarah, if we can make it work. We can certainly give it a go."

I check my watch; it's 5pm.

"Can you be ready in two hours?"

He smiles again and stands up.

"Why not? I'm on my way."

Two hours later and I'm down in the basement. Henry took care of dinner. It was spaghetti bolognese, as it's all he can cook and he's inordinately proud of it, so he acted hurt when I told him to leave mine in the fridge as I had work to do.

I've told him and Finn not to disturb me but, just in case, I put the catch on the basement door.

At 7pm exactly I text Mo.

Are you in position?

Less than twenty seconds later I receive a reply.

Yes. Perfectly placed.

I launch Twitter and unblock Frenchie. I type a tweet and then cast it into the murky waters of Twitter.

@Frenchie1066 @therealskelly you took pictures of my child. Are you a paedophile is that what your rage is about?

Almost straight away I start receiving tweets from supporters asking me what is going on and whether my family and I are okay. Sometimes the waters aren't so dark and I marvel at the part of the community that supports and protects each other and wonder whether I have become too cynical, and then Frenchie bites.

@Frenchie1066 replying to @therealskelly Too easy, you need to know the fear WE all have of murderers of girls, you liberal elite support #rotherham #Allahwasapaedo

I'm typing straight away in reply.

@therealskelly replying to @Frenchie1066 by taking pics of kids at school in detail? No girlfriend I bet.

@Frenchie1066 replying to @therealskelly successful, married with children, I want to protect them, not surrender like you #quisling #traitor

I check my phone there is a message from Mo.

Go!

I launch the Facebook Live app on my phone.

@therealskelly replying to @Frenchie1066 that's not true is it, though? You live at home with your mother.

By the amount of re-tweets and likes, our conversation is being watched by lots of my hundred thousand followers.

What if he doesn't respond? I needn't worry.

@Frenchie1066 replying to @therealskelly ha you loveless bitch you is wrong I am everywhere, I am here, I am legion #nosurrender

I check my phone. It's working perfectly and there are now over one hundred people watching.

@therealskelly replying to @Frenchie1066 but you're at home right now with your mum.

@Frenchie1066 replying to @therealskelly whatever bitch maybe next time I won't just take photos you feel like Lauren's mother then bitch #murderer #guilty

@therealskelly replying to @Frenchie1066 you know what dark places need?

@Frenchie1066 replying to @therealskelly? Fuckface?

@therealskelly replying to @Frenchie1066 plight – take a look out of your bedroom window.

I check my phone again. Mo's Facebook Live feed is coming through clearly and I can see the box room, the computer and the thin man, really just a boy, as he looks from the screen to the window.

"Go on," I whisper to the screen.

I tweet the link.

He's standing stock still at the window, looking directly at Mo, who is standing on top of a VW transporter van filming him with his phone.

The boy looks terrified and almost seems to shrink inside himself, and then he snatches the curtains tightly shut.

@therealskelly replying to @Frenchie1066 Marcus Evans, 124 Quarter Lane, North Cross, troll, child stalker, misogynist – enjoy the light!

I check the recoding of the live link; it's all been captured perfectly with Marcus framed in the window typing on his laptop. I save the file and then I post that together with a tweet to the Metropolitan Police PR department.

"Game over dweeb," I find myself saying, and I close my computer and turn off my phone. And just like that Frenchie is gone.

CHAPTER SIXTEEN

10

Henry's face is twisted in the same sort of shape that it adopts when he is prospecting for Lil'Bitch's turds in her litter box. This could go either way.

"I'm pleased, no I am, really pleased that you have stopped him, if it was him." He sees a look on my face and backs off. "I mean, of course it was him, so that's really good, but was it all, you know, legal? And I'm sure it was but" – he looks like he is sniffing a particularly pungent turd – "was it, is it, moral?"

Rage. I close my eyes and let it boil up and then subside ever so slightly but when I hear my tone it's dripping in contempt.

"This man turned up outside our son's school and took pictures of him and then sent them to me, threatening" – I turn the volume down as I can hear Finn moving about in the living room – "to hurt him. The police couldn't help." I just about avoid adding "and neither could you". "So I took action."

Lil'Bitch pads into the kitchen, looks up at me and Henry and then turns on her heels and heads for the sunlit uplands of the lounge with its warm radiators, stray Haribo and calmer environment.

"Look, I said I'm glad didn't I? I just worry about you and what you're getting into. It's dangerous getting involved with these trolls, can't you just go back to doing features like when we first met? It was safer."

I suck in my breath and look at my husband. I don't want to feel this way but I almost feel hatred for this passive-aggressive man standing here waving a spatula at me. How did it come to this? I know the answer, inch by inch, day by day, sigh by disapproving sigh. But hatred is the same coin as love, I keep telling myself. I just need to flip it back again.

I want to scream at him, "You want me to do twenty-ways-avocados-can-spice-up-your-life pieces for the rest of my life!" but I try a different tactic, surrender, and put on a smile.

"You're right, probably not the wisest thing to do, but at least it's one less worry for us."

He stirs the bloody red contents of the pot and then raises the spatula to his lips, from which a pointed tongue darts out quickly like a lizard sampling the midday desert air, and tastes the dripping sauce.

"More oregano, I think," he says quietly to himself more than to me. "You see, after what happened you need to leave this sort of stuff to the professionals. I'm not saying I'm not pleased to get rid of this troll, though I'm sure he was absolutely harmless." I think of the emails threatening to rape or kill me and suck in more resentment fuel. "But you never know what the consequences could be for you, for us, yeah?"

That "yeah" has me biting my lip and thinking of using the spatula on him in an unorthodox way.

"Sure, *yeah*. I'm going to check in on Finn."

"No worries, and honey?" He looks up from the pan and I can see there is some sauce in his beard. "Love you."

"And you," trips off my tongue.

In the living room Finn is sitting on the floor in front of the TV, although the sound is turned down. He is surrounded by plastic dinosaurs and toy soldiers.

"Are you playing *Jurassic Park* again?"

I'm still a bit angry at Henry for leaving the TV on a few months back whilst he took a call from his mother. I had come up from the basement to find Finn staring at the TV, engrossed in the first movie, but luckily it had only sparked an obsession with dinosaurs rather than the raving night terrors I feared.

"This" – he picked up the T-rex – "isn't my favourite anymore."

"Oh, why is that?"

Finn puts down the T-rex and picks up a much smaller dinosaur.

"This is my new best dinosaur. It's Compsognathus. Compy. It was in the movie, remember?"

I don't, but I nod anyway, not wishing to discourage him.

"And why is this one your new favourite?"

Finn grins as though embarrassed to tell me why.

"Come on, you can tell me," I hold out my hand and he places Compy in my palm.

"Because it's friendly at first but then later there's lots of them, all tiny, and they eat the hunter. Remember?"

I do remember now. I remember the German hunter character petting them and then suddenly he's surrounded by hundreds of them and they pounce and devour him.

Finn laughs and makes a short, sharp, snapping sound, imitating the jaws of the Compy, and holds it in from of my face. There's something about it, the small, sharp, tiny teeth maybe, that gives me chills.

"Put it down." I swipe the air unthinkingly and accidentally catch his hand, knocking Compy to the floor.

Finn looks at me, shocked, and I think he's going to burst into tears but instead he just turns and leaves the room and I hear his tiny footsteps ascending the stairs.

"Fuck," I say out loud. It's Henry's fault that I snapped at Finn; he left me with anger and the only outlet was my child. I follow Finn up the stairs and he obviously hears me coming because he pushes his bedroom door shut after him. I gently open it and see that he is lying face down on the bed. I sit next to him and place Compy next to his tiny hand.

"I'm sorry honey, I didn't mean to catch your hand and poor Compy like that."

He mumbles something into the sheets.

"You know Mummy is a bit silly sometimes, and it's like when you do something naughty and you're very sorry afterwards. You still did the naughty thing but you promise not to in the future.

Well, that's like me now, I'm very sorry and I promise I won't do anything like that in the future. I love you so much, honey. I'm sorry."

A sob catches in my throat and on hearing this my darling boy jumps up and throws his arms around me.

"Don't cry, I love you. Will you read me another story?"

I read to him and as usual he is asleep within a few minutes and I hope that the story, the love, will balance out the collateral damage I, we, as parents inflict upon him, but really whose to tell? Maybe the killer of Lauren could trace their anger against woe back to a parent's carelessness?

I go back into the kitchen and open the fridge door, taking out a bottle of wine.

Henry looks over and raises an eyebrow. I have an urge to grab his head and shove it into the bowl of steaming bolognese.

He must see something in my face, a defiance daring him to say something about my drinking, but he chooses his words wisely.

"Oh lovely, pour me one as well will you, honey?"

I get down two glasses from the cabinet and do so, making sure mine is clearly the larger.

I pass the less-full glass to Henry but if he notices he doesn't let on.

"Do you still love me, Henry?" I ask him.

He doesn't look up from his stirring.

"Of course I do. I know we've been through a difficult patch" – he snorts with what I think is laughter but it can't be, surely, given what happened – "but we'll get through it. I think the important thing is to focus on what matters." Now he looks up. "Our son, our family, us." He puts the spatula down on the worktop where it leaves a red smear and walks over to me, and then he hugs me and it's so alien but yet so needed, a human touch, that I burst into tears. "And our home."

CHAPTER SEVENTEEN

Garden

Cathy is so excited she lights another cigarette off the tip of the one she's just smoked down to the nub.

"I can't believe you didn't tell me, fucking master stroke. You know he was targeting other women yeah? Christ, you saw *The Guardian* website today, yeah? He's been trolling women in the media for years now, Suzanne Moore, Caitlin Moran, fuck, a regular one-man abuse factory, and you brought him down, and using the same tools as well. You are a legend, a troll slayer, and I don't even have to tell you about our listening figures; the podcasts have been downloaded like a gazillion times. I swear on Allah's tit if Khalil's appeal is successful next month you are going to be able to stand for prime minister." She sucks hard on the fag. "Well, leader of the Labour Party anyway, for what that's worth."

She's half in and half out of the kitchen, hanging by one arm from the French doors and swinging back and forth.

She swings out into the garden.

"Come on, come and join me, it's fucking lovely out here."

She's right. It's a crisp and sunny Saturday afternoon and the sun is out. Henry and Finn have gone to the zoo.

I heard Henry tell Finn that Mummy couldn't come with them because she had work to do and Finn had replied, "That's not true she just likes staying home." I felt ashamed.

Cathy is out in the middle of our small garden and pirouetting as she takes puffs on her cigarette.

"Those things will kill you," I say as filler to avoid the topic at hand.

"Life will kill us all my darling, no one gets out alive, but at least I can enjoy days like this when they come along."

There is an old dance track by A Guy called Gerald playing on 6 Music and Cathy starts to pull shapes; all the while the cigarette dangles from her lips.

She inclines her head, wanting me to join her.

Lil'Bitch looks up at me from her position by my feet and then slinks out of the door and jumps up on the bench near Cathy.

"Traitor," I mutter.

"Come on you, remember how we used to dance to this!" This is delivered from the side of her mouth, the cigarette somehow maintaining its position.

And I do remember a time when we used to dance to this tune. With a sweet, sick stab of a house beat I'm taken back to sweaty clubs, dank clothes, high times and a dark, heavy feeling that may have been the happiest I've ever felt. How did I go from that to this? Were there signs that I missed along the way, which if I had my time again I could say "ah there they are" and make different decisions, or as the determinists believe, was this always my fate – doomed by cause and effect?

The kiss. This song reminds me of the kiss. It was the Ministry of Sound long before it was shit, a chemically washed-through evening. I was young, everything was possible and there was a kiss with a girl I didn't know, probably didn't even fancy, but the exuberance, the life and the excitement of it all I do remember, and I can see Cathy does too as she dances, eyes closed, her mind half here and half two decades away. I've often, unkindly, told myself in the past that her still going clubbing, smoking, occasionally taking drugs is a bit sad, an attempt to stake out a settlement in the land of the young she has no business occupying, but watching her dance now, unashamedly, with joy, I realise it's me who is the pathetic one. I gave up and made choices along the way I thought I ought to make, that were expected and not the ones I wanted to make. I want to play, I realise, and before I know it I've stepped out into the sunshine and I'm dancing and Twitter, Snapchat,

Facebook and all the rest of the constructs seem a long way away from this moment.

I don't know how long we dance for. Maybe it's only for a couple of songs but I can't tell because it's like I've stopped right now, in this moment and for the first time in a long time I'm truly in it and nowhere else. The only other time I remember being like this in the recent past was, as sick as it sounds, when I was raped. Then, as now, I was locked mentally in a time and place and could not – nor did I know how to – get out of it. The difference of course is now I want to be here. I am simply here and it is joyous.

We collapse, eventually, into the wicker chairs, breathless and red-cheeked with exertion, sun and bliss.

"Do you miss being young?" I ask Cathy. She spits out the butt end of the cigarette that has gone out whilst she was dancing and starts rolling another.

"What do you mean, do I miss it? I'll be young when they are lowering me into the ground on the day after my hundredth birthday."

"It's all up here," and she taps her forehead with her fingertip and then she smiles at me.

And then it hits me. I'm outside and I'm not hyperventilating and my heart, other than pumping slightly faster due to our dancing, isn't pounding like it wants to escape from my rib cage.

I look around at the windows of the houses that back into our small garden and they don't seem so dark and foreboding as I normally see them from in the kitchen behind the safety of the French doors.

It's a beautiful day and my son and husband are at the zoo and I could join them. As I think this, pinpricks of anxiety land on my fingertips with the pleasant tingle that is normally followed by the fear creeping up my arms, the clenching oxygen-depriving adrenaline choke, but this doesn't arrive.

I take a deep breath, but not in the forced way the doctor has taught me; this is more instinctive, healthier. The pinpricks do not advance, which is progress undoubtedly, but nor do they retreat.

"We better get in, Cath," I say.

She takes out her cigarette and flicks it towards the borders. Henry will go mad if he finds it.

I stand up and walk towards the open door of the kitchen. I pause on the threshold and I can't help feeling that something has changed but I'm not sure what it is.

Cathy puts a hand on my shoulder and squeezes it.

"You did good, kidda," she whispers in my ear.

We step inside.

It's only later as I lie in bed listening to Henry's snores that I realise what the feeling was that I felt in the garden before I stepped back in the house. For a moment, when we were dancing, I was afraid of the house.

CHAPTER EIGHTEEN

Podcast 6

Podcast Episode 6 – by Sarah Kelly – 22/11/2018
TRANSCRIPT OF TEL. CALL 17/11/2018

TOM ELLIS: Hi, who is this?

SARAH KELLY: It's Sarah Kelly here. You called me and left a message saying you wanted to talk, so here I am.

TOM ELLIS: (pause) I suppose I better thank you for calling me, but after what you have put me and my family through it's the least you can do.

SARAH KELLY: Just so you know Mr Ellis, in the interest of full disclosure, I am recording this call.

TOM ELLIS: (laughs) Well, what else should I expect of a journalist? But it's okay. I've got nothing to hide and that's what I wanted to talk to you about. I want you to stop defaming me on your radio show.

SARAH KELLY: Podcast.

TOM ELLIS: Whatever. It's beyond a joke now and it's causing me harm, professionally and personally. People are talking.

SARAH KELLY: I've not put anything out on my show that isn't the truth and you and your lawyers know that – that's why you've not sued.

TOM ELLIS: It's not just that, though, is it? It's how you present something, spin the facts, tell a story in a certain way so your listeners' sympathies fall with or against a particular character, and on this occasion you've assigned me the bad guy role and the murderer–

SARAH KELLY: So you think Khalil did it?

TOM ELLIS: No, I'm not saying that, but he was convicted, wasn't he, and British justice is the best in the world, wouldn't you agree?

SARAH KELLY: Not for Khalil. You were his best friend at school.

TOM ELLIS: That was a long time ago. I had many friends.

SARAH KELLY: Everyone says you two were inseparable.

TOM ELLIS: We were seventeen, for god's sake; at that age allegiances change like the weather.

SARAH KELLY: Allegiances is a funny word for friendship. No one else described it as that. Is that how you see relationships?

TOM ELLIS: Don't be so obtuse. Look, I just wanted to speak to you to make it clear, to set it out for the record, that I had nothing to do with the death of Lauren Grey.

SARAH KELLY: I never said you did.

TOM ELLIS: (angry) You insinuated it! It's enough for libel, my lawyers tell me. This is your last–

SARAH KELLY: Did you love Lauren?

TOM ELLIS: (long pause) Lauren was beautiful, gifted and amazing. You'd be mad not to love her.

SARAH KELLY: Is that what happened? You were jealous of Khalil, you had a row with him, followed Lauren to tell her how you felt? Did things just get out of hand?

TOM ELLIS: (laughs) Jesus Christ, you've been watching too many detective movies. Of course I was jealous of Khalil, every boy in our year was. Do you think we all killed her, Orient Express *style? I'm glad you're recording this so you can play it to your listeners, unedited I hope, and they can hear for themselves that you set out to destroy a man's life on the basis of nothing more than an effort to drive up ratings for your fucking podcast. I suggest you stick with your original decision to give up journalism.*

SARAH KELLY: So you've been Googling me.

TOM ELLIS: Of course I fucking have. You step into my life, my world, dragging my name through the shit, and I want to know who is doing this to me and why. And it turns out it's some burnt-out hack using my life as a doormat on the way to some sort of comeback. It's fucking pathetic.

SARAH KELLY: (pause) You've got quite a temper on you, Mr Ellis.

TOM ELLIS: I've every right to be angry! My family are distraught.

SARAH KELLY: It's funny you mention your family. I wanted to ask you about them. Tell me, Mr Ellis, why did you batter your wife, leaving her with a broken jaw, concussion and two cracked ribs?

TOM ELLIS: You fucking bitch, that didn't happen like that. She was pissed and fell over, ask her yourself. I'm going to sue you for every fucking penny you have. Your fucking son will be pimping his ass for spare change on The Heath by the time I'm through.

SARAH KELLY: Was it this temper that made you do it?

LINE IS CUT

TRANSCRIPT ENDS

So, there you have it. My interview with Tom Ellis. Make of it what you will. Here's my take on it. He's right of course, I have no direct evidence linking him with the murder of Lauren and for the sake of avoiding any doubt, never mind court, I am not alleging he committed the murder. I want to go further than that. I'm not just saying this to avoid being sued but because I don't know what I believe, but I am some way, hell, a long, long way from even coming close to suggesting that Tom is a murderer.

But, what I do know and what I will say is that the police did not investigate other motives and this leaves a question the size of a Zeppelin hanging over the safe conviction of Khalil.

There's more. I've seen the arrest record for Tom Ellis after an alleged assault on his wife. They were sent to me anonymously and there is a statement in there, subsequently retracted I understand, from Emma Ellis that states that Tom Ellis attacked her because, and I quote, "He saw that I'd received a Facebook message off an old school friend who I'd had a short relationship with when we were in school. There was nothing to it so I told Tom so he wouldn't think there was; his response was to drink half a bottle of whisky and then start an argument which ended with me in hospital."*

So, allegedly, of course he was never convicted. A violent man, a jealous man who admitted he was jealous of Khalil's relationship and a man who, according to Amy Wilder, had the opportunity to cycle to World's End and commit the murder.

But let's cut the police some slack here. I can hear you saying they had no idea he was violent. The assault against his wife took place nearly ten years after Lauren's murder.

Did I mention that Tom had a police record at the time of the incident? No, neither did Khalil's defence, because it wasn't relevant to the defence, but I looked through the police file and there it was. 2006. A £150 fine and one hundred hours of community service for assaulting a bouncer who wouldn't let him in a nightclub. Maybe it means something, maybe nothing. You could say, for example, if you were an investigating police officer that here you had a partygoer, closely linked to the deceased, who had a conviction for violent behaviour triggered by not getting his own way. It doesn't mean he did it, of course, although I don't know about you, but it would want me to take a closer look.

But will any of this help Khalil get out of prison? Probably not, but then that's not our job here tonight listeners is it? Our job is to bear witness and if Tom Ellis has a problem with that then tough luck.

* (*This is a lie. Of course Mo got hold of them, but I'm classifying it as a white lie in order to avoid being sued and/or getting Mo convicted as I didn't ask him where he got them from. Ignorance is bliss, or rather not going to jail.*)

CHAPTER NINETEEN

Knocks once

I'm expecting at the very least another cease and desist letter from Tom's lawyers but in the days following the podcast nothing arrives.

Despite this I feel a weight of anxiety settle on me over and above my normal, admittedly high, levels. It feels like the phoney war and I'm just waiting for something awful to happen. But as each day passes nothing does, and by the end of the week I'm feeling better and it's not just the non-arrival of the terrible thing. Something good, well I know I should think it is good, happens instead.

Henry and I sleep together for the first time since the rape.

I'm still not sure how it happened but I am sure that the location of it was important. It didn't happen in the bedroom and now I see it never could; we've imbued that room, our bed, with too much tension and defeated expectation night after night with our backs turned to each other. There was no way we could learn to overcome that barrier that was made physical in the goose-down wall that separated us.

Instead, and I'm unsure whether this is DH Lawrence romantic or more cheesy *wah wah* porn, we fucked on the washing machine in the utility room.

Finn was out on a play date and after returning from dropping him off I heard Henry come into the kitchen and drop his keys on the worktop, and I remember thinking *why can't he use the bowl I bought just for this purpose and left right by the front door on the hall table?* And then he walked into the utility room and I said, "How was it?" but I didn't turn around to say this and maybe that was the key. He didn't have to look at me.

He mumbled something low that I didn't catch and then before I registered what was happening he put a hand around my clavicle, his fingers stretching and digging into my neck, and pulled down my tracksuit pants with his other hand and then he had unzipped his pants and I could feel his cock banging against my bare arse.

I put my right arm forward against the wall and shoved backwards, drawing him in to me, and then he was holding me tight, almost painfully so, but I liked it, deserved it, and he was thrusting furiously and then, a few seconds later, it was over.

I turned round, planning to kiss him, but he was pulling up his pants and shuffling backwards.

"I liked that," I said and smiled at him.

He didn't look up at me and mumbled something about "needing to do some work" and turned and left the room.

I should have felt deflated, I know. Used for sex. But I didn't. It's progress. If you still see your partner as a sexual being then all is not lost, I told myself.

Later that evening I stretched out a hand across the duvet wall and placed it on Henry's stomach, letting it rest there as he breathed in and out. He wasn't sleeping, I could tell by the pattern of his breathing, but then he made a noise that could have been a snore or could have been the noise a man makes when he wants you to think he's sleeping.

I moved my hand back across the border and instead I reached for my phone and sent a WhatsApp to Hannah, but she didn't reply so I lay there alone, listening to the house.

CHAPTER TWENTY

Silk

Gideon Poe remains expressionless as Mo bangs on the table so hard that Lil'Bitch takes a flying leap off it and scarpers into the hall and up the stairs so fast her legs are like a cartoon character's failing to grip on the polished wooden floors. I suspect she won't stop until she's in Finn's laundry basket hidden under a pair of his pyjamas.

It's so tense in here that I feel like joining her.

"How can it be? Eh?"

Mo is looking at me, his eyes wide with a mixture of rage and helplessness. I've seen that look on my child's face before.

"I think what Gideon is saying is that there are other options, but that what we have at the moment isn't enough."

His agitated state makes him seem bigger, more threatening, and I take a deep breath and remind myself that I'm safe here inside this house and it's only Mo.

But the anger is palpable and driven by frustration, and I've recognised that in nearly every man I have known.

"All I hear is that we have no chance? Am I wrong, eh?" Mo directs this at Gideon.

Gideon is sitting at the end of the table and has his hands clasped in front of him and his elbows on the table. On his right hand there is a small tattoo of a rose and half a skull, which seems incongruous to the rest of him: a thin late middle-aged man in a sharp-fitting pinstriped suit. He reminds me of the wooden woodpecker from a kid's TV show I watched as kid, called *Bagpuss*. He has remained impassive throughout Mo's rant.

Gideon sniffs loudly.

"You are incorrect in that assumption, Mr Bukhari. Your brother has an option."

This sends Mo bolting upright and storming towards the French windows. For a moment I genuinely think he might not stop and will smash right through them.

"Is that right, eh? I bring you evidence that the police enquiry was completely pathetic, that they overlooked the evidence of Amy Wilder that there was a bike at the party, so Tom Ellis could have been there, we know he beats his wife, is violent towards women, and then I prove Timothy Bowden knew, had to know, Khalil and that he had an issue with him, but all this, which wasn't known to the jury at his trial, means nothing, eh? He stays in prison? And this is justice?"

Gideon's head doesn't move but his eyes do and they fix on Mo like a butterfly on a pin.

"This is not justice, Mr Bukhari, this is the law." He extends a long bony index finger towards Mo. "And what you have given me, whilst interesting" – he nods towards me – "and suitable for a radio show, is not new evidence which would constitute grounds for an appeal."

Mo seems to visibly shrink.

"Do you have anything else for me, Mr Bukhari?"

Mo looks at me in desperation.

"Timothy Bowden lied on oath and said he didn't know Khalil, yet he clearly did and had complained about him to the newsagent. Surely this goes to the safety of the conviction?"

Gideon shakes his head.

"I'm afraid not. *Dubia in meliorem partem interpretari debent*."

Mo throws his hands in the air and looks at me but I shake my head.

"Doubtful things should be interpreted in the best way, and this is how the court will see Mr Bowden's evidence. You have not directly challenged it, just raised circumstantial evidence about a small piece of it, and not the identification itself."

Mo leans against the worktop. He's shaking slightly and I'm worried, as I've never seen him like this. It seems so out of character: this usually urbane, composed man sunk by the news his brother will not be coming out of prison anytime soon.

His chin is resting on his chest. I walk across and go to give him a hug but he raises his arm and blocks me from hugging him.

I'm shocked; it's such an aggressive gesture.

Gideon doesn't seem to notice as I back away from Mo.

"You need fresh evidence that either adds weight to an appeal that the conviction was unsafe, and the fact that Mr Bowden had his papers delivered by your brother does not do that I'm afraid. I take *The Times* every morning but I have no idea which urchin delivers it to my door. You have only provided circumstantial evidence that Bowden may have seen Khalil before, nothing more."

"What do I need?" asks Mo without looking up. He reminds me of Finn when I refuse him sweets, and to that matter Henry, nearly all the time. Men denied are dangerous creatures, I decide, as if I didn't already know.

"What you need, Mr Bukhari, is either new direct evidence that shows your brother could not have committed the crime or evidence that strongly – and I emphasise that the word strongly means more, a lot more, than a bicycle being parked in a garden – suggests that somebody else may have committed the crime."

Only now does Mo look at me but I refuse to meet his eye.

"Well then, that's what we need then. New evidence, eh? What do you say, Sarah, will we get it?"

Now I catch his eye but it's not with a friendly, supportive glance. It's total, cold professionalism because I've had an idea and I think I can get that new evidence. It was Mo's sulk that triggered the thought but I'm not forgiving him so easily for his attitude.

"Maybe," I say and even as I say it I know I can't take it back and that may turn out to be a bad thing. A very bad thing indeed.

CHAPTER TWENTY-ONE

Say cheese

Cathy isn't smoking and that's a bad sign.

She is picking the skin at the side of her thumb instead.

"Is everything okay?" I ask her.

She pulls hard and I can see she has pulled a big piece of skin off and tiny pinpricks of blood are blossoming in the pink exposed skin.

"Sure, sure. Our listening figures are through the roof."

She picks again and I wince.

"Are you sure? You seem on edge."

I look at her thumb and she looks down at it.

"Oh this? Trying to give up smoking. Angus doesn't like it."

The self-mutilation must be catching because I feel myself bite my lip to stop myself saying what I want to say, which is "how can you let that lowlife back into your life?"

Instead I say, "I didn't know you were seeing Angus again?"

I leave out the voice in my head which is screaming *how can you be so insane, you, my beautiful, intelligent friend, wasting your precious life, so full of interests, insights and fun, on that muscle-bound lump who ends every sentence with "babe" and who left you, telling you that he wasn't ready to be a father, and then went off and had a baby with a woman ten years his junior?*

Cathy attempts a smile.

"They're all the same, aren't they? Well, obviously not Henry, he would never, you know," I feel a burst of odd protective pride and nearly blurt out "he might", but I know that neither of us would believe that.

"But he's a changed man, I can tell. He's left her. She trapped him into that pregnancy, you know."

I want to weep. My friend, who has strong opinions on modernism, the iniquitous representation of women in culture and the patriarchy can't possibly have fallen for this tired old trope from a cheating man?

I can't stay silent. I would never forgive myself.

"I don't want to say this, Cathy, but this is friends 101 and I'll malfunction if I don't say it. So, here goes. You shouldn't take him back. He treated you really badly last time."

Cathy picks from the opposite side of her thumb, looking for fresh flesh.

"I'm not so stupid as to accept a man telling me he's changed" – the not so believable smile again – "but you never really liked Angus, you have to admit, so you're a little prejudiced, and what I haven't told you is that he really has changed, emotionally." I groan but Cathy ignores this and carries on. "So much so that he's been going to sex addiction therapy and he's signed up to self-improvement courses, and it's really working. You wouldn't recognise him, really."

I can't believe what I'm hearing and this time I snort in derision.

"Honestly, Sarah, we've been talking this through for the last couple of months and I wouldn't have entered into it unless I had his assurances" – she raises a hand, the one with the bloody thumb – "and satisfied myself that he meant them."

"Two months? And you kept this from me? We're best friends, Cathy. And what are these courses that he's been on? Will they make him less likely to fuck younger women?"

Cathy flushes. "Sex addiction. It's a real disease, but the courses have really changed him. He's so positive. I swear he's a changed man."

This is too fucking much. I can just about accept Cathy doing something downright ridiculous for love, or lust as I really think, and there is no denying Angus is a good-looking man, but for her to melt completely and change from a hard headed, rational, intelligent woman to swallowing self-justifying repackaged bollocks by savvy marketing executives is too much altogether. Against my rational judgement – the irony – I tell her this. It's a mistake.

The flush develops.

"And what would you know about happy relationships? You and Henry stopped having sex years ago. You know what, all the support I've given you since you were raped and–"

Her face sags with the weight of the word. "Jesus, I'm sorry, Sarah."

But I'm not sorry she said it because I'm too busy marvelling at the fact that the familiar emotional jolt I used to get, the weakness in the legs, the lightness in my limbs, hasn't accompanied the word. There was a time, and not so long ago, when even a story on the news about rape would make me tear up and have to leave the room, but Cathy's use of the word hasn't dented me. Have I become desensitised, lost something human, or am I recovering a little bit? I don't feel emotionally detached, I think, but how would I know? But then I see Cathy is on the verge of tears, she feels so guilty that she may have wounded me, and I know.

"It's not you who should be sorry, Cath, it's me. I'm so sorry for being a selfish cunt, come here." And I step forward and hug her.

She sobs, I think, and then I realise she's not sobbing, she's laughing, her shoulders moving up and down with each belly laugh.

I push her away from me.

Her eyes are streaming but they are tears of laughter.

"You… you said 'cunt'. You never swear, it's like hearing the queen say 'cunt'." And with that she's off again, big heaving laughs.

I can't help it and I start to laugh too.

"Listen," I say. "Why don't you and Angus come round for dinner on Saturday? I've invited Mohammed and Yasmin. We could all do with relaxing a little bit."

Cathy nods in between laughs but looks unsure.

"I promise I'll be nice to Angus."

"Okay, I'll ask him tonight."

And then we embrace once more as I swallow my feelings towards Angus.

CHAPTER TWENTY-TWO

Poems

I am nervous about the dinner party. As I'm getting ready, applying my make-up, or as my mother used to say *putting on my face*, I realise tonight will be the first time since before the incident that I've been in a room with more than three other people.

The thought makes me reach for the glass of red wine on my dressing table. I take a sip and put the glass down. Before I go down to meet my guests I decide to check my phone. I like to keep an eye on the death threat counts which have been coming in thick and fast, especially after the publicity surrounding Frenchie's arrest. I'm now a target for the free speech brigade who think by stopping a man sending me death threats I have somehow taken a big crap on Voltaire's grave. Before this all began I would have agreed with them, hell part of me still does, but I wonder how someone with a thinner skin than me would cope.

But my phone isn't on the dresser where I was sure I had left it. I look behind the bed but it's not there and a search through the pockets of the jeans I had been wearing, which I had left on the floor, turn up nothing.

"Honey! Cathy and Angus are here!" Henry shouts from downstairs. Lil'Bitch, who has been lazing on the bed, jumps up at the sound of his voice and runs downstairs, no doubt thinking that there is food in the offing.

I feel a wave of angst at the thought of going somewhere without my phone and I recheck everywhere quickly.

"Get a grip," I tell myself and I take a deep breath. It's only a phone and most times it brings me bad news or abuse, so I can do without it on my person for an evening, but still it feels like I'm naked without it.

I go and check on Finn. I knock on his bedroom door, a routine only recently insisted upon by him, his first real attempt at boundaries. It makes me a little sad although I understand it absolutely.

"It's okay, you can come in!"

Finn is lying on the bed deep in a Harry Potter novel.

"Just checking you have everything you need?"

He nods without looking up.

"Would you like me to bring you some snacks up?"

"I can't have them, too fatty. Miss Ritson says they are bad for you and multinationals do stuff." He runs out of words.

"Okay, but I've got some vegetable crisps in a bowl here for you. I'll just leave them on the side here."

He looks up now and his eyes lock on the bowl like a heat-seeking missile on a jet exhaust.

"We'll be downstairs. Just come down if you need anything."

"Okay." I wait for "Mum" but it doesn't come.

I softly close the door and head downstairs.

An hour and two large glasses of wine later and I'm wondering what I was so worried about. I'm having fun and so are my guests. We've done Brexit to death, and we all agree that anyone who voted Brexit is a racist, a bigot, but I know that Cath probably voted leave as she told me she was thinking of doing it before the referendum and she goes quiet during this conversation, the way Brexiteers do at dinner parties.

My main worry was Angus. Despite Cathy's protestations that he was a changed man I half expected him to be coked up and aggressive like the last time I met him at a bar in Soho two years ago. On that occasion he ended up accusing the owner of the place of being a "zio" for sourcing his pomegranate molasses from Israel.

But tonight he seems different, much calmer, and we've exchanged the usual social pleasantries, avoiding any conversational mines. Mischievously, I even served hummus with pittas as an appetiser and he didn't pass a single comment. And most importantly Cathy seems happy, with her arm on his shoulder, and there's no denying he's handsome with his long black hair and his open-necked green combat shirt, but seeing Cathy fawn over him and laugh at his jokes rather than make a better, funnier, more well-informed one herself is a little hard to watch. But if she is happy, who am I to judge?

I glance to my left at Henry. He and Mohammed are deep in conversation about the Labour Party and Mo is trying his best to look interested. Mo turned up without Yasmin as apparently she wasn't feeling well, but he came bearing a plate of homemade gulab jamun sweets which she had made.

It's all going well and then Angus holds his glass out and waves it at me.

"Any chance of a top up, Sarah? A man could die of thirst here, eh?" He laughs loudly and raises his eyebrows. It's meant to be a joke and I try my best to smile.

"The bottle is on the sideboard. I know you are a keen supporter of equality. Are you still handing out the *Socialist Worker* newspapers outside the Tube?"

And there it is, and it's my fault, I couldn't help myself.

His eyes narrow and for a moment I think he is going to lose his temper, but instead he smiles at me, which I guess makes us equal in the fake smile exchange.

"No problem." He stands up and refreshes his glass, to the top, from the bottle of Whispering Angel.

"I'm no longer a member of the SWP, by the way. Joined Momentum a couple of months back. We are really making a difference, not just talking about social change but making it happen at the grass roots. We have weekly meetings at the church hall on Buchanan Street; that's only fifteen minutes' walk from your house. You should come down one evening. It would be a lovely walk. You get some fresh air outside, and then come and talk to some like-minded people; you'd really enjoy it, Sarah. It's good to get out."

I glance at Cathy but she looks away. She's told him.

Mo catches my eye and breaks off talking with Henry to bring me into the conversation.

"Henry was just saying you two met at a slam poetry contest? I didn't even know what one of those was."

Cathy claps her hands with glee.

"I love this story."

I'm fuming but then I notice Henry is staring at me with a flushed affection. It's been a long time since he looked at me that way.

"It's true. I was working on the *Ealing Gazette* as their, er, arts correspondent. Well I say arts correspondent but it was actually just as a cub reporter. Cats up trees, council tax and potholes, Miriam running a marathon whilst dressed as a kangaroo, that sort of thing, but I was into the arts so I covered these shows in my own time and the editor let me slip in an occasional piece."

Angus snorts. "Slam poetry. The minced old drunks in Glasgow used to do that after a pint of Buckfast! Think of it as poetry without any talent. It was avant-garde for about ten minutes, you know how things are in this city. No offence Henry!"

Henry ignores him and just smiles at me across the table and I know he wants me to continue, it's one of the few remaining threads back to what we used to be,"There was this event at the pub near my old flat, well rather in a room above the pub, all old oak panelling, ancient plumbing that grumbled and the sounds of the drinkers below talking loudly about football and shagging."

Angus picks up his wine glass and drains it and then quickly refills it from the bottle, which he leaves next to his glass, a statement of intent if I ever saw one.

"The plebs doing their thing, their betters above them," I think Angus mumbles to Cathy, but she ignores him as well.

"Tell us what the night was called," says Cathy.

"Tongue Fu," and I can't help but laugh.

Cathy spits out some wine. "It gets me every time!"

"There was me and maybe ten other people in this room and I think six of those were the performers. You have to remember, I so wanted to be part of a scene, discover a scene, so wanted to like it but it was bloody awful. The first poet was so drunk she collapsed on stage whilst telling a story in non-rhyming verse about her cat called Jeffrey. The next two poets both did ten-minute poems about George W. Bush and then the first heckled the second and accused him of plagiarism. Then a man called Bert, who I think had taken a wrong turn from the bar downstairs, got up. He was so pissed and told a limerick."

"Do the limerick, Sarah," says Cathy.

"Oh, I can't, it's too rude!"

"Go on, go," says Cathy.

Henry nods and I oblige.

"You have to imagine this in a Scottish accent:

There was a vampire called Mabel
Whose periods were rather unstable
On every full moon
She'd get out a spoon
And drink herself under the table."

And this time even Angus raises a drunken, lopsided smile but I notice that he has refilled his glass again.

"I was just about to leave after the Mabel limerick when the door of the room burst open and in stumbled this handsome young man, laden down with a backpack and carrying a wad of notebooks under his arm and, well, I thought maybe I'll stay for a little while longer."

Cathy claps her hands in delight.

"And you haven't changed a bit, Henry," says Cathy, and everyone laughs apart from Angus.

I don't mention that at the time the thought of going back to my pokey little flat in Shoreditch, then not so fashionable, and facing an evening alone with just a bottle of Prosecco and a Facebook full of successful friends was not so appealing.

"And with a barrage of apologies and 'excuse mes' and 'is it all rights', like a regular Hugh Grant, Henry took to the stage – well I say stage, it was a plastic milk crate placed on the floor at the end of the room. Do you remember it, honey?"

There is a dreamy look on Henry's face, almost melancholic, but the smile he gives me reaches his eyes and I'm reassured that this memory at least is untarnished by all that has since passed.

"Like it was yesterday."

"Do you remember the poem you read?"

"You're embarrassing me now."

"Come, Henry, give us the poem," says Mo, and he winks at me in an intimate way that makes me unsure whether I should be pleased or annoyed at the intimacy we have clearly established being demonstrated in front of my husband and friends, but luckily Angus raises his glass and takes a long swig; he must have filled it up himself.

"Yeah, let's have the great work." His lips exhibit the bloodied residue when he removes the now-empty glass, so nobody notices the wink but me.

Henry shifts uncomfortably in his chair.

"Oh, it was a long time ago and I'm sure you don't want to hear it."

A chorus of "go on" and "we do".

"Well, I think I can remember a little of it."

Angus bangs the table. "Poetry! Your guests demand poetry!"

Henry closes his eyes.

"Movies of grey
Washed sodium lights
City of culture we never had
But dreams of steel
Dreams of worlds burning hot
Like rails to a below we will never know."

Henry looks up bashful and in that moment the young man I met in that dingy room is back. I reach out my hand across the table and Henry takes hold of it.

"That's a beautiful story," says Mo, and he looks at me in a way that makes me turn away from his gaze, but not before I see Henry's eyes glint. It may just be the candlelight catching his glasses, but Henry lets go of my hand.

"It makes me want to cry every time I hear it; they met over poetry," says Cathy.

Cathy looks as though she might actually cry.

Angus is sitting back and I notice his wine glass is empty now.

"Lovely story." He picks up the empty wine glass and wafts it like a brandy glass. "But it's not poetry, is it? No offence to you." Angus sounds much more Scottish than he did at the start of the evening. "Yer know, I can't see it being Keats, Yeats, Heaney and, er, Henry, can you?"

Cathy goes pale and I look at her, waiting for her interjection but nothing comes and instead she just stares down at the table.

"It's beautiful, and to have the courage to stand in front of a room of strangers and read out your own work takes real courage," I say.

"It's okay. Angus is right, it's just a bit of doggerel."

I feel rage performing a cerebral *coup d'état*. A small voice stages a rear-guard action, *just bite your lip*, but it's useless and when Angus smirks at me the game is up.

"It's not so much that it doesn't rhyme and is shit, it's just the sheer Waitrose, middle-class idea of what modern poetry should be. Aim for shite and hope for the best," and after he says this Angus leans back in his chair and I know that I'm doomed to take the bait he has just offered up.

Cathy places a hand on Angus's forearm.

"Ach, love, I'm only kidding with him. Henry can take a joke, eh?"

I can't see anybody but Angus now, just his stupid, drunken leer and cocky body language.

"Cathy tells me you've got a job now? What was it you said, Cathy?"

I see the pleading in my best friend's eyes but the anger panzers are rolling and there is nothing I can do to stop them.

"You're an arse wiper, sorry, carer. Presumably you're still working on your screenplay – what was it, a gangster movie set in London but with Glaswegian gangs who come down here and take over? Bit of wish fulfilment there maybe. So remind me: how long have you been working on that movie? Is it what, three, gosh no, it must be four years, and how old are you now, forty-two?"

"Thirty-nine," he snaps back, and I know I've got him.

"Well it must be a relief knowing you've got a career to fall back on if the film thing never works out. Cathy's career, that is."

Angus has a look I recognise. You can't disguise rage, but you need to direct it and control it. Angus makes a gulping noise, stands up and points at me.

"Oh yeah, well fuck you. I know about you, you fucking hermit, too frightened to leave your house but spitting your venom from inside the fucking web, eh! Cathy tells me you get death threats, no fucking wonder, eh, love!"

I turn my head slightly to one side so I know no one else can see me and I blow Angus an exaggerated air kiss. His capillaries, loaded with alcohol and fury, light up his cheeks like a road map.

"You fucking cunt!"

And there it is, a technical knockout, and I can see Angus knows it as soon as he's said it, in the gap following the collective (mine faked obviously) gasp, and he visibly deflates.

Cathy looks distraught but all I can think of is victory. I know the guilt and remorse will be along all too soon so I need to enjoy this moment.

Angus turns to Cathy.

"I didn't mean any disrespect." I want to punch him when he says that. "Just tossing around the issue. Good to get under our bourgeois veneer now and again, but" – he looks at his watch – "it's late and I've got an early start tomorrow."

"What time does the Jobcentre open?" I say and immediately regret it, not because it's bitchy, which it is, or because I may have hurt his feelings, but because it's small and not how I feel about such things, and mainly because I've won and this is just throwing that away, all for the momentary pleasure of an extra kick.

Angus smirks and turns to Cathy.

"What did I tell you? These people pretend to be of the left but they hate me, us, really. They are just posturing bourgeois fake bohemians. Waitrose socialists."

I've burnt my bridges and now I go about torching everything else.

"What are you on about, Angus? You've had every advantage life could offer, rich parents, public school, Oxbridge, and you used all that privilege to burn your nostrils to carbon so they needed replacing surgically, and you spend your days whining about the state of the world, dragging people down and doing nothing to improve things. You're a dilettante, Angus, and I have no fucking idea what my bright, beautiful friend is doing with you."

"Sarah, don't." Henry puts a hand on my arm but I throw it off and succeed in throwing both it and a wine glass off, which shatters on the wooden floor.

"We're off," says Angus, and he looks at Cathy. "Are you coming, love?"

Cathy jumps to her feet. The tears have disappeared and have been replaced by a look I've never seen on Cathy's face before: pure anger. I wait for her to tear into Angus but instead she points at me.

"You lock yourself away and this is the result. You've gone rotten. Sort yourself out and get some fucking help and until you do don't fucking bother to contact me."

Henry looks shocked but he follows them out to the hall to see them off. As soon as he is out of the room Mo stands up and sits in the chair next to me.

"Well that was, er, an interesting evening."

It breaks the tension – well, for me and Mo – and we both start laughing so hard that I end up putting my hands on his shoulder.

I'm still laughing when I hear Henry cough.

He's standing at the door, arms crossed, looking at both of us, and he doesn't seem to be seeing the funny side.

Mo stands up. "I guess I better be going too. I really enjoyed the food and the company. As they say, the best company is often the most challenging."

Henry nods.

"Come on, I'll see you out," I say, and I walk Mo to the front door. I've got Henry so well trained he has locked it completely after letting Angus and Cathy out.

I go to slide the top bolt back, but Mo leans in, blocking me.

"You know, Sarah, I don't think there is anything wrong with you. Nothing broken, but maybe sometimes it is easier to capture a wasp with honey than vinegar."

I go to speak but then he is kissing me on the lips, a good night kiss only, fleeting, but surely it's not just me who feels the sexual charge?

There's a noise in the dining room as Henry stacks dishes.

Mo pulls back and acts as though nothing unusual has happened but that kiss lasted just longer than it should have done. It means something surely, but he acts as though it doesn't. Confused doesn't come close.

"I will see you this week. We will discuss our next steps for Khalil, yes?"

I regain my composure and reach again for the bolt as though nothing has happened. I slide it back.

"It's going to be difficult without Cathy to produce the podcast."

He smiles and his dark eyes are full of understanding.

"She will understand eventually; you only care for her. That Angus is passing through, no more."

"I hope you're right."

He nods and I kneel and slide the bottom bolt open.

"So goodnight, and to the next day and all it brings. It is going to bring good things to you, Sarah, I can tell."

Slowly, I stand and, ignoring the closeness of us, I pull the door open. The night air is cold and there is a foul smell hanging over the street, presumably from the dying fatberg fifty feet below.

I don't wait for Mo to get to the end of the path before I close the door and ram the bolts home.

I take a deep breath and then go to the dining room.

"Well, I think that went well," I say to Henry, but he doesn't laugh, he just shakes his head and leaves the room, his arms full of filthy dishes.

CHAPTER TWENTY-THREE

Lost

There's something deeply disturbing about the aftermath of a party.

The house was empty. I made sure I didn't emerge from under the duvet until I heard Henry slam the front door. He was taking Finn to his mother's in Oxford for the day and wouldn't be back until early evening. From beneath the crumpled weight of the duvet I had mumbled something about clearing up and had received a grunt in reply that I assumed meant "okay", and really what else was to be said? It wasn't like I could go with him.

I didn't get up straight away after he left. I hovered between sleep and wakefulness for a grey hour, thoughts drifting into my consciousness, mostly benign, but then a waking dream of sharp violence, of Henry killing a sparrow with a knife, jolted me back into reality and the fear of dropping back down into this dream drove me from my bed and downstairs.

The kitchen smells of stale alcohol with background notes of rotting vegetables and tobacco smoke. It's the scent of decayed fun.

I put the coffee machine on – there's no sense in going in unprepared, I reason – and turn on the radio. I quickly change the dial from Radio 4 and doom, to 6 Music, and am rewarded with upbeat indie pop, the familiar soundtrack of many a post-party clear-up, and it lightens my mood a touch.

Fortified by an espresso, I load the dishwasher and place the empty bottles, of which there are many more than I recall us drinking, into the recycle box.

Bringing order to the mess gives me an immediate purpose and for a few precious moments when I'm concentrating on this task I feel almost relaxed, because all those other thoughts, of Khalil, Henry, Cathy, Angus and Tom Ellis, are pushed to one side.

I even decide to change Lil'Bitch's cat litter, a job I usually try and leave for Henry.

The cat's litter box is in the utility room and my technique is to breathe in through my mouth so as to avoid the unpleasant, bitter stench of Lil'Bitch's offerings.

Luckily, the litter tray is reasonably clear this time and I quickly deposit the contents into a bin bag and fill the tray with clean litter.

There is no sign of Lil'Bitch.

I call her name but she doesn't come. Not unusual, but I can see that Henry has put food out in her bowl, but it hasn't been touched and Lil'Bitch never misses a meal.

I shout her name three times, each louder and more shrill than the next. I rattle her bowl but nothing happens, no pitter-patter down the wooden stairs like I would expect.

My Zen-like cleaning mindset is replaced by the catastrophe factory, its default setting. I run upstairs and fling open cupboard doors, toy boxes, wardrobes. I run from room to room, even looking in the toilet bowl, half expecting to see her drowned body curled up in the bottom.

In Finn's room I dig through piles of clothes, tossing aside shorts, gym kit and underwear in my frenzy.

I continually shout her name but nothing.

At some point I must start crying because there are tears running down my face.

I run downstairs, all the time calling her name. The basement is the only place I've not checked and even as I descend the steps my heart is pounding and my mind is trying to work out when the last time I saw her was, and trying to push the violent images of what may have happened to her to one side.

I remember her brushing up against my leg as I poured a drink for Angus last night. What time was that? About 8.30pm, and then? I can't remember seeing her again, which wouldn't be that unusual – she doesn't really like strangers and would quite likely have taken refuge under a bed whilst they were here – but she's never hidden for this long. Cathy and Angus did nip out for a roll-up a couple of times. I told them not to let the cat out but I now know that this is what must have happened.

Even as I look around the basement I know she's not here. There's nowhere for her to hide. There's just my desk, a filing cabinet and the sofa, but still I open each door of the filing cabinet. Nothing.

I collapse on the sofa and I sob until I'm wailing with grief. She's outside and all the dangers of the city – cars, buses, hateful, murderous people – lie outside the door. She's gone, I know it.

I don't know how long I am like this but at some point the doorbell rings. I run upstairs and check the video monitor in the kitchen and there is the sweetest sight: a man holding Lil'Bitch. I can't see his face as he's looking at the cat in his arms, but I don't care, it's Lil'Bitch and she is okay.

I sprint to the door and bang open the locks quicker than I've ever done before and there is Lil'Bitch, wet and bedraggled, and I'm crying again as Lil'Bitch jumps down and dashes past me, meowing as she goes.

I look up to thank him and am rewarded with a flash of a perfect smile.

"I guess you're pleased to see this fellow." He proffers his right hand. "Glad to be of service. We haven't met, not in person anyway." I take a step back. "Tom Ellis, at your service."

My world contracts to one thought *I must close the door* but before this can translate into action he's stepped inside.

"It would be good to talk, don't you think?"

I step back again and he slams the door shut behind him. The door that protects me now cages me. I feel disorientated and have an almost overwhelming urge to curl up in a ball on the floor.

"You can't be in here," I manage, though the voice that comes out doesn't sound like my own but rather that of a small and lost child.

He cocks his head to one side and grins, although I can tell he's surprised at what he finds and he seems to reassess the situation.

"I'm sorry, where are my manners? I can see that I've caught you unprepared for visitors."

I can't imagine what I must look like: no shower after the party, grubby Sonic Youth T-shirt, Henry's PJ bottoms and streaked tears down my face.

"That's right, and you've just walked into my house uninvited, which is kind of creepy – especially with our relationship, such as it is. I think you better leave."

The grin again, and there is no denying he is a handsome man, tall and powerful with a rower's physique. I look round and gauge the distance to the knife drawer in the kitchen. I doubt I would make it in time.

"Sure, sure." He turns to go and then pauses mid-turn. "But I thought you might want to know the real reason why Khalil isn't guilty."

He fixes me with his cobalt-blue eyes and I can tell he's mocking me and knows that I won't be able to resist. He's right of course.

"Hang on. Stay right there. Promise?"

He raises his right hand and extends three fingers.

"Scout's honour and everything."

I run back into the kitchen, all the time listening for his footsteps behind me, but they don't come.

Lil'Bitch is nose down eating the food in her bowl and she doesn't look up as I open a drawer and take out a carving knife and slip it into my pyjama pocket. I grab my iPhone from the side and then quickly wet a cloth under the tap and wipe my face.

"Okay," I say to myself and then I calmly, well as calmly as my rapidly beating heart will allow, walk back down the hallway.

Tom is leaning casually against the door.

"Nice house," he says, waving an arm. "I'm guessing, given you and your husband's laudable professions, that you bought this place a while ago, before London started to" – he throws his arms in the air – "leave the stratosphere?"

"How do you know what my husband does?"

He laughs but not, on the face of it, in a mocking way, more in surprise.

"You've been researching me and, I might add, as you know, causing me some discomfort out there in the world, so naturally I wanted to know who I was up against. I did my research. You two should be proud. All that virtue in this city, you are positively saints."

He grins at me again.

"Just stay like that," I say, and I raise my phone and take a picture.

"Isn't it polite to say cheese?"

I'm not listening, as I'm too busy texting quickly.

"Just so we're clear, that photo of you has been sent to my producer, my husband and Mohammed Bukhari. They know you're here and if they don't hear from me in ten minutes the police will be here."

He takes a step forward.

"I could probably kill you in that time if I wanted to, but I'm sure you realise that which makes me salute your commitment to your story, to the truth, be there such a thing." He raises his hands. "But you have nothing to fear from me. I'm not the murderer of your story and I won't become one either, so you won't be needing that rather hideous-looking thing in your pocket."

I look down and the knife his hanging out of the loose pyjama pocket.

"I rescued your cat after all, and I think that deserves a cup of tea. What do you say? Tea and talk rather than knives and phones?"

I take the knife out and hold it in my right hand, letting it drop by my side.

"Come on then, let's talk."

And holding a kitchen knife, I lead Tom Ellis to the kitchen, all the time wondering how I can really suspect this man of murder if I am happy to do this. Life is a "curvy" bitch sometimes.

The strangeness of the situation seems to be ameliorated somewhat by the presence of ordinary things. The cup Tom is drinking from is one Henry and I brought back from a Klimt exhibition at the Tate and has a chip in it from when I cracked it putting it into the dishwasher. I only really use it now for pouring water into the indoor plant pots and, it seems, giving tea to a suspected murderer and certain domestic abuser. For some reason I find its presence calming; what sort of killer drinks from our crappy mugs?

"How's your tea?"

Tom raises an appreciative eyebrow.

"Lovely, thanks. I've had a thing for Darjeeling ever since the army. The sergeant major who trained us had a predilection for it, said it was the champagne of teas."

I sip my coffee.

"I prefer coffee."

"Quite right, too, bad coffee is always better than bad tea."

We are seated at opposite sides of the large oak table, an heirloom in Henry's family that he inherited from his aunt. It's covered in marks, scratches and the outlines of many a carelessly placed hot drink from through the ages, and it's completely out of place in our modernistic kitchen, but both Henry and I love it. It feels like family and although I have a cup of tea in one hand, the other is gripping the tabletop tightly as though it will confer some safety on me.

"You didn't come round to talk about tea."

He moves to put his mug down on the table but hesitates so I slide a coaster across to him.

"Thanks. You're quite right of course I didn't come round to talk about tea, but wouldn't it be nice if that were the case? I get the feeling that if circumstances were different we might be friends. We both like Klimt." He waves the mug at me.

I don't smile.

"You have a lovely house, by the way, at least the kitchen and hall. Is this where" – he looks across at my laptop on the kitchen counter – "you write your podcasts?"

"No, I have a studio downstairs in the basement."

"Ah, of course, what would a North London house be without a basement? Like a family without secrets, eh!"

And he flashes that smile again, a smile that reminds me of all the wise-cracking privileged men I've ever met who think that their existence is the sole purpose of the world.

"So you're wondering what I want to talk about?" He folds his hands in front of him on the table. "It's very simple. I want to tell you something."

I'm losing patience and I pick up my phone.

"Give me a reason to not text my husband now. If I don't, he'll call the police."

Tom leans back in his chair, the very picture of nonchalance.

"I can prove Khalil didn't kill Lauren."

It's as though the air has drained out of the room. The only way he could know that was if he killed her himself, surely? Is this a confession?

I reach for my phone in my pyjama pocket but it's not there. A quick glance around the kitchen and I see it on the kitchen work surface behind Tom.

When I look back at him, Lil'Bitch has jumped on his lap and is purring as loudly as I've ever heard her. I almost go to tell her to jump down but I realise how demented that would sound and I need to remain calm. My heart is beating so fast he must be able to hear it.

"Will you go on record?"

"Listen to what I have to say first."

"Did you kill her?"

He strokes Lil'Bitch again.

"I'm stroking a cat, so I can see how it would make sense for you to expect me to tell you all about my devious plans, but I'm sorry to disappoint you. I'm not a Bond villain, though I did trade bonds awhile, as you probably already know." He chuckles.

A phrase of my father's pops into my head: "never trust a fucker who makes puns". My dad hated puns and an early evening,

Saturday night light entertainment show could have him throwing things at the TV. I consider it good advice.

"I read that, yeah. You were struck off. Financial irregularities."

He smiles.

"You of all people, Sarah, should know that what we read online isn't always the truth."

He stares at me and I feel like he's reaching inside me. Does he know something?

"But to answer your question, no I did not kill Lauren and nor do I know who did, but I know it was not Khalil."

Lil'Bitch's purrs grow louder until to my ears they sound like a jet engine. Somewhere in the distance I can hear an ambulance siren. He's enjoying this moment, I can tell.

"How can you know?" I ask.

A trace of a smile flickers on his face, "I need you to tell me something first."

He continues to stroke Lil'Bitch, his long fingers moving back and forth.

"That's not how this works," I try to say this with an authority I don't feel.

Again the look, like he's hacking my soul.

"That's exactly how this works," and his words follow the meter of the stroking and now I can't hear the road, the traffic, the building works outside, just Lil'Bitch's sounds of pleasure.

"Fine, what do you want to know?" I ask him.

He slowly tilts his head back as though searching for a question but I know he knows exactly what he's going to ask me, which is why I am shocked when I hear him say, "When was the last time your husband made you come?"

I'm not a prude, far from it, I'd happily discuss aspects of my sex life with Cathy over a glass or two of wine. I think of it as the female equivalent of men bonding over football talk, except without the inherent homoeroticism, but I feel my cheeks redden.

Before I can tell him to mind his own business he raises a hand.

"That's not the question; think of it as an ice breaker."

The way he's looking at me tells me it wasn't anything of the sort. It was an exploratory probe and my flush has given me away. What's worse, I realise, is that I so wanted to say – had to bite my lip to stop myself saying – "a long time ago".

"The real question is this." He stops stroking Lil'Bitch. "Why did you disappear from the public eye twelve months ago? One minute you were a respected local TV news journalist, with your own show, and the next, poof, nothing."

I have my rehearsed line and it trips of my tongue with the confidence of a well-practised lawyer.

"I just wanted to spend more time with my family."

Tom nods and then abruptly stands up.

"Where are you going?"

"You're lying." He holds up a hand. "Don't bother trying to say otherwise. I'm leaving."

Panic sweeps over me; he can't leave without telling me what he knows. It will be the end for Mo, for Khalil.

"Wait. Please sit down. I'll tell you."

For a moment I think he hasn't heard me but then he turns and takes a seat at the table. He looks at me expectantly and then I start talking and Tom Ellis becomes only the third person I've ever told.

"I was attacked in my own home. I answered the front door on a Saturday afternoon. My husband and my son were out and I thought it was just a delivery from Amazon or something. When I opened the door…" I insert a well-practised break in my voice and pause. "A man pushed his way into the house and attacked me, tried to rape me. He dragged me by my hair into the living room. It's the room with the locked door you passed in the hallway."

Tom nods along in all the right places.

"It would have been, could have been, much worse had the door catch caught. He slammed the front door behind him but it didn't catch. You see, Cathy, my friend, chose that moment to call round, quite unexpectedly. She heard my screams from the doorstep and came in to investigate. Well, as soon as she walked in the room, he jumped off me, pushed past Cathy, who gave him a good dig as he passed, and he ran off. Never to be seen again."

Lil'Bitch gnaws on the knuckles of Tom's right hand.

"How awful for you. And they never caught him of course."

"He was a complete stranger, but he seemed to be prepared. He was wearing gloves and hence no DNA. I gave the police a description and then made up a photo fit, but nothing. I didn't want any publicity so we never went public with the story."

He waves his left hand airily and Lil'Bitch's eyes follow it like it's a ballistic missile escaping the atmosphere.

"So, he remains out there, unknown, unknowable. I can see why you are so security conscious now, what with the door."

I place my hands on the table.

"You can say it, people do, and so do I. I had a breakdown, became…" I pause again. What is it about this man that I suspect of killing a teenage girl that makes me feel I can tell him things I wouldn't tell my husband? "I became, well, still remain, agoraphobic."

He frowns and the barest of lines appear on his smooth skin, as though they are unused to being deployed for joy or for sorrow.

"Thank you for that," and I see the outline of his tongue on his cheek as he rolls it inside his mouth, "story. I can repay you in kind. Let me tell you a story. I was seventeen years old in March of 2006 and Lauren would be dead within four months. If you told me that then I would have shrugged and probably smoked a roll-up cigarette and made some off-hand comment informed by left-bank intellectuals and my own coagulating personality. I strove for insouciance and cool and mistook it for being uncaring, nihilistic and bleak." He laughs. "In short, I was a complete teenage dick frightened by the impossibility of choice and expectation, as I think we all were. A generation behind you, we grew up with the world, everything, all possibilities and choices displayed to us constantly in our bedrooms, our schools, our phones. The Internet connects us to all of these multitudes of futures and it's giddying and terrifying. The terror lies in the failure to make the right choice: clothes, music, partners, travel to the right places, schools, universities, jobs, a career, life choices. And do you know what a sense of paralysis this can bring on? You feel trapped by the choices, not liberated. It's why I joined the army after school. I didn't want choice anymore, I wanted to be told what time to get up, what to wear, what to do." He looks directly at me again. "Who to kill."

I ignore the challenge implicit in this statement.

"I appreciate the millennial angst, but what about Lauren and Khalil? I answered your question."

He strokes Lil'Bitch once more and the purring fires up again.

"They had the same problem but didn't realise it. Good-looking, young and with choices available. Too much choice. They chose each other and became an item immediately, subjecting themselves to the pressure of having chosen wrongly, of missing out on the endless possibilities."

I want to call Lil'Bitch over to me to get her off his knee, but she is geared to her environment and what's worse I suspect she wouldn't come, the traitorous bitch.

"They were in love, Khalil told me," I say.

"I think they were, but was it the right kind of love? How many likes would it get, do you think? How did it compare to the idea of love promulgated by film, literature and social media? That's why they argued all the time. I think they realised that the inside of love looked nothing like they expected and that's a difficult lesson to learn."

I think back to my own teenage years, crushes that seemed so intense they could break me like a dried twig, awkward kisses that made me dizzy with joy, diary entries and poetry and then cider, boys in tracksuits, sniggers, cool behaviour, confusion and loss. You didn't need the Internet to be broken by teenage love. Just ask Juliet.

"But it was still love nevertheless."

"But its value was not the same as the love they wanted." He raises a hand to stop the interruption telegraphed by my eyes.

"After the army I worked as a 'hedgie'. You, and now your audience, know this of course. I personally fail to the see the relevance to my alleged involvement in Lauren's murders" – the hand again – "or as you would say, the demonstrable example of me as to the police's incompetent investigation, but then we both know of course that it has nothing to do with them. The reason you mention that I'm a hedge fund manager in your podcasts is because we have become tainted. The modern bogeymen of capitalism, the face of greed, excess, the crash, our disillusionment with politics, all of it can be laid at the door of bankers, the hidden hands on the levers. It used to be the Jews of course, also bankers. A coincidence? I think not, but in the consciousness of the public we are synonymous with all guilt, all evil, worse than paedophiles for at least paedophiles were victims too. Us? We are just leeches, privileged, overeducated, oversexed, overpaid and responsible for everything from Iraq to food banks. That's why you repeat again and again the fact that I'm a hedge fund manager; it's shorthand for guilt. What wouldn't my ilk and I do for personal profit? Murder? Covering up a murder? Why not? We have no ethics, no conscience; we are reptiles of the money markets. This is why you mention it."

I start to deny it but what's the point? He's right. Society needs its baddies, and bankers and immigrants are the current scapegoats. Of course I mention his career, and let's face facts, if he was a charity worker or a teacher I probably wouldn't.

"Your lot brought it all crashing down," I say.

The light outside the French doors is turning, the aquamarine twilight slowly infusing with a dark purple. Henry will be home with Finn soon and I don't want my child meeting this man.

Tom laughs dismissively "Jesus Christ, when did liberals become so sanctimonious? I blame Islam, you know, it's infected the Left and made you all purists. You're the haemoglobin carrying militant Islam round the globe and, like most hosts, you don't even realise you're carrying and feeding the very thing that will kill you in the end. Is that why you're so interested in this case? I would go long heavily that it is the reason. This case must have been like an orgasm in Waitrose for you. Young Muslim boy, good-looking, framed by the police, the probable murderer now a white hedge fund manager. Come on, that's why you want it to be me, isn't it? It suits your politics." He laughs uproariously, clearly enjoying himself. "That's all there is to it, isn't there? This case is just a sum of all your own grimy little prejudices. Remember back in the day when all the villains in Hollywood movies used to be Russians during the cold war, South Africans during apartheid – and now what is de rigueur for every Hollywood movie? A rich English man, the posher and richer the better. I'm your perfect murderer, and Khalil, the young Muslim boy, he's your perfect hero. Go on, admit it, the story tells itself as far as your prejudices are concerned."

I could argue with him, but really, what's the point in wasting breath on this man-child with a sense of entitlement bigger than his ego? I have enough of this on the Internet.

"I can see you wanted to talk and I imagine with your money it's not a problem getting someone to listen." Whether this hit a nerve I don't know, but he visibly bristles. "But you did say you would tell me why Khalil didn't kill Lauren."

He sniffs and for a moment, something changes. A flicker of a line by his eye, no more, but it's as though he sheds a skin right in front of me and then the old twinkle is back.

"Because of the value he placed on that love. The prosecution hammered it home to the jury time and time again that she was going to leave him, that this is what they argued about the night of her murder and that it was this rage that fuelled the murder. But it's just not true."

His fingers work Lil'Bitch's fur back and forth and he's looking down at the cat so I can't see his face. Even if I could in the failing light, I might not see what I'm looking for, a sign he is lying.

"How do you know that if you weren't at the murder scene?"

"I know because neither was Khalil. You see, he was with me." He emphasises the "with" in an almost comically licentious way.

"You were at the party at the time of the murder – that was your evidence to the police."

He shrugs. "I was for a bit, but I did use that bicycle that Amy saw at the back of the garden. I went after Khalil. He was upset and I caught up with him on Caldy Hill and we argued, and then…" He pauses and stares directly at me, fixing me with his pale-blue eyes. "Well, you know what happens after lovers argue, don't you?"

I shiver with excitement and then look over at my phone on the worktop.

"Can I record this, get it on the record?"

"Absolutely not."

"Why didn't you mention this to the police? He had an alibi and he's been in prison for twelve years rotting away. Do you know what it's been like for him?"

Tom shrugs.

"I heard a rumour he turned to God, which is a shame; he was always such fun. As to why, I think you can guess why: he pleaded with me not to tell the police. For him the shame would have been harder to bear than being arrested for murder. You know what these Islamic types are like. It all gets a bit head choppy" – he does a slow karate chop movement with his hand over Lil'Bitch's neck – "if they dishonour the old family, and who was I to argue? I can't say I was game for being *outed* at that point either."

I can't believe it, the nonchalance of the man staying silent and condemning his friend, his lover, to a life as a convicted murderer.

"Will you give a statement to the police to this effect?"

He rolls his eyes as though I've asked to borrow a lawnmower.

"I don't think Khalil would be very happy about that, especially now he's all ISIS friendly. Are you sure you want me to do that? Would it be for you or for him, I wonder."

I slam my hands on the table.

"He's in prison for a murder he didn't commit."

"What time did you say your husband and son were coming home?"

There is something slow and deliberate about the way he asks me, as though there is something I should know but don't understand, and it makes my skin crawl. I don't know whether to tell him anytime now or lie and say they are not expected for some time. He seems darker round the edges, although it's probably the fading light, and suddenly my exhilaration is replaced by fear.

"None of your business. Will you or won't you give the statement?"

He slowly runs a long index finger across his chin.

"What would your husband say if he found me here? What would he say if I told him we had just slept together, I wonder? Would he believe me or would he believe you?"

I can feel my legs begin to tremble.

"You see, I rather suspect he may trust me more than you. I can be a rather good liar, you see."

Suddenly, I do see, and it seems my voice is coming from a long way away and I feel like I might faint.

"You're lying about you and Khalil being lovers."

"Well, fair's fair, you lied to me about what happened when you were attacked. Consider it a return gift."

Tom gives Lil'Bitch a strong squeeze and she yelps and then bolts from his lap. Tom gets to his feet and walks around the table until he is standing next to me, and he lowers his face so it is level with mine. His smell is strong, the after notes of an expensive cologne, musk heavy, and sweat. He lowers his face closer to mine so that I can feel his hot breath.

"You're an attractive woman, Sarah."

He leans in even closer and then there's a buzzing from my phone. I dodge around him and pick it up.

It's a text message from Henry. Just picking up pizza, with you 15 mins – Hawaiian good for you though you know fruit on a pizza should be a crime...xx?

"I want you to leave, now."

I stand up, the small of my back pressing hard against the kitchen worktop.

There it is again, that knowing smile, at once charming and sexually threatening, like he sees right inside of me. Then he whips his jacket from the back of the chair.

"I'm on my way." And he walks out of the kitchen. I follow him down the hallway and then when he stops by the front door I move past him. He doesn't move, meaning I have to get close, but I ignore him and begin the elaborate dance of the locks.

"You are quite afraid of what's out there, aren't you?" he says. I slide the bottom bolt back. "You are right to be. The city is full of dangers and noise, but sometimes the real horror is inside, wouldn't you agree?"

Top bolt next. Then it's the deadlocks, two of them.

"I wonder why you lied to me? If you're wondering, I lied to you because I could tell you weren't being truthful with me and what's good for the gander, eh? But the reason I chose my lie is because I know you, well, your type, Sarah."

I put the key in the Yale lock.

"Middle class, urbane, John Lewis, Danish furniture, holidays in Croatia – well, when you could step outside the door – Ocado shop, private school for Finn but staunchly Labour. Well, on social media anyway, though in the confines of the ballot box I imagine the Tories speak to you and I know what your preening virtue signalling means. Not what you think it means, but what it actually means."

The key sticks in the lock. Fuck it. I try it again. Nothing.

"What then? What does it mean?"

He extends his arm over my shoulder and gently slides the latch down on the Yale lock with a click.

"It means I know what you think about everything; you have standard-issue liberal opinions. You've traded your critical faculties for likes and upticks and I knew you'd just love a story about illicit homosexual love, particularly given Khalil's religion. You wanted it to be that so much."

I pull the door open and cold dirty air, suffused with diesel and burning tar, rushes in.

Tom takes a step forward and then stops on the threshold.

"I did tell you one true thing though. Khalil didn't kill Lauren. If you're ever interested in finding out why, then all you have to do is tell me what happened to you."

My mouth opens and this time it's not fear that stops me from speaking, but rage.

He looks at me as though he's a lepidopterist studying a specimen on a pin.

"I'm going to prove you did it," I tell him.

"Nice house, by the way," he says, and he's about to say something else but I stop him by slamming the door in his face and then begin slamming bolts and turning keys.

CHAPTER TWENTY-FOUR

Cathy come home

Cathy's not answering my calls. It's three days since the dinner party and two since Tom's visit to my house. All my texts and emails have gone unanswered as well.

I can see she's active on Facebook, posting photographs of her and Angus out and about at a Mexican restaurant and enjoying a walk by the Serpentine, so her silence is deliberate as, I expect, are her posts. She's officially pissed off with me and has gone "dark". I'm pissed off with her of course, but we've been friends long enough for me to know that I'm going to be the one who has to reach out or this will go on for a long, long time.

I may be locked behind doors, but when Cathy hides it's in plain sight, although she's just as isolated.

I would normally wait a bit longer, just out of self-respect, but Tom's visit has, and I don't want to admit this, ruffled my feathers, and I want to take him down. Online death threats I could deal with and although he hasn't directly threatened me, this is personal. I won't deny it; he got to me. What does he know about me anyway, with his presumptions about my life?

Unlike him, I wasn't born with a silver spoon shoved up my ass. Private school and then Oxbridge allows certain things to be taken for granted, such as not worrying where your life is going. I went to a bog-standard comp and had to get most of my education at home from my father and his collection of books. If I am a liberal it's because I realise that's the way I have to be to make things better for kids like Khalil. As for my tastes, I guess I'm guilty as charged, but the sneering at my acquired pretensions – reminds me of my earliest days in London, of wine-fuelled cackling from toxic friends when I mispronounced quinoa or stressed the "z" in chorizo.

He did it. Now I've met him, I'm sure. The same arrogance he was taught makes him think he can get away with anything; it's the ultimate narcissism of the public-school class. He did it and he's taunting me with it because he thinks I can't prove it, but he's in for a shock because his visit just spurred me on and when my eyes flicker open the morning after his visit it's with a renewed purpose and determination that I greet the new day.

I wake to an empty house. Henry's mad at me but his resentment runs deeper, and I can't totally blame him for it. I descend and then pad around my kingdom of one with Lil'Bitch as my only company, strangely content with the quiet and the archaeological remains of breakfast and a vanished civilisation of men. After switching off the radio, more grim news of terror and pain, I make my coffee, eat a slice of toast with peanut butter – it's the new protein I hear, but I eat it because it reminds me of being nine and being fed it by my older brother. The sweet salty sensation had been unlike anything else I had ever tasted. I can still find vestiges of that powerful feeling of newness and excitement every time I eat it.

After my toast, I open the French doors and stand, looking outside, whilst I finish my coffee. It's sunny outside, that diamond hard light of a November morning with the smell of cordite in the air.

If Cathy won't answer then it makes putting the next podcast together harder, but I know now what I want the subject of it to be. I want it to be the burial of Tom Ellis and if I have to do it without her then I will.

Lil'Bitch brushes past my leg on her way to the utility room and the linen basket, one of her favourite places to sleep. It's what she does best, and what I do best is broadcast and it's time to get back to it.

I open my Mac and stare for a while at the blinking white page and then slam it shut and pick up the phone. This time I am determined to make it work.

Emma Ellis answers on the third ring.

There is a pause after I introduce myself and I wait for the familiar sound of the phone call being terminated. But this time it doesn't come.

"Emma? Are you still there?"

I hear a baby crying in the background – it must be Tom's son – and I wonder for a second about the characteristics the young child has already inherited and whether psychopathy is genetic.

"Yes, I'm still here, but I've told you already, I don't have anything to say to you."

But the very fact she is talking to me tells me something had changed. I just need to push carefully.

I try not to let my excitement sound in my voice but my heart is beating faster as I carefully consider what could be the correct form of words to avoid her slipping off the hook.

"I know I can be a pain sometimes. Sounds like you've got your hands full there. How old is he?"

A sigh and then there is the sound of a pacifier being given to the baby. A sound that fills me with a sick feeling in my stomach as I recall my horror days of post-natal depression and the suicidal feelings of worthlessness that accompanied it.

"He's three, but mentally stuck in the terrible twos."

I laugh, aiming for a collaborative chuckle, but to my ears it comes out like the insincere laugh of a talk show host on hearing a well-worn anecdote from a faded Hollywood star. If Emma thinks the same, she doesn't let on.

"I remember Finn being the same and wondering why no one had told me that I couldn't hand them back."

Emma snorts with recognition and my stomach contracts with excitement. The first stage of a good interview is obtaining rapport and a snort counts; it most definitely counts.

"Yeah, I feel guilty when I feel that way, but Jesus he won't stop crying sometimes."

"You sound like you could do with a break. Do you fancy a coffee? Where are you? I'll buy you a coffee and the worst-case scenario is you get a free coffee, some time out and I promise you will never hear from me again."

I know she lives in Holland Park.

There is a pause, a pause in which I feel Khalil's future being decided.

"Holland Park. I suppose I could do with a break, and if it gets you off my back then it would be worth it, I suppose. Do you know Carlo's on Nelson Street?"

"I'm actually at home right now. I'm waiting for a delivery. I tell you what, I'll send a cab round to pick you and…"

"Ben."

"To pick you and Ben up. Come here and I'll make you a better coffee than Carlo's. I'm a bit of a barista at heart and I can stick it on my expenses. Oh, and I have a book that may help you. A friend gave it to me when Finn was playing up. I found it quite useful. It's a bit Californian self-help but it did help me a bit when combined with industrial quantities of Pinot Grigio."

There's a pause and then the sounds of muffled talking. I guess she had her hand over the receiver as she speaks to Ben.

"Okay, why not, where are you?"

"Hackney. I'll send the cab now if that works for you?"

"Why not? Your coffee better be good, I warn you."

"Give me your address. I promise it will be."

She gives me her address, although of course I already know it, and with that it is done.

"You're mine, Ellis," I say aloud. Lil'Bitch looks up from her position lying prone on the worktop and meows lazily at me in response.

CHAPTER TWENTY-FIVE

Monkey say

Emma Ellis takes a sip of my coffee and then nods in approval.

"Well you were right about one thing. You do make a nice cup of coffee."

"It's the beans. I get them delivered direct from a little place in Honduras. A foreign correspondent pal I used to work with still strings out of there and sends them to me. Good eh?"

"Super."

I can't quite believe she is sitting here at my kitchen table drinking my coffee. Emma Ellis is a beautiful woman, of that there is no doubt. Her hair is long and luxuriant, her nails polished jewels, her face evidences the complete absence of lines that can only be achieved by chemical obliteration and her make-up is discreet but heavy in a stealth-bomber way. It's the kind of beauty that requires serious money to keep it on the road and its effect is almost overwhelming. Emma Ellis glows with the aura of applied wealth.

Her baby Ben is asleep in the Louis Vuitton cot next to her. Contrary to what she said on the phone, there hasn't been a peep out of him since she arrived.

"Ben seems a lovely little boy."

She sips her coffee again.

"Yeah, he's super except when he's being a little shit. Just like his father in that way. He's better when he's off his face on Calpol, another trait that he shares with his father."

She laughs bitterly and I try to smile back in a way that is empathetic.

"Yeah, Finn was the same, but trust me, they get better with time. Now he's only badly behaved seventy-five per cent of the time."

"Such as?"

"He doesn't call me mum, for example; he calls me Sarah."

Emma's hand pats an invisible hair that must have gone AWOL. Her perfume is rich and potent and I suspect mood altering in both men and women.

"Like Bart Simpson."

"Sorry, oh yes, exactly, so I guess that makes me Homer. Doh!"

She smiles at my feeble attempt at a joke. She is maybe ten years younger than me, early thirties say, and I feel like a ditzy schoolgirl around her. I'm the professional but her composure is like the gravity around a supermassive black hole, sucking away all of my confidence.

"Well, you don't look like you eat a lot of doughnuts. I remember you from that programme you used to do on BBC2. Science wasn't it?"

"Not quite science, and it was local TV. *Egg Wars*. Teams of kids designing robots that carried eggs and did battles. I had to do an eggy pun every week."

"Ah yes, you were good."

"It wasn't eggsactly challenging."

My dad rolls in his grave.

She laughs and who knows, it may even be more than just a polite conversational waymark. What I notice is the absence of wrinkles around her eyes and her forehead when she does. *What a bitch*. That is what me and Cathy say to each other when we find ourselves discussing other people's appearances. Maybe that's what's happened to me, as I stay here at home. Maybe I'm rotting and becoming a mean old hag.

"What do you do, Emma?"

She waves towards Ben. "I look after him. I think I'm just a glorified health and safety consultant making sure he doesn't die or injure himself. Of course I have some help."

I think of the large Holland Park house and I can only begin to imagine the retinue of Eastern European assistance that must be enlisted to keep little Ben safe and well. *What a bitch.* As if I wouldn't if we could afford it.

"I believe my charmer of a soon to be ex-husband came to see you. He seemed quite pleased about it when we spoke. Did he try and rattle you? I wouldn't take it personally. He likes to think he is the intellectual superior to everyone he meets and that he has them all worked out, and invariably crushed beneath him."

I need to step carefully here, I know, and I decide to go with some more bonding, perhaps discuss schools. But before I can ask her where Ben will be going – and I fully expect for there to be a plan mapped out for him for the next eighteen years at least – she blindsides me.

"You know he killed that girl."

My heart swells and drops. I feel sick and light-headed but I try and stay calm.

"Emma, are you saying your husband killed Lauren Grey?"

She looks at me as though I'm stupid.

"Of course. Why do you think I came round to your house?" She looks around and then laughs. "Trust me, it wasn't for the coffee and small talk. Yes, he killed her; isn't that what you thought anyway?"

I take a deep breath. I thought Tom may have been a psychopath – you would have to be to kill someone and let your best friend take the fall for it – but Emma's matter-of-fact demeanour is scary. She announced her husband was a murderer much in the same way I would ask for a coffee at Starbucks.

"Well, I suspected it. He had the opportunity certainly. But, how do you know this?"

She shrugs.

"How do men normally let out their dirty little secrets, their affairs, their gambling, their schoolboy fantasies? He got drunk and blurted it all out. You know he has lost everything, and I mean everything, on cryptocurrency speculation. We are going to lose the house. Did he tell you that? I bet he didn't. He's normally so buttoned up, in control. It was the death of his mother last month that set him off. He blames your podcast, by the way, for the stress it caused her. The night after she died he drank a bottle and a half of Balvenie and by the end of it he was sobbing and telling me he had to confess something. The confession, it turns out, was to the murder of Lauren Grey."

I can feel myself shaking. Most of it is due to the revelation but I'm also thinking of a tearful Henry, wearing a Rudolph the Red-Nosed Reindeer jumper, still stinking of booze, tobacco and Chanel, telling me how sorry he was that he had spent the night with Alison, a volunteer at Earthvisions, a charity he used to work for, and how nothing, well nothing really (later established to mean a blow job, "nothing" in this case being straight from the Bill Clinton lexicon), had happened and how it meant nothing. Absolutely nothing. A nothing that had led to me, however indirectly, to never being able to leave the house.

"How did it happen? Did he tell you?"

She turns to Ben, who is mewling in his sleep, and places a hand on the little bundle and makes soothing noises.

"Shush my love," she whispers.

Ben settles down and the mewling changes to the gentle breathing of an innocent soul.

"Oh yes, he told me everything. It was very much as you hinted at in your podcast. He was furious when you broadcast the episode about the bike because he did use the bicycle to cycle to World's End; he got on it as soon as Amy returned to the party. He cycled to World's End and met Lauren and that's where it happened."

Ben continues to make soft noises, a counterpoint to the horror Emma is describing.

"What happened, Emma?"

She rocks Ben's pram ever so gently and doesn't even look up as she gazes adoringly at her son.

"He put his hands around her neck and strangled her. Squeezed the life from her. He knew he was going to do it as well. He told me he had picked up a pair of plastic gloves from the garage before the party."

I think of the times I've pulled the same type of gloves, thin blue plastic, from the dispenser at the forecourt to prevent oil getting on my hands and I can see Tom's hands and long fingers shrouded in the same gloves, almost like a surgeon's gloves.

Ben coos and she puts her face close to his and rubs her nose on Ben's rosy, soft cheek.

"Why did he do it?"

"I asked him that but he couldn't give me a reason, not one that made any sense. He just said she was there and he had to do it. I think now that maybe I married a sociopath or a psychopath, although to tell you the truth I'm not sure of the difference."

"I read recently that psychopaths do very well in the financial services industry."

"If you'd ever met Tom's friends, you'd understand why I'm not surprised."

Ben mewls and she leans over and presses her face to him in his cot and starts singing, low and hypnotically. She is singing softly, and I think the nursery rhyme is "Three Blind Mice".

My adrenaline is pumping now and everything has sharp edges and feels hyper-real. I'm not sure whether Tom is a psychopath but Emma's detached manner and lack of empathy as she describes the father of her child makes me wonder whether Tom might not be the only one who has a hint of psychopathy in the family.

"He killed her for no reason?"

"Oh no, I think there was a reason. It was because she was sleeping with Khalil. Tom couldn't have that, Khalil having the best-looking girl at school. He thought she might go for him. He had asked her out the day before the party but she had told him that she loved Khalil."

"He was jealous?"

Emma's eyes dart up and to the right.

"Not in a sexual way, no. My theory is that he couldn't bear someone else having a better prize. Everyone wanted to be Lauren or be with her, and Tom couldn't stand the fact that his best friend had the prize. What do you think they are doing in the city? The money is just a way of calculating who is winning, who gets the top prize."

"Why are you telling me this?"

She raises her hand and pulls back her hair, revealing what first just looks like a darker patch of skin. She begins to rub at it with the palm of her hand and slowly reveals an ugly purple bruise.

"Foundation can only do so much. He's bankrupt, you know. Once you started broadcasting his remaining clients ran. Well, that's what he says; the truth is that they've been gone for some time. He's very good at getting clients in, not so much at delivering. What you don't know is that he has lost his approved person status with the FCA, shorthand for he's fucked and can't trade. But like all spoilt boys he can't blame himself he blames you. Just like he can't accept he is at fault for having his affairs. The affairs I could stand but being poor, never."

Her finger traces a pattern on Ben's stomach.

It starts to fit into place.

"The oldest motive."

She looks surprised. "It's not revenge."

"I meant money."

"There's my son to consider now. My lawyers need an excuse to freeze his assets before he starts to liquidate them to cover his debts, as I know he will, and this would seem to fit the bill, wouldn't you say?"

I want to ask everything at once but luckily my journalistic instincts kick in.

"Would you go on the record with this?"

Emma leans in to the pram and adjusts Ben's blanket and then looks directly at me.

"If I tell you that my husband confessed to murder it will have consequences for me. I may never work again. If I go on record, will you guarantee I will be recompensed for my story?"

My mind is whirring. Legally, I can pay her. By me I mean the production company; they are going to have to pay and I'll need to get Cathy on board for that, but how can she resist, this is a scoop? The listening figures will go through the roof and this sort of turn around in a case could very well end up becoming an international story, never mind big in the UK We are talking movie potential, and of course a wrong will be righted and an innocent man freed. Of course Cathy will sign it off.

"If you go on record, I will make sure you are paid for your story."

Emma taps the side of the pram. It is the first visible sign of stress.

"It has to be six figures at least. That will tide me over until the maintenance is ordered."

I put my phone on the table and bring up the voice recorder app. Even though I have got professional recording equipment in the basement, I can't risk her changing her mind, not now. This fish needs landing right away.

"Look, Emma, you've got nothing to be ashamed of. He's the father of your child, violent and abusive, and he only recently told you all of this, if it was after my podcast. You've done the right thing coming to me and if you tell me what he told you and" – I shift my phone towards her across the table – "let me record you, I can guarantee you six figures at least, and it will be a weight off your conscience that will be worth a lot more than that. Trust me on this one."

She sucks her bottom lip and looks down again into the pram. Once again, she reaches into the pram and adjusts Ben's blanket and he coos in response.

"Okay, but only if you promise me the money."

I'll get it. The ads we sell for the next podcast after her confession will pay for it alone.

"I promise you'll get the money."

She nods. "How do you want me to begin?"

"Tell me, how did Tom Ellis kill Lauren Grey?"

An hour later and I'm bolting the front door, having waved Emma and Ben goodbye.

In the kitchen, I check the recording and then send a copy of the file to my own email address.

"Gotcha," I say aloud, causing Lil'Bitch's ears to bend back and glance at me from her place on top of the radiator, but she looks away when she realises "gotcha" is unconnected to food.

My phone pings as I receive a text and I pick it up, hoping it's a reply from Cathy, but it's not. It's from an unknown number but I know the sender.

You lied to everyone. You're a fucking whore and you lied to save yourself. I'm going to tell the world what you did so they know what you are. Monkey say. I know everything. Your ever living Frenchie.

I try not to let my stomach roll on the sea of adrenaline flooding it, but I can't stop the yawing and I have to put my hand to my mouth as I think the turmoil down below may escape.

I immediately call the victim of crime officer who was assigned to me when they arrested Marcus Evans. She answers on the third ring.

"I just got a text from Frenchie, from Marcus Evans. I thought you were charging him; why is he still doing this?"

I swear I hear an exasperated sigh.

"Well, here's the thing, Mrs Kelly. We have charged Marcus Evans with offences under the Telecommunications Act. He has been threatening a lot of women on Twitter, not just yourself, as you know, but here's the thing, and this is good timing, as I was going to call you."

"Go on."

"We mapped his devices, phone, laptop, tablet and all of his online accounts, hence the aforementioned charges, but it turns out he couldn't have been the person who took a picture of your son because he was in Brighton at a gaming event that day. But don't worry, I'm sure we will get a conviction on the offensive tweets to the other women."

"I don't give a fuck about the tweets, I want the man who took a picture of my son found!"

"I really don't appreciate your tone, Mrs Kelly, in fact I find it quite offensive."

I slam the phone down.

Frenchie is still out there. Cathy is still not responding so I message Hannah straight away.

Hey are you there?

Sure am Fucktart no.2 – how's it hanging?

He's back, Frenchie's back, I'm terrified, not for me, but for Finn.

There is a delay and when the reply comes I know why. Hannah has set out my choice clearly.

Well, I hate to say it, but you could stop the podcasts. You have a nice home, and a family (with all its problems I know) but you have them – is it all worth the risk? What if Frenchie is more than a troll? Sorry hun, I know you won't want to hear this and I wish I could come to you and give you a hug but su casa non mi casa.

My response is curt because I know she is right, this is my choice, but I also realise something else. Hannah doesn't know me, not really, not like Cathy. She would never have suggested giving up on a story and that realisation makes me remember something. It makes me remember who I am.

Sure, I hear you x.

And then I put my phone down. I've made my choice.

CHAPTER TWENTY-SIX

Monkey do

Despite my worry about the return of Frenchie, I work quickly.

Finn is at Henry's mother's house and Henry is away all weekend on a training course. I'm ashamed to say I'm not even sure where it is. He did tell me, of course. Henry tells me everything. The picked-over corpse of his day is one of the safe conversational areas. I participate in these conversations with the appropriately placed "yes" and "did she really" etc. but at most it has as much hope as sticking in my long-term memory as an episode of *Loose Women*. I suspect that this is something that a lot of couples experience and that it may just be an evolutionary trick designed to stop us from sticking a bread knife into our partner or ourselves.

Andover, I think he said Andover, or maybe Exeter? Either way he's not back till late Sunday evening so until then it's just me and Lil'Bitch.

Cathy is still not responding and this is damn unusual. I know she's mad with me but for Cathy to ignore a text that will have stimulated every journalistic instinct she has shocks me.

Emma will testify that Tom told her he killed Lauren – just saying you may want to call me back. Love and more apologies than there are hairs on Angus's chest. xxx

And no reply to my chaser emails. I contacted her on Facebook and WhatsApp but nothing, and I can see that she hasn't posted anywhere on social media in the last twenty-four hours which also rules out the possibility that she has taken a last-minute holiday as the first thing she would do is post an image of her hotel room or the evening's cocktail.

It's as though she's disappeared from the planet. I realise the only way I can find out if she's okay is to leave my house and go to her flat, take a cab (the Tube is totally out of the question even in this fantasy trip out of the house), but I won't leave the house so it's academic. Without electronic communication I am stranded here alone.

The problem is I need Cathy to sign off for the money that I promised to Emma.

Emma was very clear that I can't broadcast without confirmation that she will be paid. The figure we agreed upon was £100,000 with her getting five per cent of the ad revenue generated for the rest of the series on the basis this will be spectacular, as it will lead to the release of an innocent man, and this sort of breakthrough will attract top-end advertisers; Apple, Mercedes and BMW love injustices righted. I think it's a corporate guilt thing.

Emma emailed me this morning already asking me if I got confirmation that the payment will go through.

But I can't get hold of Cathy. I should wait, I know that, but what if Tom talks to Emma in the meantime and she changes her mind? I know how things are when relationships come to an end. It's a rollercoaster of emotions and sometimes you just say *fuck it* and stay with the comfortable slippers even if they're full of broken glass. The timing is everything and I need to land this story now, with or without Cathy.

Fuck it indeed, I think, and I type her a reply confirming the deal is on and the terms we agreed on have been signed off by our production company, Bulldog Productions. It's a lie of course. Cathy deals with Bulldog, and this deal would need signing off by their CEO, and clearance from the lawyers, but I know they would pay out. It's a no-brainer, and the listening figures are going to go through the roof.

Hopefully, Cathy will come back to me before the podcast is due to go out and hell, even if she doesn't, then once she hears it there will be no doubt that what I have is incendiary and worth more than we are paying. The book deal alone will hit the high six figures. So I hit send.

Emma replies straight away.

As soon as the deposit lands in my account I'll give you Tom Ellis's head on a plate.

There is also an account number and sort code and I don't allow myself to think about anything beyond the task at hand as I transfer the full amount of the deposit, £25,000, from the joint savings account I hold with Henry, into my own account.

A few clicks and nearly every penny we have put away over the last five years is gone.

I send another email confirming that the transfer has been made and whilst waiting for a reply pick the skin on my thumbnail until it bleeds. Luckily the reply comes through as fast as before.

Let's get him.

CHAPTER TWENTY-SEVEN

Podcast 7

Podcast 7 by Sarah Kelly – 29/11/18

Never forget through this that there is a victim and a victim's family. Whatever Khalil and his family have been through, it pales in comparison to the trauma suffered by the Greys. They have seen the daughter, sister, they loved brutally murdered and then once they have some closure on the conviction along comes a journalist suggesting that the conviction is unsafe and rips off the sticking plaster of that conviction. To them I apologise for what I have put them through but I hope they understand why.

So, I've been sitting on the fence so long I positively have splinters on my ass, as our American cousins might say. But there's a good reason because I never set out to prove Khalil was innocent. What I wanted to look at was the way in which he was convicted. How a police force under pressure after arresting an innocent man saw a suspect, based that suspect on a degree of unconscious racial profiling in a climate of Islamophobia and ran with it, ignoring other lines of enquiry and leading to an unsafe conviction. Unsafe, but not necessarily untrue. I believe in the rule of law and this mattered to me and should matter to you.

But I've got a confession. For a long time I thought Khalil probably did kill Lauren. That's where the evidence points, but it does so in an airy wave-of-the-hand way, not with a certain jab of the finger. And I wonder whether this vague belief in his guilt has got in the way of me pursuing the story? Did it make me hold back in some way, influence me in the same way that it influenced the police and the CPS?

Maybe.

But no more. You see, something has happened. I no longer have any doubt. Khalil Bukhari did not kill Lauren Grey. How do I know, I can hear you ask?

Because I know who really did kill Lauren Grey. It was Tom Ellis.

On 8 July 2006 Tom Ellis attended a party at the house of his friend, Shona Cunningham. He was accompanied by his best friend Khalil Bukhari and, as we already know, and it is a fact that is undisputed, they had a row sometime between 10 and 10.45pm. They both said the row was about who had brought what alcohol but this was a lie.

What they argued about was Lauren Grey. You see, Tom Ellis was jealous of his friend's relationship with Lauren Grey. She was the prettiest girl at school, the cleverest, the most charming, and for Tom Ellis's sense of entitlement she was his natural girlfriend but he couldn't have her. What do they say about close friends? I think it was Gore Vidal who said "every time a friend of mine is successful a little part of me dies", and so it was for Tom Ellis. When Khalil started to date Lauren a little part of Tom Ellis died.

The argument they had wasn't about beer like they told the police; it was about Lauren. Like boys their age, hell, boys at any age, they argued about beer but it wasn't about that at all.

I know what you're thinking. So what? This isn't evidence of a crime, never mind murder, so how about some evidence?

Three days before Khalil's final A level examination his family became aware of his relationship with Lauren Grey. Which is odd given the lengths they went to, to hide the relationship from his family, but there you go. It's possible, I guess, but here's what happened.

Khalil's mother Yaminah found some things. The "found" deserves an adjective and it's "conveniently". Searching through her teenage son's pockets, perhaps telling herself that she was helping, making sure there was nothing in there before it went in the wash – at least that was always my mother's excuse – she came across three things.

The first was a receipt from the cinema four nights previously. It showed two tickets for Harry Potter and the Order of the Phoenix.

The second was a more damning receipt for an observant Muslim. It was a receipt from two nights beforehand and it was for a round of drinks. Two pints of Stella and a glass of white wine from the Moby Dick, a pub popular with the sixth form crowd in West Kirby, a seaside town not far from Heswall, the scene of the fateful party. The third item left no room for doubt: it was a set of passport photographs of Khalil and Lauren fooling around in the booth. You know the sort, we all did it when we were kids. In one he is pulling his hair whilst she looks at the camera, in another they are both gurning and Lauren is pulling her hair up and in the last, Khalil is looking adoringly at her as he kisses her on the cheek.

Yaminah told the police she was reasonably relaxed about these things. It was nothing she wouldn't expect as a second-generation Pakistani British herself, but still not something to let slide by, and so she confronted Khalil. Not in a super aggressive East is East *way but more in a motherly "I'm disappointed, son" way. Of course she would say that, but when I checked in with Khalil and his brother Mo, both of them agreed that their Mum didn't fly off the handle. She was used to dealing with two boys in the absence of their father, who had died five years before of a heart attack, and she didn't punish Khalil in any way but just reminded him of what it was to be a Muslim and gave him that most damning of parental judgements: "I'm disappointed in you."*

Khalil listened politely, agreed with his mother and then a week later was at the party, drinking, smoking and hanging out with Lauren. So what has this got to do with Lauren's murder?

I'll tell you. It was impossible for Khalil to have had those receipts in his pocket. For the record, the police had only asked him about his parents' attitude to his relationship with a non-Muslim, nothing else. He told them about the row, but it didn't really figure in the enquiry other than in passing remarks as the prosecution tried to hint – another lazy stereotype – at a motive of familial disapproval for the killing. A hint, as there was no evidence.

But something a new witness (more of this to come) told me got me thinking about those receipts. Here's what I asked Khalil: "Did you go the cinema and did you go to the pub and buy those drinks?" His answer was yes to both. The first occasion was to see the movie on a date night with Lauren and the second was an evening in the pub with Lauren and Tom Ellis. They had all been celebrating the end of their exams in the time-honoured English tradition of getting pissed up.

Khalil went into great detail when I asked him about this night out and he was laughing as he told me the great lengths he and his cousins went to in order to avoid their parents finding out that they had been drinking. Masking agents, or strong mints and mouthwash as we would call them, were high on the agenda and an essential part of any drinking kit, then the corroboration of stories and finally the disposal of any tangible evidence, the top of that list being receipts. He was adamant those receipts shouldn't have been there. He was always so careful to dispose of any evidence. So, maybe he just made an error?

I went back to the trial bundles and checked. The receipt for the cinema was for a card transaction as was the receipt for the pub. But what struck me, but didn't occur to anyone at the time of the trial – why would it when this was a passing issue – was the card numbers differed. If this sounds a little esoteric, take a look at the next receipts you get when you buy something. Your full card number isn't there; there's a series of asterisks and then the last four digits of your card number. So, for these receipts, found in Khalil's pocket, you would expect them to be the same last four digits.

This to me is huge. The equivalent of a knife with bloody fingerprints on it. Why? Because what teenager in 2006 held more than one card? I checked, of course, with Khalil, and he recalls only having one: a NatWest current account. His brother pulled his statements and the account details matched the card used for the cinema. There is no way of checking, but here's what I think. I think the card used to buy the drinks was either Lauren's or Tom's card. If it was Lauren's then that could explain Khalil having the receipt. Maybe she passed her card to him to pay. Probably not though, as this was in the days before chip and PIN so he would have had to sign for it. But isn't it more likely that it was Tom who bought the round? I know it's old-fashioned but it's statistically more likely that the guys bought the drinks. Feminists shoot me now! So, I had to check.

I checked Lauren's bank statements, part of the unused protection material at trial, and they cover the night of the pub, and you can see that nothing was spent on her card although she had withdrawn £20 earlier that evening. She paid for her drinks with cash, which leaves Tom Ellis as the likely purchaser of the drinks.

So Tom Ellis bought a round of drinks and then somehow his receipt ends up in Khalil's jacket pocket, the jacket he routinely checks for such incriminating items, together with the photograph and the cinema receipt. How did that happen?

Khalil recalls checking his coat and he just assumed that he was forgetful, perhaps because he was a little tipsy when he went through his routine. It's possible, but isn't it a tad unfortunate that he also picked up Tom's receipt? I guess it could have been left on the table? I have an alternative suggestion.

I think Khalil did check his coat and I think there was nothing in it. His mother only found the items the day after and there was always the possibility she would ground Khalil so he couldn't go to the party later that evening. And guess who had called round earlier that day to see Khalil and spent an hour drinking tea and listening to records in Khalil's bedroom? Top marks if you said Tom Ellis. So he had the opportunity to drop the receipt into Khalil's jacket and to take the photographs from wherever Khalil had stashed them and put them there too.

But why would he do that, and isn't all this wild speculation? I can hear you shouting at the radio.

It would be yes but for the fact that I have a witness. A witness who will testify on oath that Tom Ellis told her, many years later, that this is exactly what he did.

The why? The why is the same as it always has been. One man wanted something that another man had. In this case Tom Ellis wanted Lauren Grey.

Some background you may know from previous podcasts. Tom Ellis and Lauren Grey had never been an item but they had both been on a date together. This was some two years before Khalil hooked up with her and by all accounts it was Tom who had not followed up after they went bowling and grabbed a burger together. According to friends neither of them was too cut up about this. It was just one of those things at high school, and when I spoke to Khalil he confirmed that this was never an issue between them and could only remember it being referred to once in the early days with Lauren when, over a beer, Tom had made a comment that Khalil shouldn't jinx it and take her bowling.

But Tom Ellis is a proud man so maybe back then he was a proud teenager, and pride stings. I spoke again with some of their friends from the time and asked them about this date and none of them could remember it. Who would? It was one date that didn't work out, but they all could remember that Tom never talked about it so assumed it was unimportant. But what if the opposite was true: what if he never talked about it because he really liked Lauren and she, to save his feelings, told people that they didn't hit it off that way rather than mention the weeks of phone calls and pleading which, according to my witness, was actually what happened? I'd be no journalist without checking and hey presto, guess what, there is a record. BT keep an archive and if you go back and check – thanks again to the Greys – the list of incoming calls for the weeks following the date, there were five phone calls all from a number registered to the family home of Tom Ellis in the week after the date. Each shorter than the last.

What if he pleaded with her to go out with him? He pestered her, the calls getting shorter, because she was putting the phone down on him. But she didn't publicly humiliate him, didn't embarrass him. Two years later she did start to date his best friend.

The party would be one of the last times they were altogether before they went their separate ways to university, one of the last times that a man carrying around the burden of unrequited love can plead his case – but that would have been impossible with Khalil there, so he tried to sabotage him and get him grounded.

Which is what happened. His mother grounded Khalil. The prosecution went big on this, trying to show he was in an aggressive, frustrated state of mind and also angry with her that she had still attended the party even though he couldn't.

As we know, he defied the grounding and went to the party.

He never suspected that it was Tom who had set him up but when he arrived unexpectedly it drove Tom wild with rage. He covered it up of course, and instead picked an argument over who brought what beer. This was the row that everyone saw and which caused Lauren to storm out. Did she leave because she intuited that the row was about something else, her, and she didn't want to get in the way? We will never know the answer to that question. She took it to her grave, but for what it's worth, I believe that she did.

She left, followed shortly thereafter by Khalil. The court of course found he left to meet her at World's End. But the truth is he never went there. He walked the streets, smoked a spliff and got home late.

Amy Wilder has already told us about the bicycle in the garden, the method that would allow Tom to get to World's End, kill Lauren and get back before anyone noticed he was missing from the party. I now know for certain that this is what happened.

Khalil has always been clear on this point: he had no idea that Lauren was going to be there. The jury didn't believe Khalil's protestations that she didn't tell him because of the witness, Jack Martindale. Remember him? He said that he saw and heard Lauren tell Khalil that if he wanted to talk then he knew where she would be and, given they regularly hung out there, that must have meant World's End.

But Khalil always denied that that conversation took place. And here's something interesting about that night. I am looking at a photograph taken earlier on in the evening of the party, before the row, in the back garden – I've posted it on the website – and what's interesting is what both Tom and Khalil are wearing. They are both wearing hooded tops, I guess that was the trend back then maybe, but Tom's is black and Khalil's is blue. Is it possible that Jack was mistaken and the conversation took place between Lauren and Tom instead? Unlikely, I hear you say, clinging at straws, but if you drive ask yourself this: how many times have you arrived at your destination and not remembered anything about the journey, the thousands of decisions, the speed, the lane, avoiding other traffic, following signs, taking account of the weather, all of them vital and necessary? If you're like most people I'm guessing you'll say a lot. And yet we arrive safely, and this is because of something called the filling-in phenomena; the brain builds a picture not just of what it sees, in fact far from it, but it builds a picture of what it expects to see. Jack was taking a pee at the side of the house when he glanced towards the front gate and saw what he thought was Khalil and Lauren talking, but that's what he expected to see.

He was only interviewed after Khalil had been arrested, and I'm not saying they led the witness on his evidence, but would you be surprised if Jack, wanting to be helpful, expecting the person talking to Lauren to be Khalil, had said exactly what he thought he'd seen? Of course at the trial he was cross-examined on this point and he was adamant it was Khalil who he saw talking to Lauren. But here's the thing. Age tends to bring a lot of things, bad knees, poor eyesight, terrible dress sense, but also it gives you perspective on your own existence and experience. I spoke to Jack this week, the Jack who said he was one hundred per cent certain it was Khalil he saw and I asked him, given he was drunk, and it was dark, given I had a witness who said that Tom had confessed it was him who had this conversation, wasn't it just possible that what he in fact saw was Tom with his hood up, having the conversation with Lauren? Jack, he's a dentist now, was admirably honest. He said he still thought it was probably Khalil but he if was to take to the stand again he wouldn't put the chances of it being Khalil at more than seventy-five per cent. Reasonable doubt anyone?

Maybe she asked Tom and Khalil to meet her at their meeting spot, the World's End, and Tom chose not to pass the message along but instead go himself and plead his love?

What was it like that night in the darkness of the car park? Well the police found a roach outside the car, with only her DNA on the cardboard so she was probably smoking this alone just before Tom arrived. I imagine the car was full of smoke and I think when she saw a blurry figure approach in the dark and then heard a knock on the passenger door window, she may have thought it was Khalil. But it wasn't. It was Tom Ellis. She may have realised it wasn't Khalil but it doesn't matter. What does is that she unlocked the door and he got in.

What really happened next, I don't know, but I do have Tom Ellis's self-serving version of events given to my witness.

He told Lauren that he had always loved her since the moment he set eyes on her, that he couldn't believe she was seeing Khalil, but that he forgave her, and then he tried to kiss her.

Tom told my witness that she pushed him off and then slapped him and that, in an instinctive response, his hand snapped back and slapped her and her head flew back and hit the hard metal pillar of the VW. And she started to scream at him, demanding to know what was he doing, and then Tom was trying to calm her down and was squeezing harder the more she screamed, just to stop her being so upset. And the she was quiet. That was that. It was an accident. Nothing but a terrible accident.

But of course the version he told her doesn't accord totally with what we know of how Lauren really died. Lauren had hands placed around her neck and pressure applied until her carotid artery broke. A painful, terrifying, cruel death inflicted by someone she thought was a friend.

Tom didn't wait around but instead jumped out of the car and cycled back to the party. He told my witness that he panicked but thought she was probably okay, that she was just unconscious, and everything would be fine once he saw her again and apologised. But I don't buy that; you don't leave an unconscious woman you love to her fate.

The next day brought a hangover and the news of her death. He said he was too frightened to confess and as each day went by it got harder to do, but also easier to accept that his life shouldn't be ruined by what was nothing but an unfortunate accident. Then the arrest of Brownhill, but he didn't come forward as it seemed clear that Brownhill, according to the press, was an oddball who was probably guilty of something terrible anyway. And then Brownhill was released and Khalil, Tom's best friend, was arrested. Yet the reason for it all, the reason why Lauren wouldn't go out with him, the reason his love was unrequited, and the reason he lost his cool and then his temper, was Khalil taking what was rightfully Tom's. Wasn't it actually justice that Khalil was convicted of her murder? If it wasn't for him stealing his girl, then none of this would have happened and Lauren would still be alive.

So he kept quiet whilst his friend was convicted. He kept silent when he was sentenced and he kept quiet until I started these podcasts, threatening me through his lawyers and then turning up at my house to charm and again threaten me, but he can't remain silent now. He will have to talk to the police and then the CPS because Tom Ellis is guilty of the murder of Lauren Grey.

CHAPTER TWENTY-EIGHT

Triumph

Even another email from Frenchie can't totally ruin my mood. It came in before the podcast was uploaded so that can't have triggered it, although I didn't see it until afterwards. It's the usual themes of anger, sexual abuse and misogyny but I don't feel as shocked as when I received the last message. So Frenchie, or a Frenchie copycat or one of a hundred Frenchies, is out there but I can rationalise that. If you walk in the jungle there may be noises that scare you but you rarely see a really dangerous beast, and that's what trolls like Frenchie are, scary noises in the night. And eventually the messages bring self-diminishing returns. Once you've received a hundred such treats the hundred and first just doesn't cut it.

The only concern I have is Finn, but I had another call from victim support, this one a little more sensitive than the last, assuring me that those who make such death threats, even take photographs, very rarely go on to do anything physical. I'm sure she's right but Henry is under strict instructions to walk Finn into school and pick him up from the teachers in the school premises. There will be no more dropping off at the school gate.

Frenchie's tweet, from a new account, was the usual self-pitying poisonous word vomit. I guess his mother didn't get him the Xbox game he wanted.

Frenchie7899: You have fucked up everything, it's all broken, sluts like you can't keep your legs shut hey! I will fuck you dead soon just watch.*

Nevertheless it does trigger something in my mind, like the tipping over of an egg timer. Maybe it's the "hey" at the end of the first sentence. I could swear I've seen that somewhere before.

I delete the message. I've reached a decision; my days of feeding the trolls are over.

And I have bigger and better fish to fry. The phone calls start less than five minutes after the podcast drops.

The editors of *The Guardian*, the *Mirror* and the *Daily Mail* are among the first to call. Not their assistants but the editors. This is a big story, probably the biggest I have ever broken. I even take their calls and listen politely to their entreaties for exclusive deals and refer them to Cathy. If anything will flush Cathy out it will be a call from them.

I take three calls and then put my phone on silent and watch the green message notifications appear and then disappear on the screen like flashes of luminescence in an inky sea.

Twitter is going crazy. The hashtag *#TomEllisMurderer* is trending. It's only 2pm but in the wave of euphoria I open the fridge, grab a bottle of champagne left over from the dinner party and pop the cork.

I can't find the champagne flutes and then remember we put them in the basement so I use the chipped mug that I bought from the National Portrait Gallery, the same one Tom Ellis drank tea from. It will add to the sweetness of my victory sip. I remember buying it for Henry when I was pregnant with Finn. I think that was the last time I was at a gallery.

"Sad cow," I whisper to no one in particular.

The champagne tastes delicious and decadent at this time of the day and I take two quick gulps. Lil'Bitch, sitting on the radiator, looks at me, I imagine, with disdain.

"Drop the attitude cat, you shit in a box," I giggle and Lil'Bitch yawns.

And then I feel slightly deflated as I think that I'm drinking alone – well if you don't count Lil'Bitch – and how much fun it would be if I could just go out, go to a bar and order a real drink mixed by a bartender, but as soon as I think this my bright bubble contracts a little further. I pour myself another drink and then after that is finished another one in the hopeless chase of that initial euphoria.

I realise what's bothering me. It's Cathy. Why hasn't she called? I've blown apart the story we've been working on, made headline news, and nothing. Nada. It's so unlike her so when the doorbell goes I run to the door assuming it must be her without checking the video screen first.

But I'm not so completely out of it on champagne and triumph not to check the spy hole before opening the door. Standing outside, his face elongated and shrunken like the image on the back of a spoon, is Peter the fatberg guy.

I pull open the bolts, turn the two deadlock keys and the Yale lock. A click of the latch and I swing the door open. Peter starts to say something but before he can get any words out the hard white light of a TV camera blinds me and a microphone is shoved in my face.

A voice, presumably belonging to the hand wrapped around the microphone, but it's difficult to see because of the blinding light from the camera, asks me, demands of me, "Can you prove Tom Ellis is a murderer?" but before I can answer, not that I intend to, questions are shot at me from the rest of the journalists that are crowded into the narrow pathway that runs from my gate to the front door. "Why did his wife talk to you? Will this mean Khalil Bukhari is released? Are you a recluse, Mrs Kelly? Where have you been? Have you had a nervous breakdown?"

I feel dizzy and I take a step back and stumble on the threshold but luckily I don't fall.

My sight is less compromised now and I can make out the camera crew behind the beaded presenter holding the mic.

"River Jones." He emphasized the "s" more like "zzz". "*Vice News*. Can I just ask you a couple of questions about this morning's podcast?"

I pause with my hand on the door, ready to slam it in his face. At the bottom of the path I can see Peter cowering behind a gate pillar. He sees me looking and ducks behind the pillar. I'm guessing he trousered £50 or so for his little deception. That was the going rate when I used to pull the same stunt as a junior hack.

There doesn't seem to be any other press present. The old media sent me interview requests by email and on social media. The denizens of the new media turned up on my doorstep with a camera crew. New dogs learning old tricks indeed.

And this thought stops me from slamming the door. River Jonze is a small man and he looks like a dog waiting for me to throw him a treat.

It's cold out here and the heat of the house behind me feels as though it's pulling me back into its maw but I don't move. A motorcycle drives past, loud and brash, but my breathing continues normally and I can't feel any tightness in my chest or the paralysing pins and needles that usually accompanies any time spent outside my safe space, and even the dizziness is receding. I don't slam the door as I had fully intended to.

He jerks the microphone forward again.

"Will you answer a couple of questions?"

I breathe in the cold air but to me it doesn't seem cold; it seems fresh, new and full of possibilities. It's probably just the champagne giving me Dutch courage but I surprise myself by nodding.

"Sure, why not?"

Later, when Henry and Finn get back from swimming they arrive to a house that I can see in their faces they struggle to recognise. It's the locks of course.

Henry, I think, was panicked when he found the deadlocks slack and the only barrier to his entry the Yale lock, and he ran down the hallway to be greeted by the smell of baking bread and me, sans tracksuit, wearing a dress.

I just smiled and said, "Welcome to the 1950s," and proceeded to lay out before a bewildered Henry and a delighted Finn a freshly made lasagne – early dinner.

Finn dove into it with gusto but Henry's fork hovered over the plate whilst he eyed me with barely concealed suspicion.

I smiled and then gave him an elaborate wink.

"You didn't listen to my podcast today?"

"No, sorry about that. Finn did so well, didn't you?" He ruffles Finn's hair and Finn responds by bringing his head closer to the plate so he can speed up his already impressive plate-to-mouth time. "He won his heat and then fourth in the final, but two of those boys were in Year 3. We went and got some ice cream and then we were in the car and you know I can't play it there and–"

"I told the world that Tom Ellis killed Lauren Grey. His wife told me he did it. I have her confession on tape. He's going to prison and Khalil is coming out."

I whisper this to Henry as we don't like to talk about the case in front of Finn, but I needn't have worried. Finn looks up. "Good. You can stop worrying," he says through a mouthful of lasagne.

I look at him, my strange child, but he doesn't return my loving gaze, as he's busy attacking his food.

Henry looks staggered.

"That's great, just great," he says, but his face visibly pales.

"Which is good news," I say slowly.

He does his nervous tutting, a habit that drives me crazy. It means he's holding something in but I know him, one light press such as, "What's the matter?" and it comes out.

"It's just, I worry about…" He says "you" silently but Finn isn't interested anymore. He's picked up the iPad and his face reflects the primary colours of Candy Crush or whatever game he has downloaded without our consent.

This would normally have been the spark that set off an argument in the old days before the incident. Post that, I've mostly just been able to zone it out. I do feel something, fire, when he says this, but it's different from the old anger or the newer depressed state. I can see his comments for what they are: genuine concern and not a dig or an attempt to keep me down.

Something is happening to me, something good. Either that or he's been slipping Diazepam in my coffee.

But it's not that. It's the lightening of the load. I realise the stress, Mo's worry, Khalil's innocence and all that goes with it – the trolls, the misogyny, the abuse – has been holding back my recovery. I needed something outside of myself after the attack and I found it, but it's become self-limiting and now it looks like it may be resolved I feel lighter and dare I say it, happier.

So, I smile at Henry instead of barking a "what do you mean by that?" and tell him that I'm fine, I've never been better actually, which is a lie of course, I've been a lot better, hell I used to be able to leave this bloody house but I do feel better than at any time in the last twelve months.

Later that evening when Finn is in bed we watch *Vice News* together on YouTube and marvel at me standing outside and speaking confidently to a camera and asserting Khalil's innocence and Tom's guilt. I don't even go on any social media and I ignore Mohammed's texts asking me to call him. I don't even text Hannah and unusually she doesn't text me. It can all wait till tomorrow because I realise that if I don't take advantage of this moment, this chance, then my marriage, which is as delicate as a dried wasps' nest, will crumble.

We watch the video three times.

It doesn't seem like me on the screen but there I am each time, standing on my doorstep, the door wide open behind me, winter sun on my face, saying, "The truth is clear. Tom Ellis murdered Lauren Grey."

And after the third play Henry leans forward and kisses me and I kiss him back and soon we are making love and it's just like it used to be, which isn't brilliant but isn't not brilliant, and isn't that the best that can be hoped for sometimes?

CHAPTER TWENTY-NINE

The runes

The morning after the night before is beautiful and bright and brings with it an unexpected surprise.

When I turn on my phone there are fifty-two unopened text messages. The tweets and the emails are off the charts and will need to be dealt with later, deep into espresso time.

The surprise is a message from Cathy.

Outstanding work, S. You got him.

But no 'x'. I know this is behaving like a teenager and is deep Kremlinology but the lack of an "x" is clearly a sign she is still mightily pissed off with me. Cathy's standard is three 'x's so I have a way to go yet but I'm cheered; at least she is speaking to me and this is progress.

Another nice surprise is the lack of any messages from Frenchie. My Twitter feed still has the usual nut jobs, racists and swivel-eyed loons commenting but nothing unusual there. There is currently a new theory that Khalil is not actually Muslim but rather Jewish and this explains how the "new" evidence came to light, as Jews are able to manipulate the justice system. Sometimes, I hate the Internet.

I quickly check the holy trinity: the BBC, *The Guardian* and the *Daily Mail*.

The BBC runs with "Rough Justice? Journalist claims new evidence proves convicted murderer is innocent". *The Guardian* goes with "Islamophobia behind conviction of Muslim man?" and the *Daily Mail* carries a picture of Tom Ellis holding up his hand as he leaves a restaurant with the headline, "Former model accuses hedge fund husband of murder!" and there are smaller thumbnail pictures of a young Emma Ellis in a bikini in the sidebar.

Unusually for me, it's the *Daily Mail* headline that brings me the most pleasure. The sight of Tom Ellis being harassed gives me a frisson of sheer pleasure.

The bedroom door opens and Henry comes in. He's holding a tray laden with his idea of a breakfast treat: bacon, eggs and charred bread. He gives me a schoolboy grin, places the tray on my bedside table and sits down next to me on the bed.

"Thought you might be hungry after last night."

For a moment I think he's talking about the podcast and the media storm but then he runs a finger gently down my forearm and I realise he's talking about the sex.

"Finn's playing video games in the lounge. I thought we might jump straight back in the saddle?"

He smells of toothpaste, Listerine and burnt toast. I remember reading somewhere that the smell of burnt toast signifies something bad. Brain tumour or stroke maybe?

"This looks delicious," I say and lean over and grab the tray, putting it on my lap.

There is a fleeting look of disappointment and then he smiles again.

"I made eggs as well, the way you like them. They're under the bacon."

I use my fork to nudge the pile of bacon to one side; it was covering a poached egg that looks like the autopsy of a jaundiced eye.

"Perfect. What are you and Finn doing today?"

Henry bites his top lip. "I thought maybe, and just say no if you don't feel up to it, well I thought" – he looks down and then back up eagerly – "we could all go to the park. You know, it's a nice day. We could wrap up all cosy and grab a hot chocolate and maybe even try the ice skating rink. Finn always wants to go but I've got two left feet and I know you were – are – brilliant at it."

I place my hand on his arm and shake my head. "Not yet, honey."

He nods slowly.

"But soon enough, and anyway today I'm going to be busy. I need to speak to Cathy and do some more media stuff; my phone has been buzzing non-stop since I turned it on and they won't go away unless I throw them some more meat."

"Of course." He gets up and heads out of the bedroom but then pauses by the door.

"Would it be easier if we stayed in and kept you company?"

"No, no," I say too quickly, but he doesn't seem to notice. "You two need to enjoy the day. I'll be just fine."

He picks his thumb with his index finger.

"Only if you're sure?"

"I'm sure."

I want him gone, not for the usual reason of work, or because I find his presence difficult, but because I want to conduct an experiment and I can only do this alone.

But before that I have one last appointment on the case.

Mo's arms are full of pastries and his eyes are full of tears.

I take the bag of pastries from him and put them on the kitchen table. As soon as I've put them down he embraces me in a hug that makes me feel safe in his familiar scent of Chanel Bleu, underlying manly sweat and a distant spice. It feels like home and I sigh.

He doesn't notice, or at least I don't think he does, but he doesn't push me away either so reluctantly I step back.

He shakes his head but smiles.

"I don't know how you did it, Sarah, but you did. My family will be forever grateful."

I flick a strand of hair from my face from where it fell during our embrace.

"I didn't really do anything. I just pushed until Emma had to tell me."

Mo pulls back a chair and takes a seat. This is unusual. He normally waits to be asked, his manners always impeccable. Not that I care. It was just nice to see a man who was still refined with a touch of old-school chivalry. I can hear my younger self screaming at me for being a silly woman with no sense of gender equality and I want to tell that younger self she doesn't know everything about being a woman and nor will she ever.

"This isn't true. I knew you were the right person for this all along. It's all a question of tenacity and you have that spirit. I knew it from the moment we met. May I?"

He reaches for the pastries before I can reply and takes out a large cream slice.

"Yasmin won't let me near these at home so I have to eat them here." He chuckles and takes a large bite out of the slice, forcing custard out of the sides, and a large dollop, unnoticed by him, flops on the floor. The effects of such a big man, such a masculine man, eating like this is disconcerting, and in turn, amusing.

I stifle a giggle that also goes unnoticed.

"I spoke with Khalil, you know," he says.

"How is he? He shouldn't get his hopes up too much yet. It has to be looked at by the lawyers and–"

Mo puts the slice back on the table.

"I totally understand, Sarah, and you know I contacted Gideon, and he is clear that an application for an appeal can be made as soon as Emma makes a statement to the police. He contacted DS Pearson and he said he will speak to her today. It is all in hand." But Mo is no longer smiling.

"How is Khalil taking it?"

"He has been in prison for twelve years and has seen so many false dawns, so he wasn't as pleased as I thought he would be and he has fears, you know."

I look at the pastries and the half-eaten slice and my stomach does an involuntary roll.

"Fears?"

He shrugs. "Khalil is more of a thinker than me." He raises his hands. "I prefer to make things happen, fix them. Maybe that's why I became a doctor. I see a problem and I want to find the solution; if the solution works then I am happy. Khalil is different. He wants to know all the time why it works."

"And he thinks this about Emma?"

A frown and a roll of the eyes. "Yes, it is so typical of him, you know? I told him it doesn't matter but he wants to know why she would say this after all these years. He wanted something more scientific, some sort of DNA proof that it wasn't him. I told him it doesn't matter, that this is better. That her reasons are her own and we shouldn't worry too much about such stuff, you know. I think I reassured him but we shall see, eh?"

"And you?"

He runs his fingers over his stubble.

"Me, I don't ask questions. You know I don't believe, but if ever there was an inshallah required then now is the time." He laughs heartily.

He is almost nonchalant in his attitude but I can sense that there is something else there too. It's in the corners of his eyes; in the manner he is holding himself. A tension almost imperceptible, but it is there. I know because I feel it too. I realise it's been there ever since I unveiled Tom as the murderer, but it's only seeing it in Mo that makes me acknowledge it, and as soon as I do a tight feeling of anxiety blossoms in the pit of my stomach. Its cause is a mystery to me, but one that is just under the surface. I just need to ask the right questions for it to be uncovered but I don't because I'm scared of the answers.

"Your family has such a lot riding on this, on Emma's testimony."

Mo nods. "This is true for sure, but you know we have long been convinced of Khalil's innocence, so this to us is a formality. He has his honour but not his freedom. I think for you, Sarah, it is the same, yes?"

Honour and freedom. I know that I have little of either but without knowing it, he's right, and with this act I can make amends. Emma represents my jailbreak.

We eat some more pastries, drink some more coffee and the conversation is lighter: his family, all doing well, especially now they have this news; his work, doing even better, but the cuts are hurting him; and his wife, beautiful and patient. He plans to take her on holiday now that this is over and any spare cash can be put to something else other than legal and investigatory fees.

When he leaves there is another hug but the erotic charge I felt before isn't there now. It's simple really. The return, however fragmentary, of intimacy with Henry has changed everything, I tell myself, hoping I'm not engaging in self-deception, and I bundle him out into the cold winter morning.

He pauses at the bottom of the path.

"Shall I come round tomorrow? We can talk about the next stages in the case?"

"I'll call you," I say, but I know already that I won't. Something has changed. I sniff the air. The smell of diesel, wet pavement and rotten leaves is almost overwhelming in its life-affirming beauty and filth.

"Goodbye then, Sarah. I knew you would succeed. You can do anything, you know that, don't you?"

He doesn't wait for an answer.

CHAPTER THIRTY

Out

I'm watching Mo's back as he strides off purposefully down the road, heading towards his real life. And as I think that I make a decision.

Tonight I'm going to cook a perfect dinner for Henry and Finn, but more importantly I'm going to leave the house, walk to Waitrose three blocks away and buy the food myself.

I realise that I have to seize the moment and ride this unexpected wave of bravery and I run back into the hallway, grab my big puffer jacket from under the stairs and then I quickly walk outside with not even a look back, as I fear I'll crumble and turn back to the warmth and safety of the hall, and slam the door behind me. I'm going out and as I pass the gate my stomach feels like it gives birth to a million adrenaline tendrils that surge and tangle around my body.

The street is different from how I remember it. I'm not talking about the fact that there are the orange work tents and barriers around the manhole, where they descend to tackle the fatberg, but there is a deeper change. It takes me a moment then it gradually dawns on me: the street is the same. It's me. I'm looking at it with the eyes of a prisoner who's been incarcerated underground for over twelve months.

I pass some pedestrians: a young black guy wearing headphones and then a pair of what I assume are Chinese tourists laden down with cameras and brandishing a guidebook in an attempt to attract every mugger between here and Peckham. They don't give me a second glance, which I marvel at, as I feel as though my anxiety must surely show on my face.

It's cold and I'm conscious of my breathing. It's not bad so far. Big deep lungfuls of the crisp December air and not the shallow accelerated pants of panic that I fear.

A man is approaching. His head is tucked downwards inside the collar of his large grey overcoat but he's looking straight ahead and, as we pass each other, I catch his eye and smile. He immediately looks away.

Am I invisible, I wonder, or is this just paranoia? I've been inside for nearly a year and hiding has made me invisible. My body language, my movement along the street, is that of a hidden creature and the shadows I retreated into are now around me.

I frown at this thought.

"No," I say out loud. This won't be me and it's not. The daylight will burn off the shadows and it starts in the supermarket. Not the most romantic place for the beginning of the new me but at least I can pick up some pomegranate molasses as well. This thought causes me to giggle and then the thought that I am outside walking and laughing makes me break into the biggest grin and then a man, not bad looking either, walks past and winks flirtatiously at me. Oh my days!

When I get to Waitrose five minutes later it's another story, however. It's busy, as always, and it's bright, so fucking bright, with added lights and dazzle from the tasteful but bland Christmas decorations that are positioned just inside the open doors.

I pause outside by the bike racks and reach for a pack of cigarettes in my jeans pocket that haven't been there for over five years.

It's just a fucking supermarket, girl, don't be a pussy, goes my internal monologue, but an old dear and her husband pass by and she tuts and says something disapproving to him. I must have been muttering again. It's a thing we solitary, agoraphobic types do sometimes.

Okay, I'm going in. *Who dares wins, Rodders.* I keep my lips sealed as I think this.

I head inside.

The first few steps are terrifying and I keep my eyes half closed to avoid focusing on any one person in the throng, moving in and out of the store, and then I feel the warmth of the air conditioning system and my nostrils fill with the smell of baked, artisanal bread and roasting coffee beans and I slowly open them and I'm in heaven.

I walk slowly down the nearest aisle, which is the fruit and vegetable section, and it's like looking through a kaleidoscope. Peppers in greens, reds and yellows, next to a dozen shades of green avocados, kale, spring onions, the royal sumptuous purples of beetroot and the exquisite plump red tomatoes and flouncy lettuces. I find my threatening panic retreat in the face of a sumptuous Victorian-style Christmas cheese and port stand that after a year inside my house appears to my eyes as the most beautiful thing I have ever seen,

It's all I can do to stop myself opening my arms and mouthing "wow".

Composing myself, I pick up a basket and start to gingerly place some of the glorious bounty inside.

It's going to be a lasagne so tomatoes, onions, garlic and one of the tarty Italian lettuces get picked.

"Would you care to try one of our speciality cheeses? It's a cheeky Manchego."

I look up, no longer invisible for sure, into the smiling eyes of a young girl holding a tray of tiny pieces of cheese on cocktail sticks.

"Very 70s," I say and she looks back and smiles harder. "Before your time. Go on then, why not?" And I pop a piece of cheese in my mouth where it melts and writhes in a death spiral of pure pleasure.

"Jesus." There's no doubt I said that out loud.

"You like it?"

Henry has been doing most of the shopping for the last twelve months and as I don't really cook it's been a diet of ready meals and pasta for some time.

"I fucking love it. Give me three packs."

It didn't seem possible but her smile gets wider and she hands over the cheese.

I glide down the dairy aisle and add some Icelandic yoghurt and some Parmesan and ricotta for the lasagne.

The meat counter lies at the top, sandwiched between the more aloof fish counter and the pastry-covered delights of the deli counter.

There is no one serving when I arrive but through a thick plastic curtain I can see the butcher raise a cleaver and then bring it down with a muffled thump. It slices through bone, muscle and gristle. The air above and around the meat is colder and I shiver slightly.

I peruse the blood-red cuts, fillets and mince and try to remember what Henry's favourite would be. It's the type of thing a good wife would know.

"It's amazing to think that only a few hours ago these desiccated carcasses were living breathing animals with no idea of the fate that was about to befall them."

The slight shiver becomes a spasm in my gut and all the air in my lungs seems to crystallise.

My knees begin to buckle and I steady myself by putting a hand onto the counter. The cleaver comes down hard into flesh again.

"Are you okay, Sarah? Being outside can be frightening."

I push back with my hand and turn around.

Tom Ellis smiles at me.

"Surprised to see you out and about. There are a lot of dangerous people in this city." He steps forward, forcing me backwards, so I press up against the counter. "You need to be careful."

"What do you want? I'll scream if you come closer."

He laughs and he's close enough that drops of spittle land on my face.

"What do I want? I want to thank you, that's what I want." And then he leans in and I swear he snarls.

I squirm backwards and then he steps away from me and laughs again.

"What are you talking about? You're going to prison, you know that, yeah?"

I can feel the air lighten in my lungs and some of the adrenaline being put to good use at last. I'm shaking but it's anger not panic now.

He grabs a tomato out of my basket and takes a bite, juice falling on the floor.

"Oh, I don't think so. In fact, the only place I'm likely to be going is your house. I did like it very much and I am so looking forward to owning it."

"What are you talking about?"

He checks his watch and then tosses the half-eaten tomato back in my basket.

"Hmm, I don't think I want to spoil the surprise. I must be going now. I have a date and I definitely can't keep her waiting. See you soon, Sarah."

He turns on his heels and strides off.

"Are you alright, love?"

I turn around. It's the butcher and he's still holding the cleaver.

"Where were you when I needed you?"

"Eh? You want something?" He gestures at the meat but I don't want anything but to be at home.

CHAPTER THIRTY-ONE

Run

I run back to the house and this time people do give a second glance to the middle-aged woman sprinting towards them, but it's just to make sure that they can step aside from the crazed vision of panic pounding towards them. As I run the rhythm of my mobile phone buzzing in my pocket seems to match the pounding of my heart in my chest.

When I reach my front door I press myself against it and wait for a moment for my heartbeat to slow and for my breath to return.

"Hi. I just wanted to apologise for that thing with the reporters."

I turn around and there's fatberg guy looking apologetic.

I ignore him and try to use my Yale key to open the door but my hand is shaking so much that I can't insert the key in the slot.

How could I have let my guard down and left the door just on the Yale lock? What was I thinking?

"I just wanted to say sorry."

The key slides into the slot. "Fuck off!"

And the door yields and I stagger over the threshold and slam the door in fatberg guy's face. Lil'Bitch is sitting in the middle of the floor looking at me curiously.

I bolt the door and lock every lock and then slide down the back of the door and sit down on the doormat. Lil'Bitch pads over and throws herself on the floor next to my leg and begins purring. I stroke her and my breathing starts to slow but then my phone buzzes again and I pull it out and check my messages. There's one from Henry. I click on it.

What have you done? We'll lose everything. Call me!

What can he mean? Before replying to Henry's text I see that Cathy has also texted me and despite my shaken state I can't help but feel better for knowing my friend wants to speak to me.

Cathy's email contains a link to a BBC article and two words: *read this*.

I click on the link and all I can register is the headline and the sense of shock and loss that it immediately brings on. I read it again.

"Ex-BBC journalist accused in bribery murder scandal."

I read on. Emma has retracted her statement. She says I offered her money to make it and she went along with it because she knew I had previously tried to frame her husband in my podcasts. The article says she recorded me making my offer and now I think back. I can remember her fiddling with the baby as he slept. Was that where the recording device was hidden? I can't recall exactly what I said but I know deep down I chased the story because I wanted it and now she's trapped me.

And then the full reality of my situation hits me. Tom Ellis is going to sue me for libel. He is going to win millions, claim his reputation has been ruined and he is going to take my house from me, my sanctuary, and the only place I can *be* in this world. I know that there will be a solicitor's letter coming, one that says I have defamed Tom Ellis by accusing him of being a murderer, and I know the costs and damages awarded to him will bankrupt us and we will lose this house. I've been played and in my eagerness to damn Tom Ellis he has damned me and my family.

"Fuck!" I scream and Lil'Bitch jumps up and her legs move faster than her body as she tears away down the hall her paws sliding on the wooden floor.

When Henry gets home he doesn't say anything to me for over an hour until he puts Finn to bed. And when he does come back downstairs and into the kitchen his face is a colour that if described in a Farrow & Ball catalogue would be "Aubergine Eruption".

He starts to talk but instead of words his mouth twists as though there aren't words yet invented, which could do adequate justice to his rage. When the words do start to flow I worry he won't make it through the next five minutes. He's so enraged his voice seems to have changed; it's deeper with the timbre of desolation and despair.

"We're" – he struggles with the next word and takes a huge gulp of air as though gathering fuel for the scream that follows – "going to lose our home!"

Henry is standing in the kitchen, a large glass of wine in one hand and a letter in the other.

He looks older than usual and the stress or wine or both is causing his capillaries to work overtime, providing the rich colour decorating his face.

"Defamation, libel and a claim for punitive damages because of the nature of the allegations you made. Calling the man a fucking murderer, for Christ's sake!"

I don't mention the email from IPSO as I don't imagine the press complaints commission and their sanctions will bother him right now. I've put our house, our home, in jeopardy. Without it, what are we?

The thought of losing my safe space is too much so I've not examined it, accepted it, in any way. Denial is my new watchword and even as Henry quite understandably rants and raves, I can't really come to terms with the fact that this place, this kitchen, the air with its own scent distinct to this house, everything that surrounds and protects me, is under threat.

Henry looks at me with wide eyes. "What are we going to do?"

This last plea isn't in anger it sounds like a child pleading with his parents.

"Well?"

I can't and don't answer and this makes him furious.

"Well?"

He screams, "Fuck you, Sarah!" and slams his glass down on the kitchen table, and it shatters. Red wine pools on the oak and

I get up to get a cloth from the sink cupboard but Henry pushes past me.

"I'm going out."

"Where are you going?"

"Out, remember that?" and he storms off.

I follow him, still mute, but I need to make sure he closes the front door properly, as if he just slams it, it may just bounce back off the frame, leaving the house vulnerable.

Henry grabs the Yale catch and pulls it down and then yanks hard at the door. It doesn't yield of course. His shoulders drop and he kicks the door hard.

"Fucking hell, this stupid fucking door!" He turns keys and pulls back the bolts. "No fucking more, this all stops!"

He gets the door open. Cold air and night fumes, the smell of diesel and burnt grease on the wind, rush inside.

Henry pauses on the threshold. He looks so much smaller and older than the image of him I carry around in my head.

"You have to make this better. Or…" He looks to the heavens as if in search of inspiration but it doesn't come and in lieu of divine inspiration he lets out a sob.

I stay silent.

He shakes his head and I can see the tears blossoming in his eyes. What is there that I can say that won't enrage him further?

Slowly, I push the door shut until it clicks shut and then I bring home all of the locks and bolts. Peace.

When I've finished I turn round and there, sitting in the gloom at the bottom of the stairs, is Finn, his pale face surrounded by the darkness.

"Honey." I go to him and sit next to him on the staircase. "Are you okay?"

He isn't crying. He doesn't look upset, even, and this I find more concerning.

"I'm fine. Are you okay, Sarah?"

This jars as it always does.

"I'm fine. It's just sometimes grown-ups have rows. It doesn't mean me and your dad will be breaking up or anything like that." I instantly wonder why I said that but he just nods sleepily.

He nods ever so gently. His big brown eyes are emotionless and I feel despair at not knowing my own child. He stands up.

"You should," says Finn, leaving me shocked and overwhelmed and then he pads off upstairs to bed, leaving me sat on the bottom step.

I sit there for a minute, what's left of me, and then after a minute or maybe ten make my way back to the kitchen. Lil'Bitch is perched on the radiator and she jumps off when I enter and walks out of the kitchen into the utility room.

"*Et tu*, Lil'Bitch?"

The house is quiet save for the underlying noise of it breathing, the movement of air in the pipes, the soft creak of the joist like a whisper in the night and the caress of the wind on its windowpanes.

My phone is on the table and it buzzes. I grab it without looking at the caller, hoping it's Henry or if I'm truly honest, Cathy.

Instead there is a silence so different from the comforting silence of my house; rather an absence of sound filled with malice and darkness.

"Who is this?"

But I know of course. There is a sound, like wet lips being dragged back over sharp teeth.

"You deserved to be raped."

The voice is metallic, a psychotic electronic speech at once devoid of emotion and at the same time so utterly chilling because it speaks of an effort, use of resources, to hide in the shadows and strike. This is no ordinary hatred and it has just escalated again.

"Is this you, Frenchie?"

I close my eyes and see a hand pressing my face down into the abyss.

"I've sent you a message. You will want to read it."

The line goes dead and then almost straight away there's a ping as an SMS message lands on my phone.

It's from an unknown number of course. I know it's dumb but I need to know and I open the message. There's just a link in the message. I shouldn't, but I click, and a page opens in Safari. It's a site called *datadumppowned*. The page that opens is headed "ASHLEYDATADUMP" and underneath is just a list of email addresses, thousands of them. This can't be happening.

I do a page search for SarahKelly76@hotmail.com and there it is, highlighted for me by the guiltless computer, my email address, in a list of users on a website recently hacked and its users "outed". A website that proudly advertises itself as "the world's number one adultery website".

And then I'm in front of the sink dry heaving. He knows.

CHAPTER THIRTY-TWO

Breach

They've gone.

Henry must have come home and put me to bed. I couldn't sleep and had taken two sleeping tablets, washed down with quarter of a bottle of Absolut, and woken twelve hours later in my bed. The last thing I remembered was the glass of vodka falling from my hand as I watched some late-night television turn into a kaleidoscope of primary colours and warnings. I'm still in my clothes so Henry was able to resist undressing me. No surprise there.

The house is quieter than it should be for a Saturday morning. I assume that Henry has taken Finn out to the park, their normal Saturday morning routine, but when I get downstairs there's an envelope with *Sarah* written in ink on the front, waiting for me on the table. Letters are bad; nothing good comes in a letter these days. A handwritten letter is the equivalent of a phone call at 3am, a signal of loss.

But before reading it I have to check something first and I run down to the front door and click the locks in to place as I knew, and I was right, that he would only leave the Yale lock engaged. I can't decide whether he is forgetful or trying to mentally torture me. All I know is that he gets more forgetful the angrier he is with me.

Back in the kitchen I open the letter. He's even sealed it. Henry is always so fastidious even when delivering bad news.

Sarah,

I can't be around this toxic atmosphere and neither can Finn. I'm taking him to my mother's.

We have to get back to where we were. You need to come back to us and you need to save the house. It is who we are and it binds us all, you, me and Finn together. You have to sort this out but I'm sorry I can't be around you right now.

Your husband,

Henry

The "your husband" makes me want to puke. It's the very worst of Henry, self-pitying and cloying sentimental. I throw the letter in the pedal bin.

I also cry at the thought of my boy, his innocence compromised by me and no one else, me, who should be his protector. I have visited all of this upon him.

My phone is pinging, demanding attention like a hungry toddler. I go to look but then a weariness descends on me and I realise I can't take anymore, anymore Frenchie, Tom, Henry or Mohammed. These men and their demands are just too much right now. All I know is I feel drained and in need of rest so I turn it off, go back upstairs and then climb into my unmade bed. I fall asleep straight away.

When I wake up I'm unsure of the time. I hadn't drawn the curtains so I can see that it's dark outside but at this time of winter that could be any time after 3pm. I turn my phone back on. It's only 5.40pm. The house is silent and I can't think of a single reason to get out of bed. I text Hannah and wait for the usual instant reply, but nothing comes so I hug my pillow and fall back into a deep sleep.

A dream wakes me some time later, or so I think. I awake in the dream in the same house, the same bedroom, to the sound of my phone ringing and when I look "Drallo" is the name on the caller ID. I don't know anyone by that name so I don't answer but then there's a knocking on my bedroom door and I know that it's Drallo come to pay me a visit. The knocking is loud and persistent, like the sound of a staff on a cathedral door, and I know

I can't answer, but he knows I'm inside. And I want to wake but I can't and I start to shout as I realise that this is not a dream and Drallo is coming and the door starts to swing open. I scream and then I'm awake screaming out loud and lying in a pool of sweat and my phone is ringing. I reach for it but the ringing stops. I pick it up anyway and see I have four missed calls from Cathy.

Relief that I am out of the dream, away from Drallo, is tempered when I check the time.

It's 3.15am so I assume Cathy's hard into a Saturday night and maybe the combination of booze, drugs and weekend *joie de vivre* has made her sentimental and wanting to connect with me and bury the hatchet. But a call at this hour? I ring her mobile but it goes straight to answerphone the way it does when a battery is dead. I leave a message asking Cathy to call me back as I'm worried about her.

I lie back onto the damp bed sheets. I know sleep is never going to come now. And that's when I hear it. The unmistakable high-pitched squeal of a cat. It's Lil'Bitch, I'm sure, but it's a sound I've never heard her produce before.

Goosebumps lay claim to my flesh.

I lie silently, listening to my breathing, and then there it is again: the sound of a cat, a cat in pain.

The urge to pull the covers up and over my face is almost overwhelming. I know I can't do that so somehow I swing my legs out of the bed and gently place my feet on the wooden floor.

Slowly, I lower myself to the floor until my eyes are level with the underside of the bed and check if it's still there. It is, and I reach my hand under the bed and my fingers fasten around the handle of the claw hammer that I keep there. Henry called me paranoid when I insisted on putting it there but he soon changed his mind after I was attacked; not that it helped me then.

I get back to my feet and walk out of the bedroom onto the landing. I pause there and hang over the balcony to listen. The house is suffused with dark blue shades and the stillness of night, an atmosphere in which sound and strange things travel more easily.

There is nothing and then Lil'Bitch, far below, begins to cry again.

There is nothing for it. I am going to have to go downstairs, so carefully I begin padding down the stairs step by step. Each footstep sounds as loud as a gunshot to my ears and I wonder who else is listening. What eyes are glancing upwards towards the sounds?

When I reach the bottom of the stairs I pause again and my finger hovers over the light switch. My eyes are adjusted to the gloom now though and if I turn the lights on, what then? I lose any element of surprise for very little gain. *The dark is your friend*, I tell myself. I take my hand away from the light switch. In my other hand the claw hammer hangs heavy and ready.

The kitchen is drowned in the inky blue of night before the dawn begins to bleed and diffuse the bruised darkness. There's no one in here but I can hear her cries clearly now and they are coming from the basement. This should be impossible. I always lock the basement door when it's not in use. Can I have forgotten because I fell asleep during the daytime? My breathing becomes shallower and to my ears as loud as a jet engine.

Sure enough the door is ajar and I can hear her clearly now. Cries of pain mixed with a feline snarl, and there's another noise, the sound of something large, and a smell, a bad smell, of decaying meat.

I pull the basement door wide open and then put my right foot forward on the top step. Once it's there I transfer my weight onto it and luckily there's no squeaking board so I bring my other foot forward and then slowly begin to descend into the dark.

I reach the bottom of the stairs. The LED in the Internet router which is under my desk casts a pale-blue light on the concrete floor.

Lil'Bitch is in the middle of the room. She's low to the ground, her fur in jagged spikes along her coiled spine, ready to pounce, and staring into the corner of the room.

"Lil'Bitch," I whisper, and she quickly turns her head and I can see her eyes are black pools of murder. She registers me and then turns back to face the corner. I follow her gaze and see she's hissing poison at the huge rat that is gnawing at the Ethernet cable.

The light from the router makes the rat look irradiated like a demon vision from a 1950's B movie, as a metaphor for the power of the atom, and this effect is heightened by its pus-yellow eyes which swivel now and focus on me. The rat is bigger than any I've seen before and my mind brings up a montage of urban myths and headlines proclaiming invasions of giant rodents.

I can see a small crack in the corner of the basement behind the router. The gap doesn't look big enough for the rat to get through but I remember reading that only the pointed conical head has to get through and the body will follow, however large. It must be the works on the street sewer; the vibrations have caused a crack in the basement wall. This rat must have come from there, from the fatberg. That's why it's so big; it's been feeding on kebab and burger grease, and the contents of a million wet wipes.

It goes back to gnawing at the cable, seemingly unconcerned by me and Lil'Bitch.

There's a smell: damp, animal and rank. I take a step forward and Lil'Bitch looks back at me so I take another and then I'm level with my small brave cat. She hisses at the rat again as though to signal our solidarity and this time the rat does turn its pointy head as though noticing us for the first time and it glowers at us, almost daring us to do something.

The claw hammer hangs by my side and now I raise it to shoulder height.

"Shoo!"

The rat stares at me. It clearly has no intention of *shooing*.

I pat the claw hammer in the palm of my other hand as I've seen thugs do a thousand times in movies and on TV, but the rat remains unmoved.

I take another step forward and this time the rat changes its posture. It rises slightly on its hind legs and sniffs the air. Then it bares its two, saliva-covered long incisors that look like sharp, broken lollipop sticks against the pale pink cotton candy of its mouth, and it makes a barking sound.

It moves forward and away from the hole behind it.

A realisation dawns on me that the rat isn't cornered, it just sees something it thinks it can defeat and it won't back down. At the same time I also come to the conclusion that I won't be able to kill it.

And that's when the rat jumps at me.

The thing uses its hind legs to project itself up and at me and I swear to God it's going for my eyes.

Everything happens at once. I swing the claw hammer and Lil'Bitch leaps in the air and swipes at the rat, knocking it away from its trajectory to my pupils and into the arc described by the claw hammer.

The head of the hammer connects with the skull of the rat and there is a sickening sound of bones splintering and then a thud as the rat hits the floor.

It twitches once and then stops moving.

Lil'Bitch takes an exploratory sniff and then I poke the rat with the hammer and am rewarded with no signs of life.

A wave of exhilaration chases my anxiety away.

"Sisters doing it for themselves, eh, Lil'Bitch?"

This seems to satisfy Lil'Bitch and she insouciantly glides off up the stairs looking for further adventure or somewhere to sleep. I follow her to get a plastic bin liner in which to place the rat and to find something more solid to cover the crack in the wall and stop any other fatberg rats from breaching my defences.

And then I realise I feel something I haven't felt in a while. I feel confident and powerful and I can't help but wonder: is this how murderers feel?

CHAPTER THIRTY-THREE

Free and bound

After I dispose of the rat in the garden waste bin I come back inside and I notice something peculiar: there's a spring in my step. Killing must be good for me and that's not the most comforting thought I've ever had. I pat Lil'Bitch and she follows me back upstairs to the bedroom where I crash out, but as I plummet into a deep sleep as though strapped to an anchor, there's a small voice shouting something, a voice that is soon drowned.

When I awake it's to that same voice, but it's no longer quiet. It's screaming, *Cathy*! The call was in the middle of the night. What if it wasn't a drunken late-night call? What if she really needs me and I was too busy killing rats as therapy?

I grab my phone from the bedside table and call her but it goes straight to voicemail. I leave a message asking her to call me back.

There are no messages from Henry. I wonder how long my punishment is to go on for? I know Henry's usual tolerance for staying with his mother is three days and we're only on day two now, so I tell myself not to start panicking until day four.

I can see half a dozen texts from unknown numbers but I don't open them. I suspect they will be fresh text messages from Frenchie but I haven't got the time for him today and I wish that I hadn't indulged him previously. Pick a scab and it tends to grow back bigger than before. I delete them all without opening them.

I'm relieved I've actually woken up in the morning and even though I feel stretched thin after a day and night of turbulent sleep I decide I need to impose routine so I wander downstairs and make coffee, orange juice and toast and sit in silence as I have my breakfast.

But I can't eat. Cathy is an early riser even with industrial-size hangovers and I'm worried. I put down my toast and pick up my phone and try Cathy again.

This time after four rings the phone is answered, but not by Cathy.

It's Angus.

"Oh, it's you. What do you want?"

I'm taken aback by his rudeness. How is that like the majority of the population – certainly the online one in which I mainly exist – I am desensitised to violence, can observe with detachment a beheading video in between browsing clips of piano-playing cats and Mumsnet, but everyday rudeness still shocks me? Is it a naive attachment to the middle-class values I grew up thinking held the world together despite all the evidence since to the contrary?

"Hi Angus, I want to speak to my friend. Is that okay with you?"

He makes a noise that sounds like a growl.

"Yeah, well, she doesn't want to speak to you so I guess you've got a problem there."

"Why are you answering Cathy's phone?"

He takes a bite of something and in between chews answers me. "I do a lot of things for her you don't know about" – there's a loud swilling sound – "and she doesn't share everything with her friends, especially those that put her career in jeopardy."

"I want to speak to her. Right now, or I'm calling the police."

Angus laughs.

"Be my guest. You've got form, and quite the reputation as an hysterical woman making wild allegations against innocent men."

There's a smack of lips and I imagine grease running down his chin. That's unfair, I know, but hell it's my imagination and that's the image it provides.

"Something's not right, just..." I take a breath and try and take out the screechy note of pleading. "Let me speak with her."

He snorts. "No fucking chance, you psycho." And there is a final chomp and the line goes dead.

Fuck. I think about calling the police, but to tell them what? That my friend and her boyfriend, who I insulted and whose career I nearly wrecked in the train crash of my own, won't speak to me?

I make another call instead. It's to Bulldog Productions and it's answered by Tomas, the young creative who reports into Cathy.

"Oh, Sarah, I am so pleased to hear from you. It's been *waaaay* too long, babe. Loving your work, such drama!"

I ask him if I can speak to Cathy and his response chills me to the bone.

"Oh, she's still sick darling. Hasn't been in all week. I thought you girls might be partying a little too hard, you know, to get over that nasty business with that Tom chappie. He seems like such a scoundrel."

"You better believe it, Tomas. Listen, if Cath does come in, could you ask her to call me straight away?"

I try to sound calm but my stomach has cramped in fear. Cathy is never sick; well she is, but she is never off work. She would need to be dying to not do the things she loves.

"*Tout de suite absolument*! *Ciao*, lover."

I check WhatAspp and there is a reply from Hannah but it's not the one I was expecting.

I read the story in the newspaper about accusing Tom Ellis and recording his wife that way – it's awful and I can't imagine what you must be going through? I know that our homes are the bulwark against everything that is out there – all the evil and the sewer of modern life, the selfishness, the trolls, the temptation. Whatever you need I'm here babe xx FT no.2

My reply is selfish – *Will you come over? I'm alone and need a hug x* – and I immediately regret it and I'm not surprised that she doesn't answer. What a thing to ask her.

I sit at the bottom of the stairs in my lonely hallway and I cry. I cry because I feel helpless and alone; I cry because I'm frightened to help my friend; I cry because I'm about to lose my house, my child and my husband; and I cry because none of this was meant to happen. This life was not the one I wanted. I look down the hallway at the door, at the locks – so comforting and strong, but which trap me here, bind me to this place, this version of myself.

Lil'Bitch appears from the kitchen and brushes herself up against my legs. She looks up at me and meows. I know what this means. It means she wants food, but we all make up stories don't we, and I decide to make up mine. I have to because I know if I don't I will never leave this house again. And the story I imagine is Lil'Bitch, looking up at me, saying we did it, we killed that rat, we can do anything me and you, and I know that if Lil'Bitch could say anything to me right now she would say: "The only way to deal with your fear is to attack it, stomp on its face, gouge the eyes out of that motherfucker because that's what it was going to do to you."

I find myself nodding along. "Lil'Bitch, you're goddamn right."

I stand up and walk slowly down the hallway until I reach the front door. I place my palm on the top bolt; its comforting heft now just feels cold and heavy. I slide it back and then drop to my knees and do the same with the lower bolt. I pull at the elastic keychain and select the correct keys, in order, for the deadlocks and then the everyman of the party, the Yale lock. I pull open the door and step outside.

Twenty minutes later and I'm sitting in the back of a cab with Hindi music blaring and listening to the woes of a middle-aged Indian man as he tells me about the trouble he is having with his daughter. She wants to go to university and become a lawyer but he thinks she is better suited to following her heart and becoming an artist like he wanted to.

"Jobs, they feed the family, yes, but what of our souls, eh, I ask you?"

I'm not sure whether I'm meant to answer but before I can decide he's moved on to world affairs ("what a mess everywhere") and 'the Arsenal' ("what a mess everywhere"). I find it soothing in some way and it acts as a balm to the anxiety I feel seeping out of every pore. This is the furthest I've been from the house in over a year and each second takes me further away from safety.

And then we stop and he says something and his body language indicates he needs a reply.

"I'm sorry?"

"Is this the place?"

I look outside. We are parked in front of the Victorian terrace which houses Cathy's flat.

My chest tightens and I manage to say, "Yes" and then pay him but my voice sounds like it belongs to someone else, someone far away, with a mouth full of cotton wool.

And then he's gone and I'm standing alone on the pavement. I look up at the top floor of the house and I can see that one of the windows is open slightly. A quick glance along the road reveals Cathy's Mazda MX-5 parked fifty yards away next to a motorcycle that I guess belongs to Angus; he never fails to mention that he rides a motorcycle.

I open the gate and walk up the short path to the front door. There are five doorbells and I hit the one marked "Morgan".

A few seconds pass and then there is the cracking sound of old electronics.

"Hello?"

It's Cathy and the shock of relief that she is alive takes my breath away.

I talk quickly.

"Cath, it's me, Sarah; you need to let me in. I'm in danger."

I feel bad lying but I know Cathy and she would never let me down. If she thinks I need her she is going to let me in. If she thinks I'm here to save her then the drawbridge will remain drawn.

Five seconds pass, then five more, and just when the anxiety is creeping down my arms masquerading as pins and needles, the buzzer goes and I'm in. I run up the stairs two at a time as I don't want her changing her mind, but I needn't have worried because when I get to her door it's already open and she's standing there with a bottle of red wine in her hand and I smile at the sight of it, and her, until my heart begins to pound as I register the black eye.

"What is it? What danger?" she whispers urgently.

I'm too outraged to keep up the pretence.

"What the fuck is that? Did he hit you? Oh God, Cath."

She shakes her head and attempts a smile.

"Christ, no, we were drinking. It got out of hand." Her hand goes to her eye. "I bashed it by accident."

"What do you mean, 'got out of hand'? I'm going to kill the fucker!" And I barge past Cath into her apartment.

She tries to pull me back but I'm powered by sheer rage and the power is both scary and intoxicating.

"Where are you, Scottish prick!"

I burst into the lounge but he's not there. Cathy runs in after me. "You're not listening, Sarah. It's not what you think!"

"Not what I think? This isn't a fucking soap opera, Cath, he hit you!"

She grabs both my hands.

"Look at me and listen. No he didn't."

My beautiful, strong friend has become a victim of domestic abuse and it kills me to see her like this, so pathetic and beaten. This thought causes my rage to go supernova and I snatch my hands away and storm out of the lounge.

"I know he's in here!"

"Sarah, no!"

I ignore her and pull open the bedroom door.

At first I'm not sure what I'm looking at; it's obvious "what" it is but I can't place this image together with the version of Cathy I carry round in my head.

"It's not what you think."

I manage to close my mouth. "I literally have no idea what to think other than I wish there was a bleach I could apply to my mind."

Angus is lying on the bed. Well, lying is perhaps the wrong word. He's splayed, arms and ankles tied to the posts with cable ties.

He's wearing nothing but a nappy, has a shower cap on his head and a dummy in his mouth. He looks like a giant baby and I can't help but burst out laughing.

Cathy is laughing too and she is also taking pictures on her iPhone.

"You were right of course, Sarah. I caught him texting some Momentum activist called Catherine. He was up to his old tricks. Excuse me." She moves around me and kneels on the bedroom floor so she is eye level with him.

"But instead of throwing him out I thought, let's be modern about this and engage in some revenge porn. I now need to decide whether to post these pictures to Angus's various social media channels. Despite however progressive old Angus here pretends to be they would rather put a dent in his tough Scots guy image."

She notices I am still gawping.

"I invited him back here, told him about my fantasy of making love to a big baby and this big baby here agreed to get dressed up. Men will do pretty much anything for sex, eh? Isn't that true, Angus?"

Cathy coughs behind me.

"Oh. Oh Cathy, I'm so embarrassed. I thought you were – well, you know – and what about your black eye?"

Angus starts to wriggle from side to side and makes grunting noises.

"Into S&M? God no, I leave that sort of suburban stuff to dear old Angus here." She checks herself out in a mirror on the back of the door. "My mascara ran because I was laughing so hard at the sight of this dipshit."

Angus shakes his head and his eyes widen. I wink at him.

"Can I send you these pictures?" asks Cathy.

"Sure, please do," I say.

Cathy hits send on her phone and then moves to the end of the bed and pulls out a key. She unlocks one of the handcuffs, freeing Angus's right hand.

"Now, provided Angus here is a good boy and leaves and never, ever darkens my door again, I will promise not to release the photographs to anybody else. Will you make that promise as well, Sarah?"

I smile. "Absolutely."

Cathy turns back to Angus. "Do you promise, Angus? And do you promise to leave now and not say a word despite how angry and emasculated you feel?"

Angus nods his head vigorously.

Cathy unlocks the handcuffs on his ankles and then finally the remaining pair, freeing him completely.

He jumps up and I can't help laughing as he looks like a massive toddler, unsteady on his feet.

"Please, can I at least have my clothes?"

Cathy holds her hands up, palms out. "Sorry big guy. They hit the bins outside three hours ago; it's a bit cold out so do us a favour and don't leave the door open when you leave."

For a second I see rage try to assert itself on his face but it stands no chance against his pride, which he knows lies within our hands.

His shoulders slump and he makes his way out of the bedroom and, a few seconds later, we hear the front door slam. As soon as this happens we both collapse on the bed laughing and screaming hysterically.

"A giant baby! He is a giant baby as well!"

And we're off again until we have tears pouring down our faces and our breathing is almost manic in its intensity.

Eventually, we calm down and then I spot something on the floor and say, "Look, Cathy, he really did spit his dummy out."

This causes the laughter to roll back in and soon I'm laughing so hard that I'm struggling to take in any oxygen.

Eventually, the heaves become swells and then subside once more. Cathy gives me hug.

"I'm glad to see you, and you've left the house. Progress indeed."

"Well I'll be losing the house soon so I may as well get used to being without it."

This kills the last of the laughter.

"How do you feel about taking another baby step and grabbing a coffee down the road?"

I take a deep breath. "Why not? Today is all about surprises. Will he be alright?"

"Who gives a fuck?"

The giggles return and we are still laughing as I follow her outside.

Ten minutes later and we are doing something that for a long time I thought was impossible. We are sitting in a cafe, drinking fine-roasted coffee and sharing a large portion of carrot cake and I do not feel like I am going to have to run out, my chest pounding, and head for home, to hide behind the door.

The place smells delicious – fresh coffee, and baking bread – and although the fear is there, hovering just out of sight, waiting for any sign of weakness so it can pounce, right now, in this moment, I am something like happy.

"We haven't done this in a while," says Cathy.

"I've been tied up," I shoot back, and Cathy, for the first time I can ever recall, appears to blush.

"I'm sorry you had to see him like that. You were right all along and I'm so sorry for not listening, but when you're close to someone sometimes you just can't see the truth."

"I'm not judging. All relationships are like an alien world to those observing them."

"At least you are with someone normal, who, despite any faults, loves you."

I think back to Henry in the utility room and change the subject.

"Cathy, I wasn't joking. I do need your help. You must have seen what's happening. I'm going to lose my house. Tom is going to take everything from me."

She pulls out a pack of cigarettes and takes one out of the pack. She places it behind her ear, a habit she has when thinking.

"Yeah, I heard. You should never have broadcast – total disregard for journalistic technique, a disgrace to the profession etc. But you know what?" She puts her hand on my arm. "I'm glad you did, even if it put the shits up that evil fucker for one second. Having said that, the downside is he is going to win his libel case, that's for sure, unless…" She pulls a face.

"Unless what?"

"Well, okay, you pissed me off at the party yeah, but bygones, and, well, you know I listen to the podcast, read the reports. Let me ask you something: why did Emma suddenly change her mind and want to give you an interview? What changed, hey? You of all people say people can't change. You never tire of telling me this about Angus. So ask yourself, why did Emma change her mind?"

"Tom came to see me. He asked me things, wanted me to stop the podcasts."

Cathy takes the cigarette from behind her ear and rolls it around her fingers like a mini nunchuck. A couple on the next table shoot her looks as though she is twirling an AK47.

"And what did you tell him, beyond the expected?"

I think back to our meeting. "He wanted to know about me, about…" I pause for a second. "What happened to me. The attack."

Cathy sucks in her bottom lip.

"Go on."

"I told him what I tell people."

We exchange a look but nothing needs to be said. Cathy is the only other person who knows the truth, well almost the truth.

"I also told him, or rather he guessed, that I'm" – I smile – "was, housebound."

Cathy taps the cigarette on the table, drawing more disapproving glances.

"He wants to take your house away. Once he realised that you wouldn't stop he decided to set you up, to take what is most important to you."

And I see it clearly now. She's right, I threatened Tom and his response was to play me and ruin me. I put my head in my heads.

"But entrapment can be a two-way street."

I lift my head and look up at her.

Cathy sips her coffee. "There's only one thing for it."

I raise a questioning eyebrow and Cathy pops the cigarette back behind her ear as though it's done its job.

"We are going to have to get him to confess."

CHAPTER THIRTY-FOUR

Plans

When I get home Henry and Finn still aren't back, when I go to bed later that evening they haven't returned and when I wake up the house is still dead. Dead but not quite silent; when I pause at the top of the stairs I can hear the familiar sounds of my house, my old love, floorboards squeaking, window frames rattling and water moving in air-filled pipes providing an underlying sigh.

I do receive an email from Henry telling me that he will be taking Finn into school from his mother's for the next week and that he "needs time to process". What he is "processing" is left to my imagination.

But it's just as well they aren't in the house. I need it empty, save for Lil'Bitch. I have to fix things, make everything right, and Cathy's plan is the only way forward, however dangerous it may be.

There were fewer knocks on the door this morning. *You'll be whatever the digital equivalent of fish and chip paper is come Monday*, Cathy had said, and maybe she's right but I know this is never going away. Not only has Tom Ellis ruined my life and career but Khalil is still behind bars, and now I believe that he didn't do it. Before, it was a story, an intellectual exercise – but shorn of my journalistic trappings, now I can afford to believe.

And that gives me an advantage. I have nothing left to lose and with the tools available to anyone willing to use them I can strike out.

Tom Ellis, I am coming for you.

I call Mo and ask him to come over when he's free. In the background I can hear the sounds of a busy hospital and then someone calling his name: "Doctor Bukhari!" I suppose I should feel guilty about dragging him away from his duty and perhaps I do but at the moment all I really feel is a cold, hard fury directed at Tom Ellis. Hate trumps love, as someone once said.

He agrees to come over at the end of his shift.

I crank open the cover of my Mac and bring up Khalil's case files. Something is gnawing again.

Mo doesn't arrive until the house is full of shadows. I hadn't noticed the dark arriving as my attention has been purely devoted to the screen in front of me.

I let him in and he looks at me in amazement.

"What?" I ask him.

"The door. It was just on the Yale lock?"

I shrug.

He looks like he might burst into tears but instead he picks me up and gives me a bear hug.

"This is good news!"

I let him crush me against his chest for a moment and then he puts me down.

"Yes, but I've got better. Come on." I notice he is holding a plastic bag. "Pastries?"

He beams at me. "Danish, cinnamon twirls; your favourite."

An image of Henry pops into my head but there is no guilt. This seems to be my new default setting. It doesn't make me feel happy but it does make me effective.

"Better bring those into the kitchen. You eat whilst I talk."

Sure enough, he follows me, and I take the pastries from him, putting them straight onto the table.

"Please, eat," I tell him.

He looks at me like someone unused to being told what to do but then he picks up a fat cinnamon roll, one with the fresh glaze glistening like ice caps, and begins to eat.

"I want to say sorry first of all."

He chews quickly as though clearing his mouth to speak.

"No, please don't say anything. I'm sorry I let you and your brother down and my own family too. I'm sorry for promising too much and for abandoning all my journalistic ethics and for that, wherever happens, I am truly sorry. But sorry isn't good enough. I'm going to put all this right."

He swallows and then shivers involuntarily. I realise that I haven't put the heating on, I was so wrapped up in my research.

"Sarah, it's over. He has won."

I turn round my Mac so the screen is facing him. It casts an eerie blue pallor on to his face.

"What am I looking at?"

I get up and crouch next to his chair.

"Look. This is the DNA report on Lauren's car."

"But the DNA showed that Khalil had been in the car. How does this help?"

"Khalil being in the car wasn't a big deal at the trial, yeah? He was in the car a lot in those days, and on the day of her murder. You would expect that of her boyfriend. But look at this." I scroll down to the boxes marked "Additional Markers". "Three more sets of DNA. The CPS could only positively identify one of these; it was a mechanic at Kwik Fit who had fitted two new tyres a few days before her murder. He had driven her car onto the ramp leaving traces on the steering wheel. He had been convicted of an assault, a pub fight I recall, and had to give his DNA as per the practice back then."

Mo turns and holds my arm. "This was all dealt with at the trial. He had a rock-solid alibi."

"Yes, it was, but what about these?" I jab my finger at the other two DNA profiles. "What if one of these belongs to Tom Ellis? He was never tested, his DNA wasn't on the police database, but he does" – I lean forward, tap the keys and bring up Tom Ellis's witness statement – "say that he wasn't in her car in the days leading up to her death. In fact he was away at Cadet Camp, running up and down the Brecon Beacons with all the other keen soldier types eager to lay down their lives in the desert."

Mohammed sighs and moves one of the pastries around the plate. "So, we get some of his DNA and what? Ask the police to test it? They will never do that; it would be a criminal offence, you know that."

"No, we, or rather I, get some of his DNA and then we test it. If there's a match we give it to Khalil's lawyers, drop another podcast and force the police to look at him again."

"But if it is his DNA, it proves he was in the car but not that he was the killer."

I move away from him and pull up a chair next to him. All I can hear is the soft hum of the Mac's fan and his slow, steady breathing.

"But that's not really what we are going to do. We will get him here and get him to confess. I think he wants one more thing from me."

"And what is that?"

"He wants to know what happened to me and" – I blush and look away – "I saw the way he stared at me. I think he wants me."

Mo shakes his head. "Never. I won't allow it. It's dangerous."

"No, it's not. We rig the house with cameras and record it. If I can get him to confess then great, but if not I will get some of his DNA, his hair," I say quickly, "and we will get that tested."

Mo grunts. "He's not that stupid, and so what if he does confess? He'll just say you are obsessed with him, that he said anything to please you. It's like that Wimbledon Common murder all those years ago – classic entrapment – and you have already been on the receiving end of that."

"But we'll still have his DNA and it will match one of those samples. Can you carry out the DNA test at the hospital?"

My voice goes up at the end of the sentence, propelled, I realise, by the knowledge that this plan, this plan I know that is ridiculous and far-fetched, is my only hope of keeping my house and my family.

Mo gives another long sigh; it is unlike him to be so down and it worries me.

"I can, yes, but I feel that this may be another dead end. Khalil is going to rot in that place, or" – he puts his hand to his face covering up a sob – "worse, much worse: it will kill our mother."

I put an arm around him and let him cry. I get the feeling that this may be the first time he has cried for a very long time and his despair makes me more determined.

"Don't worry," I whisper, "this injustice can't stand. Tom Ellis will be punished for what he did to your family and to mine. Will you help me, Mo? I can't do it without you. It's the only hope Khalil and I have left."

Mo looks up at me with an air of sadness that I will only come to understand much later and then he reaches out and takes hold of my hand.

"I am so sorry I involved you in this, Sarah, but I see now that you are right, this is Khalil's only hope, and for you and for him of course I will do this."

That night I can't sleep. Not with worry about Henry and Finn; they will be fine and I will sort any issues out with Henry once I have damned Tom Ellis and put our home out of his reach. I can't sleep because my mind is filled with fabulous visions of the ways in which I am going to hurt Tom Ellis. I want to destroy his career, his life, take away his liberty and punish him for what he did to Lauren and Khalil and only when I have exhausted all these thoughts do I manage to sleep and I sleep well.

My awakening is, however, the opposite of "well". The first thought I have as I re-enter existence is that I have woken to a massive cardiac event and the second is fury that this myocardial interference will prevent me from bringing justice to Tom Ellis.

I breathe in and nothing comes but fear, which causes me to jerk rapidly and then for Lil'Bitch, who has been sleeping on my face, to tear off into the en-suite bathroom, legs pumping like Wile Coyote.

"Lil'Bitch, you bitch!"

She doesn't look back and I imagine she will have ensconced herself deep in the laundry basket. Once in there she will sleep, surrounded by the memories of us, her family, carried in our scent.

Relived to be alive I bound out of bed and head after Lil'Bitch into the en-suite bathroom. A quick shower and then I will be ready to put my plan into action and destroy Tom Ellis.

I throw cold water on my face and dip down to do so again. When I raise my head from the sink I catch my reflection in Henry's shaving mirror and something else, something that's not supposed to be in here, something in the bath behind me.

My breath leaves me in a cold rush of pure fear but I force myself to turn and look.

In the bathtub are hundreds, maybe thousands, of pieces of paper.

I drop to my knees by the side of the bath and then dip my hand into the paper, which lines the whole of the bottom of the bath. I pick up a few pieces. There is writing, handwriting, on the pieces of paper. It's my handwriting. It's my case files for the podcast, the scripts, the police report copies, cut up and destroyed and then placed here whilst I was sleeping.

Dizziness hits and I have to hold tight to the side of the bath. He was here, in my bedroom.

"Fuck!"

How did he get in? I think back to Tom's visit, or maybe it was Emma. Did they have an opportunity to take a copy of my keys?

A loud shrill laugh makes me jump. It's coming from the bedroom; he's in here right now.

I look around for a weapon but there's nothing but the toilet brush. It will have to do. I grab it and slowly, acutely aware that I am naked, step towards the bedroom door.

"Ha ha ha ha ha!"

The laugh is demented, like Mr Punch in his fury, and now I am listening for it I can tell it's not from a human source.

I push open the bedroom door and see my phone on the bedside table move as it plays the lunatic laugh.

I pick up the phone and see that I have a new message. It's from Frenchie.

You look so pretty when you are asleep – if you weren't such a whore I would want you. Hope you kept a backup, fuckface. Hope you like your new ringtone. Kiss kiss bang bang.

I throw the phone on the bed as though holding it any longer could cause me to become infected. Terror, that's what this feeling of being out of time and space must be. I catch my breath just as I think I may pass out.

He came into my house, went to the basement, found my notes, destroyed them and then stood over me and changed my ringtone whilst I slept. My fear goes, replaced by anger so crystalline hard it makes me blink. Tom Ellis is Frenchie. I know this now. The messages started when I began the broadcasts and it was his first salvo in a war that has culminated in him taking everything from me. He doesn't just want my house, my career. He wants my sanity.

I sit on the bed and I notice something peculiar: the anger has gone, just as quickly as it arrived. There's an absence of emotion that scares me, because without my fear and my anger I don't know who I am.

I call Henry and to my surprise he answers on the third ring.

"Hi," he says.

I can hear Finn in the background shout, "Is it Sarah?"

"Henry, how are you?"

My voice is steady but Henry's sounds strained.

He clears his throat. "I'm fine. Finn's fine considering everything."

I let the unsaid reproach float by me.

"Is everything okay at the house?"

"Yes, it's quiet without you two here though." I cast a look at the bathroom door. In the bath are the soggy remains of three years' worth of work. I don't mention the intruder, as Henry hates the podcast, the time I spend away from him, and he may even welcome the destruction of my work. But I have another motive for not telling him. He may worry, and worse he may come home, and I need the house all to myself for the next few days.

"I need a few more days here though. It's doing Finn, and me, good to get out of the city and clear our heads. After everything that has happened."

"Sure, sure, take as long as you like."

He seems surprised that I'm not pestering him to come home and his tone becomes petulant.

"We will. Maybe we won't come back at all. There's been a lot of water under the bridge."

I'm listening but my mind is elsewhere. It's on Tom Ellis and a mental image of the front page of *The Guardian* splashed with a picture of his face.

"Yeah, if you think that's best," I say but my tone is flat and Henry picks up on it straight away.

"What? Stop it, Finn! Do you mean that? Did you hear what I said?"

"Sorry, Henry, I was miles away."

I hear a splutter of unmistakable rage from down the phone.

"Our future is at stake here and you can't be bothered even listening to me. Our house is on the line and you think of nothing but yourself. You're so goddamn selfish!"

"Selfish" is one of his go-to insults when I don't do what he wants and is usually the sign that he is two insults away from screaming. Henry doesn't lose his temper often but when he does it is as predictable in its progression as a toddler's tantrum.

I act as fireman and without any remorse tap into his empathy.

I fake a sob. "I'm sorry, honey, it's just been so stressful and with you being away – and Finn – I sometimes think that I can't cope with all the worry."

I pause, allowing him to assume the role of protector and condescending husband and god bless him, Henry obliges.

A big sigh and then, "Look, I'm sorry too. I know things have been hard for you and it must get too much. By the way, have you heard anything more from that troll harassing you? What was it, the Frenchman?"

"Frenchie? No, nothing at all." I glance back over my shoulder at the bathroom. The last thing I want is for him to feel sorry enough for me to head back home.

"I think this time is good for both of us." This causes another sigh and I wonder whether I have set his temper off again but he sighs once more. "You're probably right and you know what they say about absence and the heart."

I conjure up an image of me piercing Tom Ellis's heart with a knife.

"They're right, darling."

This seems to work and we part with promises to speak to each other in a couple of days. With any luck it will all be over by then.

CHAPTER THIRTY-FIVE

Behind the door

I've dressed for the occasion. Knowing this is going to be, hopefully, broadcast around the world, I've made sure I look good. I'm wearing a Helmut Lang dress that Henry bought me for my thirtieth – and nothing I own makes me feel sexier – paired with my kick-ass Kurt Geiger black leather boots and a full face of lies. I know that I look as good as I can and, without being immodest, that is pretty damn hot.

At 7.59 I make my way downstairs and sit at the kitchen table. Lil'Bitch is nowhere to be seen. I think she can sense the tension.

I WhatsApp Hannah.

Hey Fucktart number 1.

Hey Fucktart no.2, what's going on? Quiet night in, bottle of Pinot Grigio and a Midsummers DVD?

Better than that, I've invited Tom Ellis round. I'm going to get him to confess to the murders. I have to, to get the house, Henry, my family back.

The cursor blinks furiously.

That sounds dangerous, he is a violent man. I don't think you should be there on your own doing this!

At 8pm I glance back towards the hallway as something clatters but it's just the wind catching the flap of the letterbox.

It's fine, I've got it covered and you know what, it's all I have left.

I shuffle in my chair and go to stand up and then sit back down again. It's not nerves causing this restlessness though, it's excitement. I am about to put things right.

Listen, I think you should call him and tell him not to come over, I've got a really bad feeling about this.

At 8.02pm there is a knock, three knocks to be precise, on the front door.

I glance at the video monitor. It's him.

I quickly type *showtime* and slip my phone in my pocket.

I walk down the hallway and reach the front door. I don't hesitate. I click the Yale latch and swing the door open. The phone in my pocket buzzes but I ignore it.

Tom Ellis looks me up and down, clearly liking what he sees.

"You've dropped the Alcatraz routine on the door, good for you!"

His cocky tone makes me want to punch him hard in the face but instead I wave him in.

"Well, they're really just security theatre. If someone wants to get in, then they always can can't they?"

If he realises this is a reference to him destroying my notes under the guise of Frenchie then he doesn't let on.

I step aside and he comes in. I give the door a gentle push and it slams shut behind him. I don't bother locking it. For all my locks and barriers, I've invited the danger inside.

"Kitchen," he says and starts towards it.

"No," I say. "Tonight let's talk in here." I nod towards the front lounge door.

"Ah, the mysterious room. I hope there are no nasty surprises waiting for me in here? You should know that my lawyer knows that I am here tonight."

I cock my head to one side. "But not Emma?"

Before he can answer I pull out a key attached to a silver chain around my neck. I slip the chain off and insert the key into the lock and turn. For a moment I think it is the wrong key as it won't catch, but I give it a wiggle and then I feel the teeth bite and the lock disengage. I open the door.

The room is like it always was: an earth-brown leather sofa and matching armchair, a Scandi coffee table in the centre. On the wall above the fireplace is the faded outline of where a TV screen used to hang with a small dark circle towards the top of the pale outline.

The air in here is slightly different than the rest of the house; it seems thicker. Maybe it's just because Henry takes care of cleaning this room – I won't venture in, and he does it so infrequently that the air feels like it has coagulated.

I didn't feel any trepidation when planning this evening, about using this room, but now I'm in here I can't help but notice that there are goose bumps rising on my forearms and I can feel my heart pounding faster in my chest. I take a deep breath and tell myself to concentrate on the job at hand.

"Come in. We only use this room for special occasions and I think this a special occasion." I give him a coquettish smile.

He follows me into the room. I take a seat on the sofa and again my heart rate rises. I didn't mean to pick this room but it felt right. Was I hoping for catharsis? Instead, it could jeopardise everything as I feel myself sweating and the first pricks of panic blossom into life in my chest.

I gesture at the other end of the sofa and Tom looks at it warily.

I go to speak but he raises a finger to his lips.

"Before we talk, I need to check something. Stand up."

I get up.

"Raise your hand above your head."

I do so, and in doing so feel more exposed since – well, since the last time I was alone with a man in this room.

Tom takes a step forward and places his hands either side of my hips. He runs them up along my ribs and then into my armpits. I can smell a faint tang of whisky hidden behind his cologne.

"Turn around."

I do as he says and he repeats the process, his hands meeting at the small of my back.

An involuntary shiver of pleasure shoots up my spine.

Tom drops to his knees behind me and his hands are on the inside of my thighs and then slowly he moves them down, his grip strong against my leather boots.

His head brushes against my buttocks and I step forward.

"Satisfied?"

"I can't have you recording us now, can I? That would be unethical, but you needn't worry. I've not come here to blurt out a confession so you won't miss out."

"I'm not intending to entrap you – I'll leave that to you – and very well played by the way. You led me right to the pit."

He smiles. "May I?"

I nod and he takes a seat. I sit down at the opposite end of the couch. There is maybe two feet separating us now.

He sprawls against the end of the sofa as though he owns the place, and quite probably he will. Now he is here, I can see the plan for what it is, hopeless, but it's all I've got, all Khalil has got.

Tom puts the palms of his hands together. "So, when you called you said you would explain why you came after me, tried to ruin my life, my marriage."

"I think you have probably done your fair share of ruining it yourself."

Tom throws his head back and laughs.

"I do love Emma, you know. Marriage is a long-haul flight; sometimes you want to take a break, wander around the cabin. Eat some salty nuts."

I can't help it and I laugh. "So that's what I am to you, salty nuts?"

"Ha, not exactly. You are, were, a threat. But enough of that. Remember what I told you. You know I know about what happened to you. Why do you lie about it?"

My eyes instinctively dart to the space in the corner of the room where there used to be a lamp before it got smashed.

Tom catches my glance and looks to the same spot.

He slaps the arm of the sofa.

"Oh my god, did it happen in here?"

My silence answers his question.

"Shit. And now you bring me in here. I feel – I was going to say honoured, but I think there is something a little darker than that going on."

I shift forward along the sofa, narrowing the distance between us.

"You know, I felt there was something between us the moment I met you. These things don't follow logic do they? Here you are, about to sue me, destroy my life, and yet I can't help being drawn to you and wanting to–"

There is the sound of a crash from somewhere in the house.

Tom reacts with a start. "What's that? Is there someone else in the house?"

I put my hand on his arm. "No one but us. It's just the cat in the basement chasing rats. They are coming up from a crack in the floor."

"That's awful. I swear this city is sinking into its own filth."

I get up and switch the table lamp on and then turn the main light off. The room shrinks in on itself, the sofa subdued in the half-light.

I re-join him on the sofa.

Tom leans forward. "So, the thing that happened to you. An attack, you called it. I know what you told me, what you told your husband, was a lie."

He looks at me and then smiles, a malign glint in his eye. "I knew it. He didn't suspect, did he, though maybe he knows deep down – don't we all often conceal secrets from ourselves?"

"Know what?" I say and I lower my hand and feel for the scissors I taped to the bottom of the sofa. The plan seems awfully shaky now. What do I do if he just takes the hair sample back from me?

"That you invited your attacker in, that you weren't raped by a stranger. You were having an affair, weren't you? I can see it in you, Sarah, that longing for adventure, for excitement. It's why you stay locked up in this house isn't it? It's not because you're scared of what's on the outside; you're scared of what you will do if you go outside. You can't trust yourself, can you? You long for that danger, the thrill of the forbidden. That's it, isn't it? You were after a hook-up behind poor old Henry's back and it went wrong."

"Frenchie," I whisper, but he doesn't react.

I lean in and kiss him deeply. He kisses me back, his tongue curling round mine. I run my fingers through his hair and then he pulls me close and my hand drops to his lower back and massages him there as we kiss.

He pushes me back and then I'm lying down and he's on top of me.

And then something strange happens. I can't help it but I start to kiss him passionately. I surrender completely to my body and what it wants, not what it needs. It's been so long since I felt real desire and had it reciprocated. I realise now that I can't live without it, that living without it has nearly killed an important part of who I am. *Whatever happens, never again*, I tell myself.

Tom's pelvis grinds into mine and I feel his hardness crushed against his jeans.

And then it's not him but it's Rupert above me, holding me down. Rupert, the "something in media" who I met on the Ashley Madison website. The man who wrote funny and charming emails that made me laugh and feel young and carefree. Rupert, who was married and cared for his disabled wife after she was catastrophically injured in a car accident. Rupert, whose messages arrived and made my tummy tingle when they did so. Rupert, whose two beautiful teenage daughters – one at Durham University, the other a precocious sixteen year old – he adored, who depended on him for everything. The same Rupert who came to my door one evening, despite me only wanting to chat online, the one who, after I shut the door in his face when he wouldn't take "no" for an answer, kicked the door open, breaking the simple chain lock, and who chased me into this room, who forced me back onto this sofa and who then raped me and took away the secret of me, leaving a "me" disassembled and without a map of how to put the pieces back together. It's that Rupert who I see on top of me and suddenly I can't breathe and my chest is tight.

I push back against Tom's chest.

He ignores me and carries on kissing me.

I jerk my head to one side and shout, "Stop!"

Tom sits up and holds his hands up.

"What the fuck?"

He looks at me like I'm crazy.

He scowls at me and I can see violence in his eyes.

"That's what happened last time, isn't it? You're just a silly little prick tease and you got what was coming to you."

I turn my head to one side and look at the fireplace. Isn't that what the boys at school used to say about the ugly girls at school? *You don't look at the fireplace whilst poking the fire.* I giggle involuntarily and this seems to enrage Tom more.

"Maybe you're right. Is that what happened to Lauren? Was she teasing you, Tom? Did you get a little rough? An accident? You didn't mean to kill her, I'm sure."

He pulls his arm back as though to strike me and then with a "fuck" he drops it by his side.

"I thought that you believed me? I didn't kill Lauren."

"Then what about the evidence?"

He throws his arms in the air. "What evidence? You mean Amy saying that she saw me jump on a bicycle? Did you not think that it was funny that she mentioned this to you after all these years? You know she became a heroin addict after she left school? Did you pay her for her story? Have you ever thought about her motivation?"

And I go to reply and I can't because something clicks in my mind, a voice screaming "murder". I don't know exactly what is yet but the feeling is powerful enough to make the panic surge through me again. I reach down and grab the scissors from under the sofa.

"What have you got there?"

I hold the scissors up in front of me.

"For your hair, your DNA, I was going to cut your hair."

Tom's eyes go wide and then he jumps up.

"I'm leaving. This was a massive mistake. I came here to tell you I wouldn't be suing you. I reckon ruining your reputation is enough, but you are a fucking maniac and need professional help."

"Heroin," I say, and as I say it I realise why it strikes a chord. Mo works with heroin addicts. His clinic provides methadone to addicts in Hammersmith. I will have to check my notes, those that remain, but I already know that they will show Amy lives near Hammersmith.

I stand up too and Tom backs away. I realise I'm brandishing the scissors still so I slip them in my back pocket.

"Listen, I'm sorry. You have to listen to me right now. We're being watched. There's a camera in that hole on the wall." He turns to go. "Mo, he's in the house. Downstairs."

"What the fuck?" He spins around and spots what used to be a screw hole for mounting the TV but which now contains a miniature camera and microphone. "I don't care, that's your business. I'm leaving."

And now I see it. I've been manipulated all along and the end becomes grimly apparent.

"I think we're in danger."

But he ignores me and opens the door, striding out into the hallway. I follow him.

"It's Mo. He wanted to set you up, get his brother out of prison, and he's used me."

"I don't care. I'm sick of your conspiracy bullshit."

I cast a look down the hallway. Has Mo heard all of this? Is he even now making his way up from the basement?

Tom has reached the door and he pulls at the Yale latch and clicks it open but when he pulls the door nothing happens.

He tries again but nothing.

"Did you lock the door after I came in?"

I shake my head.

He looks a little afraid now. "Where are the keys?"

"There's a spare set in one of the kitchen drawers."

He nods slowly. "Right, let's go and get them."

And then with a hushed click the lights go off.

"Shit," says Tom and I can hear fear in the cracks of his voice.

"Follow me, and be quiet." I walk to the end of the hallway, towards the kitchen.

As I pass the bottom of the stairs I hear a thump from somewhere upstairs. It's probably Lil'Bitch, I tell myself, although my adrenaline is telling my brain a different story.

When I pass the basement door it's open. Is Mo still down there or has he come upstairs? Is he watching us right now?

Tom nods.

I take hold of the door handle and slowly turn it and push the door open.

The kitchen is in total darkness. The blinds to the French doors are closed. Did I close them before Tom arrived? I can't remember doing it but it's the kind of thing you do subconsciously.

Even though it's nearly pitch black, I know my house well and I skirt around the table and find the right drawer.

"Fuck!"

Tom, however, is stumbling round and bangs into the corner of the table. It scrapes on the tiles and sounds as loud as a jet climbing out of Heathrow.

"Shush!"

Finding the drawer was easy but I can't make out the contents. The drawer is deep and it's the place where all our kitchen crap ends up. I'm scrabbling through the pens, multiple charging cables, packs of Aspirin, plugs and boxes of fridge magnets, like I'm hacking through vines in some vast subterranean forest.

"Hurry up," hisses Tom. "I think I can hear something."

My hand grips a set of keys and I pull them out. I hold them up to my eyes and can tell right away that these belong to the shed.

"Shit."

"What is it?"

I ignore him and put my hands back in the drawer. A thought occurs to me: what if I put them somewhere else? Even as I have this thought my fingers close around some more keys and I can tell right away that these are the right ones; my muscle memory for them is perfect. I've carried them with me for so long that my fingers close around them in the same pattern as they always do.

"Got them." I hold the keys up.

Everything happens quickly. Tom turns toward the noise of the kitchen door opening and then I see a dark mass slam into Tom, knocking him to the floor. I run for the door but as I pass the struggling men, someone kicks out a leg, catching my ankle, which causes me to stumble and then fall face first on the floor.

The keys go flying into the darkness of the hall and my head's spinning, but I know if I lie here then I may never get up, so I push my hands down and lever myself up. I feel like I'm going to puke with the pain and the disorientation. Behind me the noise of a struggle suddenly stops and all I can hear is a man's heavy breathing and a gurgling sound that makes me think of an abattoir.

The front door is only ten feet away but I can't see the keys anywhere and now I can hear heavy breathing and steps behind me. In panic I run upstairs. Blood is pounding in my ears and when I reach the first landing I risk a look back but can't see anyone pursuing me. There is noise though, coming from below, and it sounds like dough being dropped onto the floor and it makes my stomach roll.

My hand goes to my pocket but of course my mobile isn't there. Mo had said I should give it to him, as Tom would undoubtedly ask for it to make sure he wasn't being recorded. And then a thought hits me; there is a telephone socket in the bedroom. We don't have a phone attached but I remember Henry putting the old phone in a box – he's such a hoarder – when we decided to remove the bringer of gloom, as Henry called the landline. I think I know where the box might be.

I take the next set of steps three at a time and run into our bedroom.

I pull the chair away from the dressing table and position it next to the wardrobe. I jump on it and reach up to the top shelf and sure enough there's a cardboard box. I take hold of it and pull it back, but it won't come loose. It's packed in so tightly that it is jammed tightly against the insides of the unit. I pull hard but the cardboard is thin and has somehow gotten damp and bits of the box come off in my hands. I totter backwards before grabbing the shelf and pulling myself forward.

I look round but there's nobody there. I strain my ears but there's no sound; the house is quiet, or is it? Can I hear footsteps on the stairs? I listen but there's nothing. I fight the urge to lie back on the bed and await my fate.

There is only one way the box is coming out so I straighten my hands and jam them between the sides of the box and the inner wall of the unit. I can feel the skin ripping as I plunge my hands further in. Once my hands touch the back wall of the unit I lean back and yank the box as hard as I can. It comes loose and this time the inertia sends me flying and I fall down onto the bedroom floor, the contents of the disintegrated box following a split second later. And amongst those contents is a blue plastic phone, with the wires wrapped tightly around the case.

I can't afford to think that he is on the way up the stairs. My trembling fingers start to try and unwind the cord but the shaking is so bad I can't get any purchase.

Get a grip, I scream silently.

It seems to help and when I try again the cord unspools easily and then it's free. I scramble across the floor and plug the phone into the socket and when I pick up the receiver I am rewarded with the most glorious sound: a dialling tone.

I dial 999.

"Hello. Emergency services, how can I assist you?"

"I need help, right away. There's a man in my house and–"

There's a noise on the line, "Miss, how can I help you? Are you alright?"

And then the line goes dead.

I look round. Apart from the bathroom, the only place to hide is the built-in wardrobe but I've seen enough horror movies to know how that ends. I could open the window and hope that someone hears me shouting but how long would I have before he dragged me away and killed me? And I know that's what he has planned, how plausible it will be: the obsessed journalist killing the man threatening to take her home away and then killing herself, is that how he will make it look? Hell, her medical records will show PTSD following an earlier attack. She wasn't all to blame, her condition was. She's a victim, and Tom Ellis – well, his DNA – will be tested, taken as part of the crime scene investigation, and what do you know? It will match the DNA in Lauren's car, and whilst his guilt will still be in doubt, it will be enough to raise serious concerns about the safety of Khalil's conviction. Or will he just make it look like Tom Ellis is the killer, a murderer now and then, who was fatally wounded after coming to my home to kill me?

This goes through my mind in a flash. But he has to find me to make this work. Was this his plan all along or did it just evolve as he saw Khalil's chances of an appeal evaporate? I find myself hoping it was the former as that would mean I was always disposable before he had the chance to know me. As quietly as I can I make my way down to the next landing and slip into my son's bedroom and stand behind the door. It will be a fifty–fifty chance that he goes upstairs and chooses my bedroom first. If he does I will have an opportunity to run down the stairs; if not then I will die in this room.

I hear footsteps on the landing. Each creak is like the splintering of bone and I think of Tom Ellis. And then they stop and Mo starts talking, slowly, deliberately and with no trace of what he has in mind for me in his voice.

"Sarah, I had to do it. He was going to take everything you have. I couldn't let him do that, I couldn't stand by and let that happen to you. Not after everything. He killed Lauren and my brother went to prison for his crimes."

He's nearly at the top of the first landing, maybe less than five feet away from me. I hold my breath.

"He's okay. I only knocked him unconscious but he's breathing just fine. Let's talk about what we should do next. I think we should carry on with the plan and take a cutting from his hair. We can still make this happen. I'll tell the police it was self-defence or, if you want, just tell them that I lost my temper and hit him. We can make this work."

The door moves back and I can hear Mo pause and I know he is peering into the box room.

My lungs start to ache and I swear I can hear the sound of my skin and muscles tightening. And then there is a bang from the floor above. It's a bang I recognise well; it's the sound of Lil'Bitch jumping down from her perch on top of the wardrobe and landing on the bedroom floor, but to Mo it sounds like his quarry.

He slowly moves back and I hear him slowly and deliberately start to make his way up the stairs towards the second landing.

Through the gap between the hinges I see his dark mass moving up the stairs and I catch the flash of what is unmistakably the large Santoku butcher's knife from my kitchen.

My hand goes to my mouth, stifling a stillborn cry.

I watch him disappear from view as he climbs the stairs to my bedroom.

"Move," I tell myself, but my legs refuse to obey.

If I stay here I'll die, I know this, but my body remains stuck.

"Fucking move."

Nothing. I'm not sure how air is getting into my lungs, as I feel frozen in time and space, already dead but for the formalities.

I whimper and my head sinks to my chest and in so doing it brushes against a piece of paper stuck to the wall. Even in the dim light I can see that it's one of Finn's drawings. It's a picture of our house. Finn is pictured in his bedroom playing on his Xbox and in the room above there is a bed and two figures – me and Henry – are lying in it and we are both smiling.

I hear footsteps from above. How many seconds until he checks the wardrobes and then the en-suite bathroom? Ten or thirty? The difference between life and death. I think of Finn. I need to live for him.

"Move," I whisper.

And I'm moving, out onto the landing, and I pause and listen. Nothing. Is he above me, ten feet or less, doing the same, listening for movement like a snake waiting for its prey?

I move towards the stairs and then start down them quickly as I can without making too much noise.

I get halfway to the bottom when the house reverberates to an almighty roar.

"Sarah!"

And then the footsteps are thundering down the stairs behind me.

I jump to the bottom of the stairs and look at the floor. The keys must be there or I'm done for, but I can't see them. The only place they could be is under the console table and I drop to my knees and feel under the table. Nothing. Maybe there is a spare set in the drawers of the table. I stand up and take hold of the handle.

There is the unmistakable jangle of keys and I look up.

Mo is standing on the landing above me.

"Looking for these?"

He holds up my keys and shakes them in the same way that he always presented the cakes and pastries he brought me.

"Let me guess, you want me to ask you how you killed her?" I say.

Mo shrugs. "If I tell you it was an accident would you–"

Before he can say "believe me" I pull the console table drawer free and throw it as hard as I can at Mo. I don't wait to see if it lands but the cry of pain I hear confirms the hit.

I burst into the kitchen and try the French door handles. Locked. I spin on my feet at the same time as Mo comes crashing through the kitchen door. His momentum takes him careering into the table and then he falls to the floor. I leap over him and pull the basement door open.

I slam it shut, slam home the top and bottom bolts.

I put my ear to the door and listen but it's quiet. Slowly, never taking my eyes from the door, I retreat down the stairs one at a time to prepare for my last stand.

CHAPTER THIRTY-SIX

Sisters

I wait for the door to splinter and for Mo to come crashing through, bringing me my fate, but nothing happens.

My hoping heart leaps at the possibility that Mo has gone but then I hear something soft and low: it's Mo's voice, and he's talking to someone.

Pressing my ear to the door I can make out the word "soon" and then abruptly he stops talking and I know, just know, he is looking at the door.

Slowly, so slowly, I back down the stairs until I submerge myself completely in the dark pool of the basement.

I take a step back and my foot catches against something heavy and I fall awkwardly, landing on the point of my elbow with a crack, but I ignore the pain because even though it's dark I can make out the crooked body and crushed head of Tom Ellis, like a deflated Christmas balloon, lying on the floor of the basement.

But I don't scream, not even when I feel the sticky wetness of Tom's blood seeping into my jeans, but I do gag when the smell, iron and shit, hits me. I dry heave but I push myself backwards, moving easily on the slippery floor.

I wedge myself in the corner of the basement where the rat got in. Perhaps because subconsciously I know that this crack leads to the outside and to safety.

As I crouch there a memory comes to me. It is of a day before Finn was born; just before I found out I was pregnant. I had gone on holiday on my own. I was freelancing back then and could come and go as I pleased and I loved to travel. Henry, with his fledgling career as an accountant, soon to be abandoned for teaching, couldn't accompany me, so I travelled around Europe whilst he worked. Too old for the inter-rail crowd but still young enough to pass for a student, I enjoyed a magical summer of cities, hostels and late-night wine-fuelled conversation with bright young things from all over the world. And I think it was the last time I was really happy. Finn brought something else, a purpose, a magnificent event, and a sublime one, but it was not the happiness of your soul chiming when you are true to yourself.

And towards the end of that holiday I met someone else. In the Black Mountains of Languedoc in the sleepy village of Labastide-Esparbairenque. There are two churches at either end of the village. For as long as anyone in the village can remember these churches have pronounced the hour with their bells – the first five seconds before the real hour, according to my iPhone and tradition, and the second church four seconds after the hour. And in those nine seconds, between the chimes of the first bell and the beginning of the second, lying in bed with Charlie, I finally felt I had found my real life, the real me and my joy. From the moment we first met I wanted him and he wanted me. For one week I would write during the day and then as the sun began to dip behind the black mountains there would be a knock on my door and I would slip the catch and let Charlie into my room. When the week ended and I returned home it was with the intention of leaving Henry.

On the ferry from Calais to Dover, in a toilet cubicle that smelt of shit and disinfectant, I pissed on a cardboard stick and my suspicions of the previous two weeks were confirmed and I found out I was pregnant. At the age of thirty-four, I was not going to have an abortion and so Charlie and my dreams of becoming a novelist were discarded. I told myself that I could love Henry if I tried, and I did try, but it wasn't enough and hence Rupert and eventually this, me, cowering in the corner of a basement.

In the dark, waiting for Mo, this glimpse of the real me brings me to tears and even as it does so I'm filled with a mother's guilt that my fondest memory is not one of my son.

My son, who I will never see again. My son, whose last memory will be of me arguing with his father.

There is a metallic clank, the sound of the door handle to the basement being turned. I take a step backwards towards the corner of the room and then trip as my foot catches on something light and plastic, sending it flying across the basement floor.

As I scrabble round in the dark there is a louder sound as Mo tests the door with his shoulder and I frantically lie on the basement floor and stretch my limbs out like a starfish searching for something that I can't see but that I know is there. Another bang as Mo slams into the door. I flail around and my foot knocks against something light and plastic. I fling myself towards the object and then my fingers close around it with a sense of relief. It's my mobile phone.

I turn the phone on and the screen lights up but something is wrong; black cracks like spider legs cover the glass and the back of the phone case is cracked and sharp. Mo must have crushed it or thrown it to the ground. The screen is open to the last message from Frenchie. It reads: *I hope you die by a thousand cocks you slut, it's all you deserve.* I click on the back button but nothing happens. There is a thud as Mo's shoulder bangs into the door.

I try the home button but nothing.

Another thud and this time I hear the crack of wood as the frame starts to give way. I shove the phone in my pocket and back towards the far corner of the room.

And then there is a huge crash as the basement door splinters and gives way followed by a silence that is punctuated by first the sound of heavy breathing and then slow deliberate footsteps on the stairs. It sounds like he's dragging something heavy. A beam of light from a torch pierces the dark and grows wider as Mo descends.

When he reaches the bottom of the stairs the beam cuts through the blackness like a lighthouse searching for a doomed ship and though I crawl as far back into the corner as possible it finds me and blinds me temporarily. He throws something heavy on the floor in front of me and it lands with a soft splat. For a moment the torch beam passes over the broken bloody face of Lil'Bitch.

I stifle a scream but the beam of light finds me.

I hold my hand up and block it. Mo is a dark silhouette behind the glare.

"Why are you doing this? I thought we were friends. I did nothing but help you."

He snorts with laughter. "Everything you did also helped yourself. It's the way of the world, is it not? Let's not pretend otherwise."

"But this. Why? How does killing me and Tom help Khalil?"

I know, or can guess, the answer already. He wants it to look like Tom killed me, that Tom is a killer and I was about to expose him so he killed me.

"I watched her, you know? I watched her kissing Tom. He used the bike to get there but nobody saw him but me and I was unable to come forward as a witness. He lied; he was there."

"You killed her because she was pregnant and you thought it would ruin Khalil's life. An honour killing. I thought you were better than that."

Mo laughs again. The sound is thin and so different from the laughter we shared in my kitchen not fifteen feet above us and I can't help but wonder: which is the real laughter? Which is the real Mo?

"An honour killing? Is there anything more reductive and racist then the English liberal middle classes? I couldn't give a fuck about religion but she was pregnant and cheating on my brother."

The funnel of light is focused back on me but my eyes are getting used to it now and I can make out the outline of Mo's face.

"I saw him kiss that slag and then leave and jump back on that bike."

"But no one at the party saw him do that, but you knew Amy Wilder had spoken to him, so when she turned up at your clinic, an addict, you saw a chance to put things right. You told her to say she had seen him take off on the bike. She lied – for what? More methadone?"

"Amy believes what she thinks is true. She didn't need much in the way of suggestion to remember the bike. She believes it now but it doesn't matter any longer. You've given me a better way to set Khalil free."

"You won't be able to tell him, not ever. He's a good man and he'd turn you in, you know that. He would hate you for what you've done, are about to do."

Mo steps forward and the torch beam dips and catches the light of the long-bladed knife in his right hand.

"He'll never know. I saved him from being humiliated. I only wanted to talk to her, make her understand she had to leave him, but she wouldn't listen and then she started screaming." He holds his hands up and examines them. "I owe him this much, to save him, and you should be glad Tom is dead. He was an evil man who would destroy you. At least this way your family keep their house and, well, when I came to and looked in the basement, I could see you were dead and when someone charged up the stairs I pushed them and Tom broke his neck."

He takes another step forward and starts to raise his right hand.

"The police will have to take a DNA sample from Tom, of course, and it will match one of the DNA samples on the car dashboard and, well, grounds for an appeal will be strong I'd say, particularly given the gruesome way he murdered you, the same method of strangulation."

I pull the scissors from my back pocket and leap forward, plunging them deep into his shoe. I can feel it catch something hard, bone, and then Mo is screaming and I'm scrabbling forward in the dark on my hands and knees. He has dropped the torch and the basement is black again.

My fingers touch the bottom step and then a pain unlike any I've ever known shoots up my calf into my lower back and I realise that I've been stabbed. Instinct makes me kick backwards and my foot connects with Mo's head.

I crawl forward and try to get to my feet but my leg gives way. I look down and see the kitchen knife is buried up to the hilt in my calf muscle. A dim thought about there being an artery there crosses my mind but disappears as I hear Mo groaning from behind me.

My world shrinks to the wooden step in front of me. If I can make that first step I have a fighting chance of escape. I reach out with my fingers and fasten on to the lip of the step and then I drag myself up the stairs and have gotten halfway and can see the moonlight coming from the kitchen windows and lighting the kitchen floor when I hear Mo roaring with rage and pain behind me.

He grabs my legs, causing a fresh electrical jolt of agony, and pulls me back to the basement floor.

His weight presses down on top of me, and I can smell his scent, the same scent that made me tingle with excitement, mixed with sweat and fury. Mo places his hands around my neck and begins to squeeze. *This is how Lauren died*, is what I think. *These were her final moments.*

The little light narrows and I realise that this is dying.

A roaring like thunder – my heart – fills my ears and there is something else too, a higher-pitched sound coming from somewhere off to my right-hand side.

And the blackness rushes and my fingers stretch and grab hold of the remains of the mobile phone. They close around the hard plastic case, feeling the serrated edges where the plastic has cracked, and I feel it cut my hand but the pain is nothing. I hold fast and bring my hand up fast and towards the dark mass of Mo's face above me.

His hands leap from my throat and he screams in agony.

He rolls off me and I take in a breath of air that cuts like razor blades in my bruised throat. As oxygen returns to my brain I can see Mo staggering around in the corner of the basement, one arm outstretched, the bright yellow corner of the mobile phone case sticking out of the socket of his right eye. His cries make my stomach churn and for one crazy moment I pause, thinking should I go to him and help, but then he screams again, this time in fury, and I watch in horror as he pulls out the plastic, bringing with it gore and jelly.

He screams once more and then throws the plastic, and half of his eyeball, on the basement floor. His other eye rolls demonically and focuses on the mess, before rolling once more and staring at me. There is madness in this basement, which will consume us both.

He charges but I roll aside just in time and he slams into the stairs and lets out a fresh howl of pain and rage.

I scuttle backwards and find myself under the computer desk.

In the dim light cast from the moonlight framing the basement door I can just about make out Mo's silhouette, arms outstretched in front of him. He takes an uncertain step forward and then stops.

He turns his head slowly in an arc and I realise he's listening. I guess a piece of hardened, primary-coloured piece of Chinese plastic in the eye would hinder your vision.

I feel around on the floor beside me and my hand lands on something heavy, metallic and familiar. It's Finn's metal fire truck, the source of many stubbed toes. As quietly as I can I pick it up.

Mo's head turns sharply towards me but he doesn't move; he suspects a trap and he's guarding the only way out.

"I'm not moving, Sarah." There's a new gurgle to his voice. Blood from his wounds are filling his throat. "If you come out now we can end this, if you wait there's a chance Henry and Finn could come back, and I don't want to have to involve them in this, as I am sure you know what that will mean."

For a moment I want to scream at him, and attack and claw, but I know that this is what he wants me to do.

As I think this I suddenly feel faint and have an almost overwhelming urge to close my eyes. *Blood loss*, I think through the fugue that has descended on me. How long have I got before I pass out? Seconds, minutes? I pinch the soft skin on my forearm hard and focus on the figure of Mo blocking the stairs.

"No," I whisper out loud. Mo turns to face me but I can tell he can't see me from the twitching of his head. He's listening intently, trying to get his bearings.

I spread my left hand slowly, hoping to find something else I can use but instead I feel something soft and moist. It's Lil'Bitch and I can't help it, I let out a small gasp.

Mo wipes his good eye and lets out a small sob of pain.

"Now I see you."

In the basement, in the dark, hidden, alone and afraid, I stroke for one last time Lil'Bitch, my cat, my companion, my friend. A rage, a swirling ball of bile, anger, agony, shit and unsaid thoughts, bursts, and I'm nothing but energy aimed at a point in time and space.

"Fuck you!"

It all happens quickly. Mo starts to move towards me; at the same time I launch myself up and out from beneath the desk. I'm dimly aware of the pain in my leg but all I really know and see is Mo's face, covered in blood and gore, one eye a black, bloodied hole, and the other wide in fury.

His arm is raised and the knife he holds seems to float in the air above him, before it slashes downwards, but I'm under its arc and I see the surprise on his face as my extended right arm holding the fire engine swings like a pendulum and then the corner of the truck smashes into the side of his head with a sickening crunch. My momentum brings me so close that our noses touch. He goes to say something but produces nothing but a gurgle and then he sinks to his knees and his eye rolls upwards, all life extinguished, before he collapses.. .

Even though I'm sure, I kick him with the point of my shoe, but he's dead, how could he not be, and strangely I hear laughter which can't be mine surely, because I don't think I'm laughing, but then I realise it must be me and this causes me to laugh some more and it's then that I feel the pain in my back and the dampness on my back, and blood pouring from my jeans and drip, drip, dropping on the concrete floor and now I'm on my back looking at the low ceiling – how did that happen? – and it's dark and Lil'Bitch and this house, here, now, what's the noise, who is that?

Is it you?

CHAPTER THIRTY-SEVEN

Henry

It's a bright, sunny afternoon.

The park is full of picnickers, children playing and eating ice creams and the low buzz of a London Sunday afternoon. We managed to grab a bench, although only I'm sitting at it, toying with my mobile phone as I watch Finn and Henry kick a ball to each other. Henry sees me looking and waves.

I wave back and then look down again at my mobile phone.

Finn runs over and smiles at me and I recognise the smile; it's his "I want something" smile.

"Dad says I can get an ice cream if you say it's okay?"

Sunshine, the park and ice creams. How could I say no?

"Sure honey." I take out my purse from my bag, get out a five-pound note and hand it to him.

His face lights up with joyful anticipation.

"Thanks, Mum."

That "Mum" kills me and makes me grip my phone tight. He runs off back to Henry and they start walking towards the ice cream van in the distance.

Hannah saved my life, or rather Henry did. Hannah rang Henry after I had told her that Tom was coming round to my house and Henry came home and found me bleeding to death in the basement. Another few minutes and I would have died.

But he can't explain how she got his number, just says "ask her", but she has gone silent. She's not responding to my messages. This made me suspicious. Suspicious enough to take Henry's phone from the kitchen table when he was doing the garden and put it in an old Waitrose bag and then hide it in the recycling bin under a pile of carrot and potato peelings.

I looked at it this morning.

When I saw the number of his email accounts – there were ten of them; Gmail, Yahoo, Hotmail and other more esoteric Chinese and Russian ones – it made me run to the bathroom and dry heave over the toilet bowl. But I needed to know. Once I had stopped heaving, and my breath, now fetid and foul, had returned, I made my way back to the bedroom.

They were password protected of course. I tried the Gmail account first. I tried every combination I could think of including sequences involving Finn's, Henry's and my name and birthdays. Nothing.

And then I tried Frenchie and as the star whirred I knew for certain.

Welcome

The inbox was curiously empty. I clicked on the sent items and my world collapsed once again. The various subject headers were highlighted in bold, attacking capitals.

BITCH, CUNT, WHORE, MUSLIM FUCKER, TRAITOR, PSYCHO BITCH

And on and on, all of Frenchie's emails to all the email addresses and phone numbers I had used. I had wondered how he was finding me, assuming it was some computer witchcraft that allowed him to follow my footsteps into the depths of the Internet, but it was much simpler than that and even as I thought this I remembered Henry bringing me cups of tea, looking over my shoulder at my computer screen.

I clicked on drafts. Emails that were never sent, subject headings that didn't pack a punch maybe. I recognised a couple of Henry's favourite phrases when mad: *silly woman, oddball.*

All so simple and mundane. Seeing these messages there, and some in drafts that were never sent, they lost their power. Frenchie was Henry – correction, *is* Henry. You see, the email abuse continued even as I lay recovering in hospital, even as Henry brought me flowers and sat by my bed reading to me. He loves me and he hates me.

I took screenshots of all the messages, bundled them up and sent them to my email. I then deleted that email from Henry's sent email folder. I checked the Snapchat and Twitter apps; they had the same password and same dark history. I adopted the same procedure as the emails: taking screenshots and forwarding them to my email.

But I could have, as crazy as this may sound, forgiven him for being Frenchie, for the abuse and hatred. He suspected all along that the rape was due to me seeking something. He is my husband. He knows me. He couldn't accuse me directly without us splitting up but he needed an outlet for his rage and Frenchie provided that. But what I find hard to forgive are the accounts he registered with Mumnset and the account marked "Hannah".

After I had done this I went downstairs and left his phone on a chair under the kitchen table.

An hour later I heard Henry shout, "Found it" and I could hear the relief in his voice.

And now here we are in the park with sunshine and ice creams.

I know why Henry did it. He didn't want me to leave the house. He wanted me frightened because he knew what really happened with Rupert, or rather he suspected. He had a saved website in his favourites, one that listed all the users of the Ashley Madison data dump. Truths come in all flavours in a marriage and this was one of those that he knew even when not acknowledging it to himself. I could confront him with the emails, watch his face go white and then listen to the pleading that would, I am sure, be based on a claim that it was all done to protect me, to save me from what lay outside, and after all hadn't he been right all along?

And some good has come of this. Gideon tells me that Khalil's appeal will definitely succeed now that they have new evidence, evidence that I gave them.

I toy with the phone. The email is ready to go to the police.

Henry and Finn are walking back from the ice-cream van. Finn has his face buried in a 99'er and Henry waves and then nods towards the ice cream he has bought me, a delicately balanced cone with raspberry ripple sauce spiralling around it. It's my favourite flavour.

If Henry hadn't stopped the bleeding in my leg – taken off his belt and pulled it tight around the severed femoral artery – I would have died in that cellar. He saved my life and I have the power to save his now. What would I have left if I go ahead and tell the police that he was Frenchie? Finn and Lil'Bitch is the answer – albeit she is now a three-legged cat after the surgery that saved her – and you know what? That is more than enough.

I look at the phone again and my finger hovers over the send button.

I was afraid of what lay outside, and Henry wanted it that way, but Henry was right to be afraid of what lies outside. It's me.

Lightning Source UK Ltd.
Milton Keynes UK
UKHW041428271018
331315UK00001B/21/P